# COFFEE AND CAKE AT WILDFLOWER LOCK

HANNAH LYNN

Boldwood

First published in Great Britain in 2024 by Boldwood Books Ltd.

Cover Design by Alexandra Allden

Cover photography: Shutterstock

A CIP catalogue record for this book is available from the British Library.

Paperback ISBN 978-1-80549-652-6

Large Print ISBN 978-1-80549-651-9

Harback ISBN 978-1-80549-650-2

Ebook ISBN 978-1-80549-653-3

Kindle ISBN 978-1-80549-654-0

Audio CD ISBN 978-1-80549-645-8

MP3 CD ISBN 978-1-80549-646-5

Digital audio download ISBN 978-1-80549-648-9

Boldwood Books Ltd
23 Bowerdean Street
London SW6 3TN
www.boldwoodbooks.com

*To Amy,*
*Thank you for being my cheerleader for over twenty years and*
*counting.*

# 1

---

Daisy May looked at the keys in her hand. This was it. Any second now, she would post them back through the letter box of the flat where she had lived for the last two years and mark the end of that chapter of her life. Not that she had any choice. The hike in rent and involuntary redundancy made it impossible to stay. Fortunately, those two events had coincided with an entirely unexpected inheritance.

When Daisy had first learned she was the owner of the *September Rose*, a wide-beam canal boat, moored at the picturesque Wildflower Lock, her mind had turned giddy with images of a beautifully painted vessel with a picture-perfect interior, complete with a wood-burning stove. Never envisioning herself on the water, she had also assumed that a quick sale of the aforementioned imagined boat would leave her with a healthy deposit for a house of her own. Her assumptions were wrong.

While a wood-burning stove did stand in one corner of the living space, hidden behind crumbling cardboard boxes, that was where the similarities between her vision and the real *September Rose* ended. From a grime-filled water tank to a hull that hadn't been tended to in years, the boat was in need of some serious TLC. Daisy's plans had pivoted when she decided to renovate the houseboat herself before she sold it. Only, the more time she spent on the *September Rose*, and the more she learned about her family's history on the waterways, the less she wanted to be separated from it.

And now, be it serendipity or simply good timing, selling wasn't an option. Instead, she was going to live in it full time.

Her phone buzzed in her pocket, spurring her to slip the keys through the letterbox before answering the call.

'Hey, Mum, is everything okay?'

'Fine. Just checking you were all okay? What time are you leaving the flat?'

'I'm outside the front door. Leaving now.'

'Good, good.' Her mother had a restlessness in her voice and Daisy envisioned her holding the phone between her ear and shoulder as she hurried about the house, trying to keep things straight the way she did when she was worried about something. 'You don't want to be hanging around for long. You want to get an early night. You've got a big day tomorrow.'

Daisy bit her tongue. After all the preparation and the sleepless nights over the last fortnight, she was hardly going to forget the significance of the next day. Tomorrow morning was opening day at The Coffee Shop on the Canal.

The coffee shop was going to be the answer to all Daisy's problems. While she owned the *September Rose* outright, boats still came with all sorts of costs, like mooring fees and electricity bills. She needed a new job, and preferably one that didn't involve too much travelling. At the same time, Wildflower Lock desperately needed a place where all the dog walkers and paddle boarders could grab themselves a cup of coffee. And so, a little over three weeks ago, she had got to work renovating a small area of the boat into a takeaway coffee shop. It had been non-stop, using every daylight hour to make sure it was properly fitted out. And now the time was almost ready to open up the hatch and start serving customers.

'Don't worry, Mum, I'm heading back now.'

'Good, good. Okay, darling. I'll see you soon.'

As she hung up the phone, Daisy took one more step back onto the pavement and placed her hand on the front door of the flat. It was strange to grow so attached to nothing more than bricks and mortar, but she had made memories in this home. Good memories.

But now it was time she moved on.

As she drove away from London toward Wildflower Lock, Daisy considered her to-do list for the following day. Like writing out a price list on the chalkboard and checking that she had enough change for a float. Despite her mother's love of food, and lifelong career as a chef, it had never been Daisy's dream to run a coffee shop. But since the idea had struck, she felt – for the first time she could remember – that she had found a role in life into which she could truly see herself settling.

The car journey was swift. After parking up, Daisy stepped outside and breathed in.

It wasn't hard to see how the lock had got its name. All along the towpath, the hedgerows were alive with colour, from the whites of cow parsley to the yellows of buttercups and the soft pinks of dog roses. And every day it changed. A covering of clouds could transform the tones of the water from vibrant blue to the darkest of greys, while swans and herons and all other forms of waterfowl made the waterway a hive of activity. And that was before you considered the people.

'Afternoon.' Daisy raised her hand to a dog walker, who was making their way through the gate.

'Afternoon.'

A few metres later, she greeted one of the paddle boarders out today.

'Have a good evening.'

'You too.' They offered a brief nod.

The people who visited the lock were some of the friendliest Daisy had encountered. Every day, she would find herself embroiled in a conversation with someone, from canal volunteers to hikers who wanted to tell her all about their day, and though the walk from the car park to the *September Rose* was only a couple of hundred feet, sometimes it could take as much as half an hour to make the distance. But despite the friendliness of the visitors, the same could not be said for the people who lived on the water – at least not all of them.

'Afternoon.' Daisy raised her hand to a man standing on the back of his boat. Given how close he lived to the towpath entrance, and the fact that his boat roof was covered with plants which needed constant attention, Daisy saw this gentleman at least twice a day, if not more. And yet so far, despite trying her hardest, she had not managed a single conversation with him. 'Your begonias are looking beautiful,' she added, hoping today might be the day.

With a small grunt, he ducked his head back down and continued to water his plants.

'Nice to see you too,' she muttered under her breath.

As excited as Daisy was for her upcoming life on Wildflower Lock, it was proving harder to find her place amongst the long-time boat owners than she'd expected. It probably didn't help that until three months ago, she hadn't known the first thing about living on the water. She hadn't known the difference between a pump-out or a cassette toilet, or why you needed to get hulls blacked, or even what a tiller was. The learning curve had been steep, and she was getting there, but obviously not quick enough to make good with all the locals.

Currently, one of the only boat owners who would greet her with more than a passing hello was Yvonne, an elderly lady who owned a beautifully painted boat called the *Ariadne*, which was moored on the other side of the canal.

Yvonne had the dress sense of a seventies' *Vogue* model and every time Daisy caught sight of her, standing on the boat with her purple ombre hair, she couldn't help but feel a deep sense of respect for this lady with a penchant for crystals and incense sticks. She was one of the longest-standing residents of Wild-flower Lock and had lived on this stretch of the canal so long, she'd been there back when Daisy's father first bought the *September Rose*. It was Yvonne who'd told Daisy about her past, or at least pieces of it. The rest she had insisted Daisy heard from her mother. Something they were still working through.

The other person who Daisy would regularly spend time with was her neighbour, Theo.

As the owner of the neighbouring boat, *Narrow Escape*, Theo was the first resident Daisy had met on the lock. Rather than the standard introduction you would expect, she had walked in on him naked in his home, though in her defence, it was her first time on the canal, and she'd thought it was her boat she was on. Needless to say, he had been less than impressed. Yet the pair had worked through their rocky start and formed a solid friendship, which had almost progressed to something more.

Right now, they were still at the just-good-friends stage and Daisy was perfectly fine with that. It had been several years since her last relationship, but the emotional scars had only just healed and the last thing she wanted to do was open them all up again by rushing into something. No matter how much her friends tried to badger her.

Sensing that today might not be the day to strike up a conversation with any more locals, Daisy carried on down the towpath towards her boat.

The *September Rose* was a long way from that dusty, forgotten vessel she had first inherited. Now painted a light, duck-egg blue, with a freshly blacked hull, it was hard not to feel an immense sense of pride every time she looked at it. Often, she would stop and take a photo, noting how the light reflected off the top so she could save the image for a painting at a later date, although this time, when the boat came into view, Daisy stopped and squinted at the figure in front of it. Then, realising her eyes were not playing tricks on her, she hurried down the path.

'Mum, what are you doing here?'

It had been four months since Daisy had inherited the *September Rose*, and during that time, her mother had visited exactly zero times. It was tough. While Wildflower Lock was a fresh start for Daisy, for Pippa, it was the opposite. This was the place she had fallen in love with Daisy's father, Johnny, and where they had first lived after Daisy was born. But there were plenty of bleak memories alongside the happy ones. Like how difficult and lonely her mother had found life with a newborn, and how at one point, when it felt like there was no way to escape that loneliness at Wildflower Lock, she had left her family to go chasing a dream.

'This isn't a bad time, is it?' Her mother moved forward and hugged her.

'Of course not. I just don't understand what you're doing here. Or why you didn't say you were coming?'

'My daughter's starting her own business. I had to come down here at some point. I was going to put it off until your opening tomorrow, but then I worried you might be busy, so I thought it better to visit now. I'll come down tomorrow too, of course, but I just needed to see the place once before then.' Her mother stopped talking and turned in a circle, slowly taking in the view. 'It's so strange. So much of it's the same. But it's aged. It's aged a lot. The canal, the lock. It's all got older. Though I suppose we both have.'

Daisy nodded, unsure of what to say next. She and her mother had once been as thick as thieves, but when the truth about Daisy's father had come to light, it had forced a wedge between them. Now they were rebuilding their relationship bit by bit, but it took time.

'Do you want to come aboard?' She reached into her bag for her keys, though her mother quickly shook her head.

'No, thank you. Not yet. You don't mind, do you?' Her voice was growing faster, the more stressed she became.

'No, Mum, it's fine. You don't have to do that if you don't want.'

Her mother nodded again, this time focusing her gaze through the window of the *September Rose*. Daisy couldn't help but wonder what she was thinking. After all, it had been her marital home and, most likely, the place where Daisy was conceived. There had to be some good memories about the place.

'Oh, I forgot why I came. I made you these.' Her mother reached down beside her and picked up two large carrier bags. 'I made scones.'

'Scones?'

'And a Victoria sponge. I know you're planning on just selling tea and coffee at the moment, but people love a slice of cake, and I thought it might help bring you a few more customers.'

'Mum, you didn't have to do that.'

'I know, but it's fine.'

'You shouldn't have.'

The issue wasn't just that Daisy hadn't planned on selling any baked goods, but that she didn't know how she was going to afford them. If she was going to run this coffee shop properly, then anything she sold had to be bought as a business expense, even if that was a Victoria sponge from her mum. And the fact was, there was no spare cash left in the kitty. She had already used her credit card to buy a decent coffee machine, knowing the deposit from her flat would pay it off when it came through, and Theo had put the hatch in as cheaply as possible, but there were still costs involved, like the hinges and the lock and the paper cups and sugar stirrers. The last thing she wanted was to owe people before the coffee shop had brought in any money.

'It's not a problem. I was going to do some baking, anyway. And you never know, maybe if it works out, I can cut down my hours at the restaurant and bake for you full time.' She laughed, as if she had made a joke, though Daisy couldn't help but wonder if there was an element of truth in what she had said. She had wanted her mother to slow down her hours and the restaurant for a while now, but her mother had been insistent she needed the work. Maybe this cafe could benefit them both.

Daisy was about to say as much when a figure appeared on the stern of the boat behind her. For a second, her eyes locked there, his silhouette cast in long shadows from the low summer sun. Then, realising she was staring, she cleared her throat and smiled broadly.

'Theo.'

## 2

Before she had met Theo, Daisy could never have imagined herself dating a guy with a man-bun, and even now she thought 50 per cent of the men wearing them only chose that style because they couldn't be bothered to get their hair cut. But the look suited Theo. More than that: it looked good on him.

As normal, he was dressed in a worn t-shirt and a pair of jeans, and as normal, somehow, he made it look effortlessly stylish. Standing as he was, with the background of trees and the water behind him, he looked like those men in the dark and moody adverts in magazines, who wore a two-hundred-pound white t-shirt with a pair of dark boxer shorts and a scowl.

Not that she was thinking about Theo in his boxers.

'So are you going to introduce us?' Her mother's voice brought Daisy back to the moment.

'Theo.' Daisy hastily tried to swallow back her embarrassment at so blatantly staring. 'This is my mum, Pippa. Mum, this is Theo, my neighbour.'

With an impressive leap, Theo jumped from the stern of his

boat onto the towpath. Then, in three long strides, was standing beside them, his hand stretched out to her mother.

'It's a pleasure to meet you.' A line like that could have been cheesy, but the way Theo spoke made it sound genuine. And it probably was. Never had Daisy known someone so happy to help other people and want nothing in return. Without him, the *September Rose* would likely still be an empty shell and Daisy would be facing months more work ahead of her. But Theo had been determined to help, and even this last week, had sourced her a full-size, second-hand fridge in perfect working condition, which was now chock-full of milk for all the impending cappuccinos and lattes.

'So you're the great Theo I've heard so much about?' Her mother smiled slyly. 'I've never known Daisy talk about a young man quite so enthusiastically. Not for a long time.'

'Mum,' Daisy hissed, sounding far more like a teenager than she'd hoped.

Yet Theo beamed at the remark.

'You talk about me, do you? That's nice to hear.'

'I talk about you because you helped with the boat, that's all.'

'Of course. I believe you.' With a smirk that matched her mother's, Theo carried on talking to Pippa. 'So, have you come to see the place before the big opening?'

'Just briefly.'

'Well, has Daisy shown you the hatch we put in? It's pretty impressive, even if I say so myself.'

'By we, he means he,' Daisy interjected. 'Theo is the one who put the hatch on the side on the boat. Just like he's the one who sorted the electricity and plumbing so I have room for the coffee machine. That would be why I've mentioned his name a lot.'

'What can I say? I like a project. Have you been inside yet?'

Her mother's easy smile faltered, and had this not been hopelessly obvious, Daisy would have shot Theo a major glare. It was a miracle her mother had come down to the lock at all. The last thing Daisy wanted was for Theo to push her too far and scare her off from ever coming back.

'Actually, I can't stay,' she said, her smile back in place. 'But I'll be back tomorrow. Probably not until late in the afternoon, though. I've got the breakfast shift. Do you know what time you're going to be open until?'

A surge of anxiety, far greater than the question warranted, rushed through Daisy. In less than twenty-four hours, she was going to open the coffee shop. It didn't feel real.

'I've checked the weather report, and it still says it's going to be dry all day, though it now says cloudy in the morning.' Since taking over the *September Rose*, she'd been checking the weather report fastidiously; a rainy weekend could entirely upset plans for painting and renovating or even just taking the boat out. But since starting work on the coffee shop, her need to check it had become borderline obsessive. After all, bad weather would mean fewer customers.

'I plan on opening as soon as I'm dressed and ready in the morning. Half past seven is the aim, to try to get the early-morning dog walkers. Then I guess I'll be open until people stop walking the lock. Or I run out of tea bags, but considering I bought two hundred, I can't see that happening.'

If there were people on the canal wanting teas and coffees, then she was going to be the one to sell them. That was all she knew. And if that meant standing at her hatch, with the coffee machine blasting out steam behind her for twelve hours straight, then that was what she was going to do.

'Fabulous, then I'll pop down after lunch,' her mother said, shifting her feet. 'Now, I should definitely get going.'

Daisy pulled her in for a hug. 'Thank you again for these.' She gestured to the scones and cakes. 'Let me walk you back to the car park.'

Her mother waved the offer away. 'No, don't be silly. You've got enough to get on with here. And don't stay up too late. Theo, it was lovely to meet you at least.'

'You too,' Theo replied.

A minute later, her mother was walking away, leaving Theo and Daisy alone.

Since a near-kiss incident less than a month before, Daisy had been doing everything she could to keep thoughts of Theo strictly platonic. But it wasn't always easy. As much as she tried to insist to the girls – and herself – that they were better off as friends, there were moments when she struggled to remember that. Like a couple of nights ago, when they had been laughing, then caught one another's eye, and the laughter had suddenly stopped and they were left gazing at one another. Or all the moments where his hand brushed up against her, causing her pulse to skyrocket and her heart to hammer against her ribs. And moments like this, where the two of them were left on their own, and her adrenaline would surge with the fear that he might turn around and disappear and leave her on her own, when all she wanted was for them to stay together, talking and laughing.

'So, are you all set up for tomorrow?' His voice broke the silence that was blooming between them.

'I think so. There's not that much to set up, if I'm honest.'

'Well, if that's the case, fancy joining me for a sloe gin?'

'Sloe gin? I thought you were a beer drinker?'

'I am, but Nicholas on the *Jeanette* has given me a vat load and keeps asking me what I think of it. I figured it's easier just to try it and give him a truthful answer than keep smiling politely. And I've got some focaccia I made yesterday.'

'Day-old focaccia and sloe gin that some random guy on a boat made? Now there's an offer that's hard to refuse.'

Her voice was laden with sarcasm, but in truth, it was hard to refuse. An evening of drinking with Theo, laughing at the stories he told her and distracting her from all the nerves she had about the following day was exactly the remedy she needed. And if there was one person she should celebrate handing in her flat keys and officially moving into the boat with, it should be Theo. After all, without him she wouldn't even be here. But no matter how deep her desire to say yes, she shook her head.

'Actually, I'm going to take a rain check. Is that okay? I should have an early night. And I've got this painting I've been working on too. I thought I might finish it tonight.'

'Sounds intriguing. Well, the offer's there if you want it. You know I'm not going anywhere.'

Offering him a smile, when what she desperately wanted to do was hug him, Daisy stepped on board the *September Rose*.

# 3

When Daisy had first entered the *September Rose*, it had been like stepping onto the set of a horror movie. Along with the cobwebs and dust so thick you could write your name in it, it was chock-full of boxes, most of which contained junk, but one or two had some hidden treasures. Sentimentally, at least.

There had been the box full of letters and cards that her father had sent to her over the years, which, unbeknownst to Daisy, her mother had returned to sender before they'd even been opened. Those had been the start of unravelling the truth about her past, and she still hadn't opened every one. After the first day of finding them, she had found it too painful to read her father's words without being flooded by a deep sense of guilt that she hadn't done more to repair their relationship. Deep down, she knew it wasn't her fault; she had only been a teen when he died. But that didn't stop the hurt or the anger she felt at her mother every time she thought about those cards. So that box was kept in the bottom of the wardrobe, covered with shoes and handbags, ready for a time when Daisy felt ready to address them ʒin.

However, the other box that struck a chord with her was the one packed to the brim with art supplies. And she delved into that box nearly every day.

For the longest time, Daisy had dreamed of becoming an artist. In particular, a children's book illustrator. In her head, she had weaved together hundreds of stories full of charming and humorous characters that she would bring to life with the strokes of her paintbrush. But a couple of bad decisions and a severe bout of cold feet meant that she had stepped away from that dream a long time ago. Recently, however, since finding that box of paints and papers, and realising the connection it made to a father she had never known, she had taken it up again.

The hobby hadn't been plain sailing. Her first attempt at getting her work shown in a gallery had resulted in utter humiliation, which in turn, caused her to crash the *September Rose*. Yet unlike before, when one false start would have seen her quit, she hadn't packed it all away. Instead, she kept going. Even if she wasn't going to be the great publishing success she had once hoped, art was part of her, and there was no denying it any more. So her dining table, which she had sanded down and varnished herself after Theo had salvaged it from another restoration project, was now covered in paint brushes and watercolour paper with stacks of dried paintings piled up on the chairs.

For a moment or two, she looked at the table and considered sitting down. Her words to Theo had been half true. There was a painting she had been working on, only she'd finished it the night before. The image of a woodpecker perched on a tree trunk above a gently flowing river was one of her favourites so far. It had been tricky to get the sheen on the bird's head and wings the way she wanted it, but for a first attempt, it really wasn't that bad. But she wasn't going to try again today. What she wanted to do was get everything ready for the morning and make the *September Rose* look as good as possible.

Although The Coffee Shop on the Canal was a takeaway business, Daisy knew what people were like when they walked down the towpath, peering in through the windows, trying to get a glimpse of life inside. She had been the same before she became a boat owner. The last thing she wanted was someone to look inside and see a load of mess, particularly if it put them off buying teas and coffees from her, and so she got about tidying up, putting items away, sweeping the floor and wiping down all the surfaces. With that done, she considered the scones and cakes her mum made. After a quick browse online, looking at a couple of local restaurants to work out how much to charge, she wrote the prices on the chalkboard. When that was done, she stood back and observed her home.

It was strange how quickly it had become that. Not a boat she inherited or a renovation project, but her home. The thought swelled within her. She may not have her friends on her doorstep, or even be on speaking terms with most of the neighbours, but Wildflower Lock was her home.

As she sat down on the sofa, she browsed through the string of messages that had pinged through when she had been tidying. Bex and Claire had both sent emoji-filled texts wishing her luck and apologising again for not being able to make it to her opening day, though they assured her they would be down later in the week, if not the weekend, to show their support. Daisy fired back a couple of smiling emojis in return. Truthfully, she was glad they would not be here when she first opened. They had both come down several times in the last fortnight, so Daisy could test her coffee-making skills, but making cappuccinos for a couple of friends when you're chatting about your lives and have all the time in the world was a very different situation to doing it with a queue of paid customers waiting. It was bound to take a couple of days to iron out any kinks, so hopefully, by the time the weekend rolled around, the coffee shop would be running like clockwork.

There was also a message from her old manager, Amanda, wishing her luck.

The last message was from Theo.

She opened it up to find a photo of his coffee table, upon which was a slice of bread and a glass of a deep-purple drink, which Daisy assumed with sloe gin.

It's really nice. Are you sure I can't tempt you?

He had written beneath the image.

Daisy stared at the photograph, only for her stomach to rumble in response. She had meant to pick up something from the bakery beneath her old flat before she left London, but her mother's phone call had distracted her. She hadn't eaten anything since breakfast.

Without bothering to reply, she picked up her phone and keys and slipped out of the *September Rose*.

At the *Narrow Escape*, she knocked on the door, although she stepped inside without waiting for Theo to invite her in. This was the way the pair of them worked now, constantly moving back and forth between each other's boat – Theo even had a key for hers.

'I knew you wouldn't be able to say no.' A grin spread across his face as he handed Daisy a small glass.

'Looks like blackcurrant cordial.' She lifted it to her nose and inhaled. 'It smells like it, too.' After another sniff, she took a tentative sip. 'That is good. I don't know what I was expecting, but it wasn't this.'

'I know, I don't know how much he makes or where he gets the sloes from, but he had two plastic crates worth of the stuff when I went past.'

'Nicholas, remind me again, which one that is? I think I need to ask for some.'

'He's the old guy who has the *Jeanette*. Right by the car park.'

It didn't take Daisy long to recall the man who would duck down into his plants each time she tried to make conversation.

'Oh, well, that's out. He shoots daggers at me every time I say hello.'

Theo took both glasses and moved across to the living area, prompting Daisy to follow.

'Don't take it personally. Honestly, all you've got to do is see through one winter here and they'll love you. You forget, we get a lot of seasonal people who holiday here and cause complete havoc. As soon as people realise you're not one of those, they'll be far more welcoming.'

'I hope so.'

Daisy stared into her glass. Why was it that making friends got so much harder as you got older? When you were a child, it was easy. All you had to do was like the same game in the playground or the same television show as someone else and you could strike up a conversation and declare yourselves best friends within twenty minutes. Adulthood was a whole lot harder.

'Have you checked the weather report?' Theo's voice broke Daisy's train of thought. 'There was something on the news about a storm coming in off the North Sea, or somewhere.'

Daisy laughed. 'Trust me, I have checked the weather report at least a dozen times. My phone thinks I want to train as a meteorologist. The weather is going to be fine.'

'Good. I wouldn't want anything to upset tomorrow. Also, while we're on the subject of the coffee shop, I was thinking, why don't you sell some of your paintings from it too?'

Daisy rolled her eyes. Theo had been the one to persuade her to take her paintings to an art gallery in the first place, which led to complete humiliation when she crashed her boat. Most people would have taken that as a sign not to bring up the topic again. But Theo wasn't most people.

'I'm hardly going to put paintings on the menu,' she said, being deliberately facetious.

'That's not what I meant and you know it. You could hang them on the walls behind you and put them in places where they're visible. If nothing else, they'd be a talking point, but I'm sure you'd sell some too.'

'I love your optimism, but let's tackle one thing at a time, okay?'

'Fair enough. I take it you want some focaccia, too?'

Theo's bread-making skills were almost as good as her mother's, not that Daisy would ever say as much to her. Now she'd lost the bonus of free pastries from the bakery below her flat, Daisy was going to make the most of whatever Theo offered her.

'I will, but I'm just having this one drink. Then I need to get back.'

'Oh yes, the good old one-drink line. How about we use the time to test your coffee knowledge again?'

While Daisy was the one opening the coffee shop, Theo was the coffee expert, and he had spent several hours between jobs, and over many cups of tea, trying to impart his knowledge onto her. Knowledge that Daisy now felt she had mastered.

She put down her drink and straightened her back.

'Go on then. Test me.'

'Cappuccino?'

'Really? You want to start that easy? Fine, one third coffee, hot milk and foam. Unless it's a double shot.'

'Fine, that was easy. Latte?'

'Single shot espresso, filled to the top with steamed milk only. No foam.'

'Macchiato?'

Daisy smiled. This was one that had caught her out at the beginning, but it hadn't been that tough to learn. 'Single shot of espresso with an equal amount of foam.'

She was feeling smugly confident now. After all, she'd not only practised saying what they were, but making them too. In the last three weeks, her caffeine intake had reached a level her doctors would probably be less than happy about, but it was all in the name of the business.

'Fine then. Dirty chai?'

Daisy's smile dropped.

'Dirty chai? I don't even know what a chai is. I don't think I'm selling that. People won't ask for that, will they?'

Theo's smirk flickered and his eyes flashed with guilt.

'Sorry, that one was probably a step too far. No. My bet is cappuccinos, Americanos and lattes are all you get asked for. And teas too.'

Daisy nodded. The smugness she had been feeling only seconds before had been replaced by a nervous churning which refused to fade, even as she finished her drink and Theo steered the conversation onto a different topic. Even when she hugged him goodnight and headed back to the *September Rose*, it was hard to ignore the gnawing, grinding away at the back of her mind.

As someone who had worked in several different places in her lifetime, Daisy was well versed in the new-job jitters that arose the night before the first day. But the fluttering that filled her abdomen was unlike anything she had experienced before. This wasn't just some job she could walk away from if she didn't get on with the manager or found the work tedious. This was her life, her livelihood. And she needed it to work.

**4**

---

Daisy bolted upright, her pulse racing. She had set three separate alarms to be sure she didn't oversleep and had checked several times that her phone was fully charged, yet here she was, already awake, and not one of them had gone off. When she'd made a decent day's takings, she was going to buy herself one of those big, metal alarm clocks. The type with a metal clanger that people had used for decades before phones had come into play.

Her heart hammered as she reached across onto the bedside table for her phone, only to knock it on to the floor.

'For crying out loud.' She dropped down, dreading to think about how much morning trade she had missed. So many dog walkers came first thing in the morning, before they had to jet off for work and there was no chance of her serving them now. Why hadn't she showered last night? Or at least sorted out what clothes she was going to wear? With her mind whirring, she picked up her phone and tapped the screen to see the time displayed there in full brightness. Six-thirty.

She tapped it again to make sure that really was the time,

then opened the alarm app. There they were, all three alarms, ready and waiting.

With a heavy sigh, Daisy sat back on the bed. With all the butterflies that had been churning through her, it was a miracle she'd gone to sleep at all, and now she was up half an hour before she intended.

Deciding to start the day earlier than expected, she moved toward the bathroom, only to stop. Life on the boat was always filled with noises, be it families enjoying a day out in the sun, an early-morning dawn chorus, or the constant rush of water as it moved through the canal, but there was something about the rhythmic sound that caught Daisy's attention. At first, she thought it was the lock. Even when it was closed, water flowed over and through it, creating a constant background babbling to her daily life, but this was different. It sounded like the lock, only it was coming from directly above her.

'You have to be joking.' Daisy snatched back the curtain, only for her stomach to plummet. Rain. 'It's fine. It can still be fine,' she said, trying to comfort herself as she grabbed her dressing gown and raced to the back door. After all, it could just be a shower. An exceptionally late April shower in July that would be gone as soon as it started. That was what she hoped until she opened the front door and stepped out onto the hull.

All above her was a thick blanket of dense, grey clouds, through which not even the smallest sliver of blue could be seen. Trees whipped their branches back and forth and ducks huddled within the rushes, while from off in the distance came the far-off rumble of thunder. This wasn't normal rain. This was a full storm.

With a steeling breath, she stepped backed into the boat and forced herself to breathe slowly. It was six-thirty. An hour she rarely saw any more. She just needed to keep calm. She would fix herself breakfast, have a shower, then see what the weather looked like in an hour's time. Or two, even. After all, eight-thirty would be a perfectly reasonable time to open up the coffee shop.

* * *

Two hours later, the rain continued to pour in great torrents that splashed up the side of the boat.

Daisy watched the weather report on her television.

'As you can see, there's some unexpected bad weather moving in from the east.' The weatherman pointed to a map of the United Kingdom which zoomed in almost directly above Wildflower Lock. 'What we've got here is a high-pressure system that's pushing in from the continent, causing heavy rain and strong winds across Essex and the surrounding areas. It's quite unusual, folks, especially for this time of year, but don't worry, it should pass soon.'

'Like I'd believe anything you say any more.'

She dropped back onto the sofa and clicked off the television. For a minute, she stayed there, staring through her large windows at the mass of grey that greeted her. No one in their right mind would leave the house in this weather. Not unless they had to.

A flicker of hope lit within her. Dog walkers. Dog walkers still had to leave the house.

The serving hatch was at the far end of the *September Rose*, in what had once been a cabin with two narrow bunk beds. Now the beds were no more, and a sink had been placed on one wall, while a large, state-of-the-art coffee machine now took up most of the counter space. When the hatch was closed, the *September Rose* looked like any other wide berth boat, but when those wooden windows were opened up, the inside was painted in a deep shade of red, which contrasted with the boat's duck-egg exterior. Theo had also crafted a small awning which folded outwards, designed to offer a minimal amount of protection from the elements. But it was no match for a day like today.

It took more strength than ever before to battle against the wind and clip the hatch doors open, but with several grunts and groans, Daisy finally got it done. The chalk board sign she'd created to fix to the outside had to stay in the dry to stop her penmanship sliding straight off in the rain and, given that a slight change in breeze would cause the water to come directly into the open hatch, she also placed a towel down by her feet, and wore a waterproof jacket.

In less than ten minutes, she was set up and waiting for her first customer. And it didn't take long for them to come, suitably dressed in wet weather clothes and wellington boots.

'Morning. Can I have a cup of tea and a slice of that Victoria sponge cake?'

'No.' Daisy's response was immediate.

'No?' Theo pouted.

'No. You can't be my first customer. My first customer has to be real.'

Theo raised his eyebrows until they were lost in the hood of his coat.

'I am real. I'll pay you. See, I brought cash and everything.'

He lifted his wallet out of his pocket as proof, although Daisy's pout remained firmly in place.

'You have a perfectly good coffee machine at home. And tea bags, and everything else. And I wouldn't let you have a disposable cup out of principle.'

A smile twitched on Theo's lips.

'Okay, at least that's something I agree with. Can I at least get a slice of cake? I was going to take some homemade bread with me for lunch. Only someone came over last night and ate it all.'

Daisy scowled. 'Fine.'

She cut him a slice of her mother's Victoria sponge, which she placed on a napkin and handed to him.

'Thank you. Now, how much is that?'

'It's fine. It's on the house.'

'Are you sure?'

'Really, after you just said that I ate your lunch? Besides, if this doesn't clear up, I won't have anyone else to sell it too, anyway.'

'Well, it's delicious,' Theo said through a mouthful of cake, which he ate with his hood tipped forward to prevent it from getting wet.

'I thought you said you were eating that for lunch? It's barely breakfast time.'

'So? You can't have a better start to the day than cake.'

Daisy groaned and shook her head. She knew exactly what Theo was trying to do: playing the fool in an attempt to distract her from how disastrous her opening was. But just as she could tell his aim, he could tell it wasn't working.

'Look, don't get stressed.' He lowered the remaining chunk of cake as he spoke. 'Just think of it as a nice soft opening, that's all. And I'm sure it's going to get better. I've got to head to work now, but I'll pop back and see you later.'

As he spoke, a gust of wind blew his hood from his head.

'No, I'm not stressed at all,' Daisy muttered.

As optimistic as Theo had been, the weather didn't get any better, and according to the app on her phone, it wasn't going to.

It wasn't the case that people weren't coming to buy teas and coffees from her; there weren't people coming to the lock at all.

When lunchtime rolled around, Daisy had seen a total of four people walking along the side of the canal, all of them with dogs. Two of them had umbrellas in one hand and a dog lead in the other and wouldn't have been able to hold a cup of tea, had they wanted to. One of them didn't even glance in her direction as she said hello, but that was probably because the wind was howling too hard for them to hear her. Then, at lunchtime, the winds changed, and brought a full sheet of rain straight in through her open hatch. At that point, she admitted defeat.

Flopped on her sofa, Daisy stared out the window and took in all the different shades of grey and purple in the sky. Normally, she would love a view like the one she was gazing at. All those deep tones created exactly the type of scene she liked to paint. And with an unexpected free afternoon, she could probably get a lot of painting done. But her mind was too preoccupied to think about art.

Still busy debating whether to head back to bed and pretend the day had never happened, she was distracted by her phone buzzing beside her. *Mum*, flashed up on the screen.

Daisy hesitated. The last thing she wanted was her mother's sympathy, but then again, maybe she deserved it.

'Hey Daisy Bear, how's it going? Can you talk? You're not too busy, are you?'

Daisy laughed out loud. 'No, Mum. I'm definitely not too busy.'

'Oh no, is the rain keeping people away? That's a shame, dear.'

*It was more than just a shame*, Daisy wanted to say. This coffee shop was her livelihood, and if she didn't make it work, she had no idea what she was going to do.

'Maybe it'll pick up later when I come down. You know, I've told everyone at work about it. They're all very excited.'

Daisy stared back outside at the impenetrable swathe of clouds that seemed to be getting even more dense. If it hadn't been for the leaves on the trees and the fact she knew better, she'd think it was the middle of winter, not one week away from the schools starting their summer holidays.

'Mum, there's no need to come down today. Honestly, it's not a good day for it.'

'Don't be silly, of course I want to come and see you.'

'Wait until the weather's better. You don't want to travel all the way down here and just be stuck inside. Unless you want to sit in the boat for a couple of hours.'

It was probably slightly manipulative. Given how her mother hadn't been able to step onboard the *September Rose* the afternoon before, Daisy knew there was no way she was going to want to feel trapped in it.

'If you're sure, love?'

Daisy breathed a sigh of relief.

'I am. According to the weatherman, this storm will blow through tonight, so tomorrow is meant to be much nicer. Fingers crossed, I'll get a bit busier.'

'Okay, my darling. Well, keep your chin up. We'll speak soon.'

Keeping her chin up was not as easy as anticipated, and by the time the evening rolled around, and Theo knocked on her door, Daisy had sunk herself into a deep well of misery and was elbow-deep in the bag of marshmallows she had bought for the hot chocolates.

'I'm going to assume you didn't hear me knocking, although you're only six feet away from the door?' he said as he stepped into the boat.

'Sorry.' Daisy groaned as she sat up. 'I was in my own world.'

'The soft opening didn't go so well then?' He took off his waterproof jacket, which was already causing a puddle by his feet. After hanging it up and removing his shoes, he crossed the boat and took a seat next to her.

'This is a ridiculous idea,' Daisy moped, voicing the words she had been afraid to say aloud. 'I have zero business experience. Why on earth would I think this was a good idea?'

'It is a good idea,' Theo stressed. 'A great idea. It was just terrible timing.'

Daisy huffed.

'It looks like you had a couple of customers at least.' He nodded towards the kitchen. 'Half the Victoria sponge has gone.'

Daisy scowled. 'I'm a comfort eater. So basically, I've made a loss. And I'll probably make a loss tomorrow and the next day and the next day—'

'Don't do that.' Theo placed his hand on hers. 'Tomorrow is going to be better. And even if it's not, this is a business. This is what happens in business. You have good days and bad days, but the only way you can make it work long-term is by not giving up. Think of all the things we'd be missing in our lives if people gave up at the first hurdle. The lightbulb to start with. You know it took Edison over a thousand attempts to make the first working lightbulb?'

Daisy emitted a strange harrumphing noise. Theo was right, giving up didn't help you succeed in life, but maybe she wasn't meant to succeed. She was definitely much better at giving up. She had given up at art school after one term. And she had given up on displaying her paintings after one rejection. Some people were meant to keep trying and succeed, and other people were meant to fail. And she was one of the latter.

'How about, to keep your mind off this, we think of something more fun to talk about?' Theo straightened his posture as he spoke.

'Okay, but I don't know what you can say that's going to distract me from how terrible I feel.'

'Well, why don't we talk about when you're finally going to let me take you on a date?'

## 5

Theo had definitely taken her mind off the failing coffee shop, that was for certain. As he left his question hanging in the air, he looked at her expectantly, awaiting her answer. His eyebrows were raised and the soft beads of rainwater that had slipped past his hood shimmered in his hair. When would she be willing to go on a date with him? That was what he had asked – outright and with no room for misinterpretation. And Daisy was terrified. Not because she didn't want to, but because of what going on that date could end up meaning.

A definite tightening in her throat was coupled with a raise in both her temperature and heart rate.

'Theo, this is not a good time for either of us. You know that.'

'What you mean is you think it's too soon since Heather and I broke up. Despite the fact I've told you I'm over her.'

Daisy pressed her lips together. It was hard to say no, given that he was spot on.

'You two were together for a long time. You had an entire life planned together. You don't just get over those things in a couple of months. I know that. I've been there.'

'No, you haven't. You had your heart broken when a relationship unexpectedly ended. This is not the same as that. Heather and I were drifting apart for years. It just took something else to make us see that.'

The way he looked at her as he said the words *something else*, made her stomach tighten into knots. He didn't mean something else. He meant her. They had nearly kissed when he and Heather were still together, more than once. The first had been when she had literally fallen on him after cleaning out the water tank on the *September Rose*, but she couldn't blame clumsiness on the second time, and she'd still not forgiven herself for that moment. For nearly kissing another woman's boyfriend.

'These things still take time to get over,' she insisted again. 'The fact that you won't even acknowledge that probably means you haven't even started grieving the relationship.'

As clichéd as she may have sounded, she believed what she was saying. No matter how relaxed and date-ready Theo felt he was, Daisy couldn't believe he didn't need more time to get his head straight around the breakup. The last thing she wanted was for them to be two months in, or with her heart on the line, only for him to decide that he and Heather weren't as over as he had thought. She'd had her heart crushed once and wasn't planning on ever feeling that way again.

'If this is something you're not interested in, then you can just say that.' Theo's eyes were locked straight onto her. 'But we spend a lot of time together, Daisy, and you can't pretend that we're just friends. You and I both know there's more to it than that.'

She couldn't hold his gaze any longer. She dipped her head and looked at her hands.

'I know it sounds like an excuse, but it's not. It isn't. Theo, the way I feel about you... I haven't felt that way for a long time.' Almost as if it was an involuntary action, she lifted her head back up and their eyes met again. She could feel the static building between them, her breath quivering in her lungs. It would take nothing to lean forward and plant her lips against his. Nothing to wrap her hands around the back of his neck and kiss away the stress of the day. But as the thought entered her head, she jerked away from him. Her pulse hammering. 'That's why I can't put my heart on the line. Not yet, because if you're not over Heather—'

'Which I am—'

'But if you're not. If she decides she wants to give things another try, and you decide you want to do that with her because you have history, or you and I are spending time together and you find out that it's her you wish you were talking to instead of me, then our friendship wouldn't recover from that. Theo, so much has changed for me in the last six months. Mum, Dad, my job, my house. I need to keep this friendship. I have to. Please, I need you to understand. It isn't that I don't want to be with you. But I don't want to be with you until I know I'm all there is for you.'

Rather than objecting, he wrapped an arm around her and pulled her into his chest. She wanted to resist, but she couldn't. His t-shirt was damp and he smelt of rain and the canal; she could breathe him in forever. Closing her eyes, she dropped her head onto his chest and allowed herself to feel the warmth of his body. She could have stayed there all night, but no sooner had she relaxed into him, he sat upright and pushed her back to an arm's length. This time when he looked at her, it was with extreme focus.

'So you're saying that we have to give this a deadline?'

'The business? Obviously. I've got until my savings run out, but I've already thought about signing up with a recruitment agent. Just to get on their books.'

'No, I don't mean the business.' Theo shook his head. 'I mean you and me. You want me to have some proper time after the breakup before I jump into this, so how much time are we talking? Daisy, I am crazy about you, and I am telling you than I am all in, but if you're going to make me wait two or three years or however long it took you to get over Paul, then I'm not sure I can promise you that.'

Daisy shook herself back into the conversation, which had taken a very different turn to what she had expected.

'No, of course I don't expect you to wait three years.' She realised how ridiculous the idea sounded as she spoke.

'Okay, then how long do you think a person should be broken up for before they consider another relationship? How long is the right amount of time, when you will be confident that I am over Heather and ready to explore what you and I have?'

Daisy bit down on her bottom lip, half wondering whether Theo was joking, but she knew him well enough to know that he was deadly serious. He wanted her to give him a deadline. But while she had been so focused on Theo needing time to grieve his previous relationship before the pair of them pursued their own, she'd not actually considered how much time that would be.

'I don't know. I guess about six months.'

'Six months?'

'That feels about right.' Daisy had zero data to base this on. She had taken three years to get over Paul, Bex was ready to move from a guy after one decent night out and Claire and Ian had been together since the start of time. Her knowledge of how long it took someone to be ready to date again was even weaker than her knowledge of narrow-boat engine mechanics, and that was saying something. Yet Theo was nodding his head, apparently in agreement with the suggestion.

'Well, Heather and I have already been broken up for a month, so it's more like five months.'

Daisy thought the timeframe over in her head. Five months.

On one hand, it didn't feel like that much time, but she knew how much could change in such a short period too. Her life had done a complete one-eighty in less. And more than once, too. Then again, putting a timeframe on when someone would be over a past relationship felt ridiculous. After all, you had to consider how long they had been together, who ended the relationship, why it had ended. With Theo, all those things felt like five months would be a minimum before he was actually ready to commit to somebody new.

As she pondered what to say next, Theo tilted his head to the side, studying her.

'Look, I promise you I'm ready for this. For us. But if you want to give it that bit of time, just to make sure, then I'm okay with that too. Trust me, you'll find out for yourself. There's only one person I'm hung up on.'

## 6

When Daisy went to sleep, her mind was still abuzz with thoughts of Theo. At least he'd kept his promise and distracted her from the disastrous first day of the cafe opening. All she could think about was how much she'd wanted to kiss him. And it hadn't been a one-off thing. Later that evening, when he'd said goodbye, she had reached up and almost kissed him instinctively and once again, she'd had to force herself to jerk away from him.

Several hours later, the memory was on repeat in her head, as she tried to justify her reaction. That was the way it was with friends, wasn't it? She wouldn't think twice about giving a hug to Bex and Claire, and while she'd never kissed them on the lips, she'd offered plenty of pecks on their cheeks. Theo had simply become a very close friend in a short space of time, that was all.

Still, her heart couldn't help but flutter as she thought about what Theo had said. How he would be waiting for her whenever she thought he was ready. The idea of a date with Theo, some-where in the not-too-distant future, was still on Daisy's mind as she finally fell asleep.

The next morning, it was the alarm that cut through her

dreams and provided a welcome relief to the stream of night-mares that had afflicted her. Nightmares about everything from the boat flooding to only having frogs to serve in her takeaway coffee cups had addled her sleep and, even though she was awake, she had to take a second to accept this was real life and none of those things had actually happened. For a moment, she lay in the bed and allowed herself to revel in the lightness that had come with Theo's company the previous evening, but then memories from the rest of the day flooded back. In particular, what a disaster The Coffee Shop on the Canal's first day had been.

Her stomach sank. She'd had such high expectations and met none of them. And now she was going to have to do it all over again.

She swung her feet off the edge of the bed, only to notice a sound coming from outside. Pausing, she tilted her head to the side, as if that would help her hear more clearly.

It was a familiar sound, though rather than rain hammering on the roof of the boat, as she had expected, this was much more welcome. Daisy May heard laughter.

Tentatively, she drew back a small section of the curtain, then a larger one still, until she looked outside.

There above her, with the sun blazing, was a bright-blue sky.

* * *

'See, I told you today would be a good day.' Theo smiled as he waited patiently in the queue to order a coffee she knew he could have made at home. But seeing him here made her beam. An actual queue had formed on the towpath, with real customers all lining up for drinks. And while there were only three people in said queue, and one of those was Theo, it was so much better than the previous day. Daisy's heart was already aching with pride.

'Are these scones homemade?' The woman at the front of the queue had first ordered a cappuccino, which Daisy had made immediately, only for her to add a latte to her order too. Though it would appear she still wasn't done.

'Yes. They're completely homemade. The Victoria sponge is too.'

'And do you serve the scones with jam and butter?'

Daisy internally cursed herself for not thinking of such a thing. 'No. I'm afraid we're out at the minute.'

The woman crinkled her nose. 'It's fine. I'll take one, anyway.'

'Great, so that's one cappuccino, one latte, and one homemade scone. That's a total of eight pounds, please.'

With that, the woman handed over the money before moving away, so the lady behind could place her order too.

The second woman in the queue wanted two cups of tea, which Daisy promptly made, though she let her add the milk herself. After all, the ratio of milk to tea was a very personal thing.

When she left, the only person who remained was Theo.

'Have you still got some of that Victoria sponge?' He leaned on the countertop as he spoke. Had it been any other customer, she might have been worried that it couldn't hold the weight, but Theo was the one who built it; she trusted he knew the strength of his workmanship. 'I think cake might be my favourite breakfast.'

'In that case, you're in luck.' She sliced him a portion and placed it onto a napkin before handing it over. 'That'll be two pounds fifty, please.'

Theo frowned. 'The last slice I got was on the house?'

'I know, but that was yesterday when I didn't have any

customers. I won't make any money if I let you have everything for free.'

Despite Daisy telling Theo that he now had to pay for his food, he grinned widely, his eyes glinting.

'I like this confident, businesswoman Daisy. Much better than the one that was moping around here yesterday.'

'It's only early. You never know, it might start raining again soon. I'm sure she'll come back if it does.'

'I don't think so. I think she's here to stay.' He glanced down the towpath, before looking back at her. 'I better get off, but I'll see you later. You can tell me how fantastically everything went.'

When she had been renovating the boat to get ready for The Coffee Shop on the Canal, Daisy had frequently envisioned how her days would go. Mostly, she saw herself wiling away the hours, chatting to customers, hearing about their days, or their dogs, or their grandchildren as she leisurely poured them cups of tea or expertly sprinkled marshmallows on top of hot chocolates. A steady stream of customers that would keep her busy, but never overwhelmed. That was what she had assumed she would face. The reality was a million miles away.

At one point, Daisy went forty minutes without seeing anybody at all, and then another ten minutes where the people who passed offered her only the most cursory of glances. The longer this silent spell continued, the more she worried the early-morning run was simply a fluke, and she was destined to have no more customers for the rest of the day, but then one person asked for a flat white, and another wanted a long black and all of a sudden, there was a mad rush, and a queue five people deep. At that point, Daisy was grateful she had gone for four extra-large bottles of milk, rather than the three she had originally planned, but she quickly learned she hadn't covered all her bases.

'What other sorts of milks do you have?' The woman had

appeared at the boat just after midday in full jogging get up, with a crop top, and sweatband across her head.

'I've got whole milk, semi-skimmed, skimmed, and soya.' Daisy was proud of remembering to put an alternative milk in for people who didn't do dairy. But the woman didn't look impressed by this.

'No oat milk? Rice milk? Soya leaves me terribly bloated.'

'No, sorry. Just dairy and soya,' she apologised.

'Fine, then in that to case, I'll take a latte without any milk.'

Daisy paused, needing to repeat the request. 'A latte without any milk? Like an espresso?'

Theo had gone through the various coffee types and this was never an option he had tested her on.

'A latte, with no milk. It's really not that difficult.'

In the end, Daisy gave the woman a long black coffee.

When she took it, she took a long sip and smiled.

'You see, it really wasn't that difficult, was it?'

Mostly, the customers were lovely and, as she expected, wanted to chat, either about themselves or the business, which they all thought was a wonderful idea. Although at four-thirty, when the paddle boarders arrived after work, and the sun was still gleaming above them, Daisy found herself facing a new problem.

'What cold drinks have you got?' a paddle boarder asked. His face flushed from the heat and the exercise, while sweat dripped down his temples.

'Cold drinks? I've got tap water?'

'What about cans? Any fizzy drinks?'

'I'm really sorry, we just sold out.' It was a small lie, she figured, as she placed fizzy drinks on the mental list of things she needed, along with jam and butter. Although as the day got longer, her brain felt less and less willing to remember them all.

Having left school after her A Levels, Daisy had worked hundreds if not thousands of long days, but in the last couple of years, she had spent those in an office. Sitting all day at a desk came with its own aches and pains. Her back, neck and shoulders suffered and by the end of a week, the cramps down the side of her body made her feel a good three decades older. But it was the soles of Daisy's feet that could take no more. She'd given up wearing actual shoes at about two o'clock and decided that, as the coffee shop was in her home, she would just wear slippers. But even that wasn't enough to ease the deep throbbing that went all the way from her toes to her heels. She didn't want to close, though, not when there were still customers to serve. Thankfully, the decision was made for her, when, at five-thirty, she ran out of coffee cups.

'That means I sold a hundred drinks,' she said to Theo that evening as he clinked a glass bottle against hers. 'I was not expecting that. Maybe on a weekend, but not on a Thursday. I'm going to need to go to the cash and carry tomorrow to get some more cups. A lot more. And some fizzy drinks. And I was thinking about getting a dog bowl and putting it out the front too, you know. Hopefully, it would encourage people to stop and give their dogs get a drink, then maybe they'd decide to want one too. What do you think?'

'I think you look incredibly attractive when you're this excited about something.'

Daisy scowled. 'That isn't very helpful. I'm talking to you about my business.'

'I'm sorry, you're right, but if you're talking about your business, why don't we talk about your paintings?'

'Theo—' Daisy's tone was a warning one. It would be great if he could go just one day without nagging about her art.

'Just hear me out. You've already gone to all this effort to set up the coffee shop, and it's brilliant. But how much do you make on a coffee? Two pounds? Two pounds fifty? All you need to do is display some of your paintings at the back. Coffee shops do it all the time. Restaurants too. If you only sell one a week for thirty pounds, that's over ten cups of coffee. Surely it's got to be worth it?'

Daisy considered the idea. She'd never thought of the money in that way, and she could already think of where to put them: on the back wall where there was room.

'Fine.'

'Sorry, what did you just say?'

'Fine. I will put them up for a week, just so you'll stop nagging me about it. But after that, I'm taking them down and this conversation is over.'

'Two weeks, and you can use the profit to take me out for dinner.'

Daisy tried to suppress her grin, but it was hard. So instead, she stretched her hand out to Theo's and shook it once firmly.

'You've got yourself a deal.'

# 7

Friday was just as beautiful as Thursday, and Daisy wished she could've opened up first thing. But with no coffee cups, there was no way she could sell any drinks, so instead, she was outside the cash and carry at the crack of dawn waiting for it to open.

Once inside, she filled a trolley with everything the customers had asked for, from fizzy drinks to small tubs of jam and little packs of butter that could go with the scones. Not that there were any of those left.

She had sent a message to her mother the night before and asked her to make a second batch for Saturday, with enough to get her through the weekend. Excited by the more positive news, her mother had replied with so many questions, Daisy had needed to call her to answer them all. But with no set timeframe for the arrival of the scones, Daisy also purchased some crisps and chocolate bars, along with a basket to put them in, in the hope they might bring in a couple more sales.

With her car boot full, Daisy headed back to start unloading. Since spending time at Wildflower Lock, she had spotted several people sporting wheeled shopping baskets, which they pushed and pulled down the towpath with their wares. It made sense. After carrying one load of shopping from the car park to the *September Rose*, her arms ached so much she nipped aboard the *Narrow Escape* to borrow Theo's wheelbarrow. The last thing she wanted was to injure her back before she had even served a customer.

Once everything was unloaded, an impressive feat of engineering was required to get everything from the fizzy drinks to the miniature packs of butter into the fridge. Some of her everyday groceries even had to be taken out and placed in boxes in the bedroom. Surprisingly, though, the sight of broccoli by her bedside table filled her with an immense sense of excitement. This wasn't just a pipe dream any more; it was happening.

The weather in the afternoon was better than she could have hoped for, with not a single cloud in the sky. Every person within a ten-mile radius seemed to be making the most of the hot weather. Shorts and t-shirts were the only garments on display – a drastic difference to only forty-eight hours ago, when raincoats and wellies were needed to be able to face the outside.

When Daisy opened up the hatch at midday, she already had a queue.

'Make that three lemonades,' a man said, taking a note out of his wallet. 'And do you have ice-creams?'

'We're all sold out.' Daisy used her tried and tested lie while trying to work out if there was somewhere she could put an extra freezer. This time, there were far fewer quiet spells, and only when her stomach growled so angrily that one of the customers heard did she realise it was three in the afternoon and she still hadn't had a chance to eat.

'This is fantastic, Daisy Bear.'

'Mum, what are you doing here? I thought you were working today?'

'Well, it was quiet and what's the point of being the most senior member in the kitchen if you can't take some time off now and again to support your baby girl?'

Her mother stood on the towpath with two large bags beside her, her face glowing with pride as her eyes moved up and down the boat, finally resting on the counter.

'And it looks like you need these, too.' She lifted the bags and hoisted them through the hatch. A quick peek inside revealed several dozen scones, not to mention three sponge cakes. 'I got to work last night. I didn't want you to run short.'

'Thanks, Mum.' Daisy placed the bags down as she hurriedly wiped the counters and checked the lids on the milk bottles. 'I'll sort out the money for it all tonight, unless you need it now?'

'Don't be silly. I'm just proud to see you doing so well.'

Daisy's stomach growled again. At some point, she was going to have to stop and eat something – probably one of her mum's freshly made scones – but she wanted to make sure everything was straight first.

'It's been great, definitely busier than I expected,' she said. 'But I need to make the most of it. It's not going to be like this every day.'

'No, that's the thing with the boats; they're very seasonal. But this is brilliant. And it looks like you've got a big group coming now.'

A number of men were walking towards them. From the noise they were making and the manner they were pushing each other, it was clear they weren't your average walkers. Add to that the fact they were all wearing flip-flops and matching bandanas.

'Thank God. Coffee.' The one leading the group placed his hands on the countertop. 'You have no idea how much I need a drink.'

'Do you have any cakes left?' Another man sidled up beside his friend and gestured to the sign.

'I've just got some in, fresh actually. Victoria sponge.'

'Great – we'll take one.'

'One slice of Victoria sponge coming up.'

'No, sorry. I meant one whole cake. And a dozen coffees. Make them quads. You know what that is?'

'Four shots of espresso?' Daisy said. The man nodded, at which point, Daisy felt the need to repeat the entire order again, just to make sure she'd got it right. 'An entire Victoria sponge cake and twelve quads?'

'That sounds right. How much is that?'

Daisy considered herself fairly adapt at mental maths, but this was a seriously big order. She didn't want to mess it up. So she used the calculator on her phone to check while filling up the coffee cups one after another.

'That'll be sixty-two pounds,' she said.

The man handed over four twenty-pound notes without batting an eyelid.

'Keep the change.'

Daisy frowned. 'Are you sure? That's quite a lot.'

'It's fine. We're here celebrating. Billy is getting married.'

Only now did Daisy notice how one of the young men was wearing a plastic veil, while receiving a piggy-back from a friend. She assumed the one with the veil was Billy.

'We've hired a canal boat for the weekend. It's brilliant. I might buy one myself.'

Daisy smiled as she continued to make the coffees. 'Are you staying here the whole time? At Wildflower Lock?'

'We hired the boat in Chelmsford last night. Stayed there, now we're down here for the night, then going to head to Heybridge tomorrow before we make our way back.'

'Sounds like you've got it all planned.' She placed four of the coffees on the counter and went back to the machine to fill the remaining cups.

'Maybe if you feel like it, you could come and join us later? I'm sure there's going to be a party on the barge.'

'Technically, I'm not sure that you have a barge, but thank you for the invitation. I'll bear it in mind.'

It took a few more minutes to make the coffees, and it was only when the men disappeared that she remembered her mother was there.

'An entire Victoria sponge cake? Did he really just buy that?' Her mother was staring at her with a look of sheer delight.

'He did. I don't think these cakes are going to last as long as we planned. I'm going to need to put you on the payroll, Mum. How long before you can make me another batch?'

'I guess I better get back and get onto it. Maybe I'll do a batch of brownies too, if you'd think they'd sell?'

'I think you're going to need to give me a cookery class,' Daisy said truthfully. 'Otherwise you're going to spend all your spare time shipping me cakes.'

'There are worse things for a mother to do.'

Given the sale of an entire cake, the fact that it was the afternoon and how truly happy her mother looked, watching Daisy in her element, it felt like a good time to persuade her onto the *September Rose*.

'You don't need to leave straight away, do you? Why don't you come in for a coffee and one of your scones? I haven't eaten since breakfast. It would be nice to have you keep me company.'

Daisy watched as her mother gazed at the boat, the thoughts and memories evidently corkscrewing through her mind.

'I shouldn't today. But how about when I drop the next batch of cakes off? Would that be okay?'

'That would be lovely. Maybe I could take you for a—'

Daisy was about to continue when she noticed a gentleman making a beeline for the boat. Not wanting to miss out on any customers, she nodded quickly to her mother, who, understanding the gesture, stood back and allowed the man a clear path to the hatch.

'Good afternoon, sir. What can I get you?' Daisy felt like she recognised him, but she couldn't think why. He didn't have a dog, and he didn't look like the average paddle boarder. Perhaps he was one of the volunteers who would walk the towpath cleaning up the rubbish. They came around often enough. Although if that was the case, they'd normally be in their uniform.

'You can start by telling me what you're doing here.' The man's tone was hostile. Daisy shifted back, prepared to reply, but he continued his tirade without giving her a chance to speak. 'This part of the canal used to be peaceful. If it's not bad enough with hen parties and thrill seekers, now you're bringing your yuppie ways and your yuppie friends with your frappu-cappuccinos and choca-mocha-lattes. Well, I'm not happy about it. I'm not happy at all, and I'm not the only one.'

It was then that it struck her. The reason the man looked familiar was because she saw him almost every day, ducking back into his boat or hiding behind his pot plants as he refused to reciprocate her good mornings, or engage in any form of conversation.

Daisy noticed several people nearby shift their gaze between her and the irate boat owner, though there was only one person Daisy was worried about. If she didn't act soon, her mother would go into Mama Bear mode and step in, and the last thing Daisy wanted was for that to happen. But it was hard to get a word in edgeways as the man was barely pausing for breath.

'Sir, if you can—'

'Did you even think about all the work that went into creating a beautiful boat like this when you cut a gaping hole in the side of it? I dread to think what Johnny would have said.'

The name wasn't one said in front of Daisy very often.

'You knew Johnny? You knew my father?' Daisy's pulse raised. Any link to her father was one she wanted to know more about, even if it came from a bitter old boat owner.

The man's eyes widened, but before he could reply, her mother was standing beside him.

'Nicholas? Nicholas Granger? Is that really you?'

The man's brow creased as he stared at Daisy's mother. His eyes narrowed before widening into a smile.

'As I live and breathe. Pippa. Pippa Arnold?'

'It's May, remember? I married Johnny.'

'Yes, difficult to forget that. Oh lord, I never thought I'd see you again. And this. I'd heard rumours about Johnny's girl taking over the boat, but I thought it was all gossip. Balderdash is what I thought. You know what I'm like, keep myself to myself.'

'By which you mean you're an utter recluse who thinks you're better than everybody else?'

Daisy assumed such a remark would cause the man to scowl and react more aggressively. But instead, his smile grew even broader.

'Pippa Arnold, as I live and breathe.'

Daisy felt like she should say something. It didn't look like Nicholas Granger was about to erupt into another angry tirade about her and the coffee shop, but if that were the case, then she'd quite like him to move out of the way. She could hear a large group of people walking towards them. Hopefully, people who wanted to buy coffee.

'Can I get you a drink?' Daisy felt rude about injecting herself into the reunion, but they were standing directly in front of her hatch.

'No, no, not to worry. I've only just put the kettle on in my place. I'm sorry, love. I didn't realise it was you. I should get out of the way.'

'I was actually going to head back to the car myself,' her mother said, still looking at Nicholas. 'Maybe you'd like to walk with me?'

'I'd like that very much.'

With that, her mother turned and walked back down the towpath with Nicholas Granger, with barely a glance in Daisy's direction.

# 8

Between Nicholas Granger and the stag do's impressive order and tip, Daisy thought she'd had her fill of surprises, but just as she was about to close the shutters and call it a day, a tall woman with a long-haired dachshund in her arms approached the hatch with a friend.

'I'm not too late, am I? Are you still serving coffees?'

'I am.' Daisy moved from where she was about to start cleaning the coffee filters to take the lady's order. 'What can I get you?'

'I'll have a half-shot latte. It's all the caffeine I can deal with at this time of day. And you?' She posed the question to her friend, while the dachshund stuck its nose on the counter, looking for stray crumbs.

'That sounds good,' the friend replied.

'Perfect. Then two half-shot lattes.'

'Just one minute,' Daisy said as she got to work.

With the coffee dripping through the filter, she was busy steaming milk when she noticed the woman looking intently at something inside the boat. Daisy's heart leapt as she realised what it was. After the conversation with Theo, she had placed one of her pictures on the back wall, not that she'd expected anyone to show the slightest bit of interest, let alone ask if it was for sale. The only reason she'd hung it was to keep Theo quiet. But now this woman was leaning in, her glasses perched on the end of her nose to get a better view.

'That is simply darling.' She looked at Daisy. 'It's a heron, isn't it? I don't suppose you remember where you got it? My godson adores herons. It would be perfect for his bedroom.'

'Oh.' A rush of embarrassment flooded through her. 'Actually, it's one of mine.'

The woman tilted her head quizzically.

'Yours, as in, you are the artist?'

'Yes. Yes I am.'

Daisy had such a hard time referring to herself as an artist, and yet here was this woman saying it and sounding completely natural.

'And is it for sale?'

Daisy's heart leapt so far up her throat, her breath caught. She hadn't even considered which painting to place on the wall. The heron had been the one on the top of a large pile, that was all.

'Yes. Yes, actually it is. All my paintings are for sale.'

She was simultaneously overjoyed and infuriated. Had she placed a few more pictures around the hatch, she may have had even more interest.

The lady nodded. She was one of those women who exuded elegance. A few years older than her mother, and her greying hair was a perfect contrast to the darkness of her skin.

'I'd love to have a closer look, if that's all right?'

'Of course. Of course.'

Daisy dried her hands on the tea-towel, then carefully removed the picture, at which point the woman handed over the dachshund to her friend and took the painting. Daisy could barely look at her, fearful of what tell-tales signs she might see in the woman's expression. Did she think it was amateur? Derivative? Little better than what you would find in an A-level art exhibition? Her heart pounded as she tried to appear impassive. The last time Daisy had offered up her paintings for a stranger's opinion, the man had come back with a less than favourable critique, and even though the woman was smiling, Daisy could feel her breath quivering in her lungs as she waited for a response.

'Well, you certainly have a talent.'

A gasp of relief flew past Daisy's lips, although she tried not to show it.

'Thank you.'

'You studied fine art, I assume?'

'For a short while.' She hated herself for the response. 'After that, I'm mostly self-taught.'

The woman hummed and Daisy wondered if that meant the woman could tell she was an art-school dropout. If she could, thankfully, she was too polite to mention it.

'I love the way you've captured the water so perfectly. The texture of the feathers is sublime, and the choice of colour... truly inspired. Yes, I'm simply going to have to take it. How much did you say it was?'

It was almost too much for Daisy to bear. She chewed on the inside of her cheek and forced herself to smile while her brain frantically tried to come up with a sensible figure. Her thoughts flicked back to the conversation with Theo and his remark about ten cups of coffee.

'I was thinking thirty pounds.'

'That seems very reasonable indeed. I'll be honest, you can probably charge more than that, but if you're happy, then I think I've got myself an absolute steal.'

The woman reached into a handbag and pulled out her purse, though the woman's look of satisfaction at securing the painting for such a cheap price faded slightly.

'I completely forgot. I have no cash on me. Do you take card?'

Daisy ground her teeth together. Getting a card machine was one of those things Theo and her mother had both told her she needed to do, but she hadn't wanted to invest any more in the business before it was up and running, and given the prices of coffees and teas, she hadn't felt it would be necessary straight away. That was another mistake she would need to put down to experience.

'Sorry, this is only my second proper day open,' she confessed. 'I'm working on it.'

'Don't be silly, it looks like you're doing a marvellous job.' She turned to her friend. 'Do you have thirty pounds I can borrow?'

'Cash? I'm not sure.' After handing back the dog, the second woman opened her purse.

'I've got six pounds.'

'We'll need that for the coffee.' She took the coins and handed them to Daisy before giving the painting one last glance. 'I tell you what, will you put it aside for me? I'm always back this way. Sasha loves her walks down here.' She nodded to the dog. 'We were going to Danbury Park tomorrow, but we'll just come back here instead. I can give you the money then. Would that be okay?'

'Of course, that would be absolutely fine.'

'Brilliant. Now, make sure you put it out of sight. I don't want you selling it to anyone else accidentally.'

'Don't worry, I won't.'

A moment later, the woman was walking away, and as Daisy finally closed the shutters on the hatch, she let out a silent scream of delight. A business owner and an artist. Life really was looking up.

## 9

By the time Daisy had finished clearing up, wiping all the surfaces and making sure everything was ready for the next morning, her feet were throbbing, her back ached and she'd decided she needed to invest in some comfier shoes if she was going to be on her feet for this many hours every day. However, even worse than all the aches and pains was the hunger that now clawed at her.

As she stepped out of the kitchenette, her stomach growled angrily, although the last thing she wanted to do was cook. There were the scones and the cakes her mother had brought, but she didn't want to eat into her profit, not when the following day was going to be her first weekend day, and probably her best day to date. Fortunately, she knew a neighbour who was a dab hand in the kitchen.

Daisy didn't even bother knocking as she let herself in.

'Please tell me you've cooked enough of that for me?'

'I hear today went well?' Theo was stirring a pot on the stove and offered Daisy only the most cursory of glances. 'And yes, I cooked for you. I figured you probably wouldn't be up to it.'

'I'm going to have to go to bed earlier each night. I thought getting the train and buses every day was hard work, but this was insane.' She reached out and opened the cupboard where Theo kept his plates, after which, she went straight to the cutlery drawer.

'You just need to get used to it. Early nights sound like a good idea, although I doubt you'll manage that tonight.'

'Why not?'

'What do you mean, why not?' Theo finally shifted his attention from the cooking to her. 'Don't tell me you haven't heard it?'

Daisy had no idea what Theo was talking about and was going to say as much when something made her stop. Something felt different. The stillness of the lock. It was then she noticed the deep thumping resonating through the walls.

'What is that? Is that music? Is there a party going on?'

Daisy liked to listen to music in the *September Rose*, particularly when she was painting, but she would always keep it quiet enough to hear what was going on outside. Normally. When she had first inherited the boat, Bex and Claire had come over to help her tidy all the boxes. When they'd finished, they'd cracked open the drinks. It had been a great night until she'd woken up to find an 'unreasonable noise' fine stuck to her window. Thankfully, Yvonne was the one who had issued it and had been quick to revoke the claim after finding out who Daisy was. At no other time had she heard even slightly loud music on the canal. And certainly not in the evening.

'It's a stag do. They hired a boat up in Chelmsford but are staying the night here. Hopefully, they'll tire themselves out.'

'The stag do? I met them. They came to the coffee shop.'

'Did they cause chaos there, too?'

'Actually, they're in my good books. They bought an entire sponge cake and gave me an eighteen quid tip.'

'Seriously?' Theo quirked an eyebrow.

'Seriously. I can deal with a bit of music for sales like that.'

'I think you'll be alone there.' Theo went back to stirring the food. 'I suspect there'll be several noise complaints coming from Yvonne soon. Personally, if it's only one night and they stay on the boat, then I'm okay with it.'

The comment left Daisy confused.

'Why wouldn't they stay on the boat? I thought that would be the point in hiring it?'

'I know. But trust me, they don't always think that way. Sometimes, after a few drinks, a night-time swim feels like a good idea or they decide to light bonfires on the towpath. And then you get the ones who prefer to use the outside of our boats as a urinal as opposed to the toilet they have inside.'

Daisy gagged at the thought.

'Okay then, I agree. I want them to stay on the boat too. But they're still in my good books at the minute.'

She took the cutlery over to the dining area, leaving the plates for Theo to dish up. Theo's narrowboat, the *Narrow Escape*, was a fair bit smaller than the *September Rose*, but there was still enough room for a dining table with four seats. Not that she had ever seen Theo have three guests on his boat. The only visitor she'd ever known him to have was his ex-girlfriend, Heather, when they were still together.

'So, what are we having?'

'Vegan carbonara. Someone I worked with gave me the recipe, so I thought I'd try it out. It's nice, actually.'

'Smells good.'

'I'll be sure to give him your feedback, too.'

He served out substantial portions of pasta onto the plates before carrying them over to Daisy, who was already sitting and waiting.

'Do you want a beer?'

'No. Yes, no.' Daisy tackled the question badly. 'I shouldn't. I need to be healthy so I can get up early. I think I'm going to do yoga in the morning.'

'And doing yoga means you can't have a beer?'

Daisy pouted. 'Maybe just a small one.'

With a sly smile, Theo headed back to the kitchen and pulled two distinctly average-sized beer bottles from his fridge and flicked off the lids.

'To your second day at work.'

'To my second day at work.' Daisy clinked her bottle against his. 'And... my first sold painting?'

'What?' Theo's face exploded into the widest smile she had ever seen. 'I told you. I hate to say I told you so, but I did. I told you. Which did they buy? Was it one of the lock?'

His enthusiasm was contagious, but Daisy was determined not to get ahead of herself.

'Before you get carried away, she hasn't actually paid for it yet. She asked me to put it on hold for her and said she'd come and collect it when she can give me the money. But you never know, she might change her mind before then.'

'She won't. She definitely won't.'

Daisy's stomach growled again. Having food in front of her wasn't enough. She actually needed to eat it.

'We should've had a proper celebration,' Theo said, twisting the spaghetti onto his fork. 'I should have brought some bubbles.'

'We can do that later.'

'What, when you finally think I've waited long enough to start dating again? Or do I get to celebrate with you properly before then?'

Daisy couldn't help but smile. 'Maybe we can have a small celebration before then.'

As they ate their dinner, they chatted about their days. Theo told Daisy about the problems that came with the sunny weather and the sudden influx of people visiting the lock, particularly with all the rubbish they left behind. As a linesman, he was in charge of a substantial chunk of the canal, and his job could be as varied as calling wildlife rescue out to help trapped swans, to assisting people with lock difficulties.

When she finished the food, Daisy sat back in her chair, wonderfully full. Outside, the music had kicked up a notch. As well as the thumping deep bass, she was also pretty sure she could hear people singing, too.

'Do you ever go out and tell them to be quiet?' she asked as she checked the time. It wasn't even eight yet. There was a good chance their party was just getting warmed up.

'Do I ever go out and accost a group of drunk men and ask them to keep their noise down? No,' Theo answered bluntly. 'Or drunk women, for that matter. It's a pain, and I don't think it would be so bad if it were local people who owned the narrow boats and were renting them out, but what can you do? It's a business. Besides, most of the people who hire them are really nice. Families or people looking for a relaxing getaway. That type of thing.'

As he was talking, Daisy let out an involuntary yawn.

'I'm sorry. Am I keeping you up?'

She knew the comment was in jest, but now she was full, her body had decided the next thing it needed was sleep. And lots of it.

Scrunching up her eyes and face, she covered her mouth for a second yawn before she replied.

'I'm really sorry. I don't want you to think I'm rude or anything—'

'But now that you've eaten my food, you're going to leave?'

'Is that really terrible of me?'

'It's no more than I've grown used to. I think I've just accepted it. You're a terrible person.'

Had she had the energy, Daisy would have protested the comment, but when she opened her mouth to reply, she yawned again.

'It's fine,' Theo laughed. 'Go to bed. Get a good night's sleep. I'll see you tomorrow. Saturday. You're going to be busy.'

'Do you want help with the washing up?' she asked, as manners dictated.

'It's fine. You need me to walk you back?'

'You know what, even in my tired state, I think I'm going to make it.'

Then, with Theo still sitting, Daisy stood up, kissed him on the top of the head, and made her way back to the *September Rose*.

Once inside the boat, Daisy contemplated whether to have a shower. She had been around steaming hot coffee and milk all day and had been sweating endlessly. She probably should take one, but at the same time, she just didn't feel like she had it in her.

Besides, the shower might wake her up, which was the last thing she wanted, given the music that was still blaring out from the narrow boat outside. By the sound of things, they were down the other end of the canal, which was good. Though she couldn't imagine what it would be like for the poor folk who lived down that end.

Not giving herself a chance to think too deeply about anything, she changed into her pyjamas, brushed her teeth and closed her eyes.

Unusually, Daisy fell asleep immediately, and more unusual still was how animated her dreams were. First, she dreamed she was at a wild party where she was being asked to make coffees as fast as possible. She only had one jug of milk, and she kept trying to tell people this, but the milk jug never seemed to run out, and people were laughing louder and louder. All the laughing was making her dizzy, and it felt as though her whole body was rocking. Then she was standing up on a bouncy castle, but it was rolling from side to side with no control. She was about to shout out when, with a loud thud, the sound of glass shattering filled her ears. For a split second, she assumed it was in her dream until she sat bolt upright in her bed and the sound of falling glass continued even when she was awake.

'What the hell?'

# 10

Daisy jumped out of bed. As soon as her foot hit the floor, she knew something was wrong. The rocking motion she felt in her dream was still there, only now she was wide awake. Placing a hand on the walls to steady herself, she inched across towards the light switch, bending her knees just as another surge hit, rocking the boat back and forth. Her head pounded and the motion continued. She was securely tied to the towpath. It didn't make any sense.

Having reached the switch, she flicked it on.

'What the?'

Several items had fallen from the shelves, including books and her bedside lamp, which, by some miracle, hadn't broken.

Still confused by the grogginess of sleep, she headed into the living room.

Smashed glass glinted all over her sofa and floor, and her eyes were so distracted by the sight that it took her a moment to notice the cold chill of summer air whipping directly into her home. She lifted her head towards the window. This time, there was no stifling the cry.

'Oh, my God.'

A tree branch, which should have been outside on the towpath, was now in her living room. It wasn't a small spindly branch, either. It was thicker than her thigh and had dozens of smaller twigs and leaves jutting off it. At least that explained where the broken glass came from.

When she finally gathered her thoughts, Daisy dashed back into her bedroom, picked up a pair of shoes and a torch that she had in a drawer, and made her way through to the front of the boat. Each step was taken with careful consideration. It wasn't just glass on the floor she was worried about. The boat was swaying as if it had been untied from its mooring and repeatedly rocked from side to side.

When she reached the stern, she pushed open the door only to confirm what she already knew; she was adrift. Only the presence of the giant branch was wedging the boat in place, and every motion was sending more twigs, leaves, and glass into the living area.

But how? She hadn't taken the *September Rose* out for days, and she was fastidious about checking that it was tied up properly. Even now, she normally got Theo to check her knots were up to par, just to be on the safe side.

The moon was still bright, although the stars were slowly bleaching from the sky. In a few hours, the sun would send the first slivers of its watery, pale light across the horizon and the birds would begin their song. It should have been a peaceful time. A slice of serenity in the busy world. But at that moment, chaos reigned.

Looking out across the canal, Daisy could see that the majority of boats had become unmoored and had drifted various amounts. In some respects, Daisy was lucky. Her place near the end of the river meant she hadn't collided with anyone else, but that was likely the reason she had an oak tree rather than a curtain in her living room.

'Theo! Theo?' she called out in the direction of the *Narrow Escape*'s mooring, uncertain if the silhouette of the boat she was staring at was in fact her neighbour's. 'Theo, are you there?'

A heartbeat later, the reply came. 'Daisy? Daisy, are you okay?'

A flash of torchlight shone across her face, causing her to flinch. There, looking right at her across the water, was Theo.

'What happened?' she yelled.

'The damn stag do, that's what happened. They thought it'd be funny to untie all the moorings. Are you okay?'

Daisy took a moment to consider the question. Her pulse was racing, and she was feeling more than a little shaky on her feet, but other than that, she didn't feel hurt and couldn't see any injuries.

'I'm okay, though a branch came through the window in the living area.'

'Can you start her up? Drive her back?'

'I don't think it will work. I'm wedged in place. The tree's got me trapped.'

She wasn't sure whether Theo understood exactly what she was trying to tell him, but his voice came back.

'Just stay where you are. I'll get myself moored up and row over to you.'

After a couple of minutes, Daisy realised Theo's arrival would not be as imminent as she'd first thought. Hoping to stave off a little of the cold, she headed into the boat and started to sweep up as much of the broken glass as she could. It was a mess. Shards had scattered across her coffee table and were sticking out of the sofa, and though she plucked out as many as she could see, she would never feel comfortable sitting on it again. Branches had scraped the top of the ceiling, which she'd only recently painted. Thankfully, though, being in the middle of the room, the branch had missed the kitchenette where she'd placed the coffee shop. It was a small mercy, but at that moment, she'd grasp any positives she could.

With the sweeping done, she switched the engine on to warm up. On the chance that Theo could somehow manoeuvre the boat away from its deciduous shackle, she wanted to get back on her side of the canal as quickly as possible.

By the time Theo had the *Narrow Escape* all moored up, light was splintering across the horizon, casting the clouds in vibrant shades of pinks and oranges. The birds had begun their dawn chorus from their posts high in the trees and Daisy even spotted one dog walker out, as if it was a normal day. For her, she knew it would be anything but.

She waited out on the stern, still dressed in her flannel pyjamas as Theo rowed across in a small wooden boat. After tying it to the *September Rose*, he climbed aboard and immediately folded his arms around her.

She breathed in the comfort of his scent, and it was only his warmth that made her realise how cold she was. But no sooner than the thought entered her head, Theo backed away.

'Are you okay?' he asked again.

'A bit shaken, but I got off lightly. It's a mess in there.'

At Daisy's words, Theo looked past her and peered through the doors into the *September Rose*.

'Jeez.' He blew out a long sigh, before tentatively taking a step inward. Daisy promptly followed.

'I was lucky it didn't get the television,' she said, still trying to see some positives in the situation, but Theo wasn't having any of it.

'Are you serious? You're lucky it didn't go through the bedroom.'

As he turned to look at her, his face was ashen. His eyes met hers. In that second, something passed between them. She wanted to reach out and take his hand. Or for him to hug her the way he had before, but instead, he whispered, 'Those hooligans. They have no idea what they could have done.' His voice cracked.

'I'm fine. We're all fine.' Never had Daisy wanted to hold someone so much.

As they stood there, she saw the reality of his morning, how he had been the one in charge of keeping his cool and helping other people without thinking about himself, and now he was here with her, his true emotions could finally release. She waited for the embrace she was sure would come, only for him to blink his eyes, and straighten his back, as if the moment had never happened.

'Okay, where do we start?'

Daisy swallowed. It felt like she should say something more. Comfort him the way he would her, but her mind was blank.

'We need to deal with the boat,' she said eventually. 'Is there any way you can steer it out of here?'

Theo looked at the branch and the hulk of a tree it was attached to. He didn't even bother with a closer inspection before he promptly shook his head.

'No, we're going to need to cut this down. Otherwise, it could end up doing more damage. How's the engine? Have you started it up?'

'Not yet, but I've warmed it. She's good to try.'

Theo nodded. 'Let's check that then, before we decide a course of action.'

Ten minutes later, Daisy was wondering if this was the worst start she'd ever had to a morning. Initially, they had thought everything was fine. The engine had warmed up as normal, and it started okay, but as the propeller began to move, a loud clunking noise rattled from below the stern.

Theo let out another low sigh as he turned the engine off.

'That's not good, is it?' Daisy asked, somewhat unnecessarily.

'We don't know for sure yet.' He tried to sound upbeat, but Daisy wasn't buying it. 'Let's get you across to the *Escape*. I'll get some tools and get that branch down. Then we can work out how to move her. I might have to tow you if the prop is that damaged.'

Prop damage. For some reason, that was even worse than the window. At least she knew what a window was made of, and that it could be fixed with another pane of glass. She had no idea how you went about fixing a propellor.

As Daisy looked across to the *Narrow Escape*, she remembered it had been unmoored and set drifting too.

'I haven't even asked how you are,' she said with a surge of embarrassment. 'Was there any damage to the *Escape*?'

'No, she was fine, thankfully.'

'And the others? Yvonne, was she okay?'

'Yvonne and the *Ariadne* are fine. It's mainly just a lot of scratched paintwork. Come on. Let's get you in the warm.'

Using Theo's hand to steady her, Daisy stepped down into the small rowing boat, quickly balancing her weight before taking a seat. Theo stepped in afterwards and untied the knot, before he sat down and took the oars.

As Daisy looked out across the fields, a perfect semi-circle of sun bisected the horizon, shimmering on the clouds with a sherbet-pink hue. It was going to be a beautiful day. A perfect early summer morning. And on any other occasion, she would have taken a mental, or perhaps even physical, photo of the scene in case she wanted to paint it later. But she couldn't think about painting right now, just like she couldn't think about the beauty of the sunrise. The coffee shop had only been open for two days and now it would be closed. Again.

# 11

As soon as Theo left, with a hefty toolkit loaded into the rowboat, Daisy was overcome by a dozen different emotions. With her head buried in her hands, she dropped onto the *Escape*'s sofa and allowed herself the cry she had been desperate for since she had first seen the mess in the *September Rose*. How could it be that after only two days of having the coffee shop open, she had to close again? If she was a believer in fate, then fate was really testing her. Not to mention her credit card balance.

Daisy was well aware how fortunate she'd been in inheriting the *September Rose*. While decoratively, it had required an over-haul, and the water tank would give her nightmares for years to come, structurally, it had been sound. Other than a new blacking, the hull had been in good shape and none of the windows had needed to be replaced. Even the engine had needed little more than Theo to give it a good clean and look over. Now it was going to need a lot more attention and a lot more money. And while she didn't know how much a new window cost, she knew it was out of her budget, and that was before she considered the propeller.

After a quick moment of concentrated self-pity, Daisy picked herself up and brushed away her tears. Right now, there was nothing to do but wait for Theo, but if she didn't find something to occupy her mind, she'd go crazy. It didn't help that outside, people were charging into action, towing boats wherever they needed to go and clearing the mess that trailed in the stag do's wake. For a brief moment, Daisy considered helping, only to remember she was still in her pyjamas, and wasn't much in the mood for meeting new people dressed in flannel.

Looking around, she scoured the boat for any tasks she could get on with.

As Theo had said, the *Narrow Escape* had lived up to its name. From what she could see, there hadn't been any damage at all. She headed over to the kitchen and emptied the mini dishwasher he'd installed, straightened up the cushions, then found herself out of jobs.

It was an agonising fifty minutes until *September Rose*, towed by the *Ariadne*, was moored back in her spot. Daisy jumped off the *Narrow Escape*. As she expected, Theo was at the back of her boat with the tiller in hand.

His look said it all.

'How bad is it?' she asked when he climbed aboard the *September Rose*.

'Well, you saw the state of the living room. It's the same. But it looks like the prop is busted. Sorry.'

'So what does that mean? Money, I guess? How much?'

'The propeller isn't as much to replace as you'd think – a couple hundred quid.'

He paused, and Daisy could hear the rest of the sentence hovering in the air between them. As the pause expanded, she finally took the plunge and said the word she didn't want to hear.

'But?'

'But we'll need to get the stern out of the water to see how much damage there is. If it's that bad, we might need to take her fully out of the water to do the repairs.'

Daisy closed her eyes and tried to fight back the ache that was burning in her chest.

'You mean we're going to need to get her to a dry dock? How? If the propeller's not working?'

She could hear the panic in her voice, and she desperately wanted to keep it in check. After all, Theo had been awake just as long as her and was working far harder too, but her eyes still pricked with tears.

'It's really not that bad. Not yet.' He squeezed her arm, though she found herself wanting a hug far more. 'I can check the propeller here. I've got a buddy that can help me winch her up. Then, if she needs to come out of the water, there's a towpath, a couple of miles away towards Chelmsford. The coffee shop will only need to be closed for a day to get it sorted.'

'Another day, after today that is,' Daisy said. ''Cos I can't open with a broken window and glass everywhere, can I?'

She hadn't meant to snap, but thankfully, Theo knew that.

'As for the window, I've got a friend I'll call, but for now, there's some tarpaulin back on the *Escape*. I'll grab that and we can tack it up around the hole to stop the draught, okay?'

Daisy nodded, struggling to find words in the muddle of thoughts that filled her head.

'This friend of yours, any idea when he'll be able to come?' She remembered when her mum had got new double glazing in the house. The process had been surprisingly quick, but it had taken months to set a date of them to come.

Theo shook his head. 'I haven't rung him yet, but he owes me and he lives close, so fingers crossed he'll make it here today. If not, you can stay at mine tonight. And I'll even let you have the bed.' He raised his eyebrow ever so slightly before he finished. 'Alone.'

Given how much he had already done for her, this offer was almost more than she could take.

'Thank you,' she said, curling her lips into the slightest of smiles.

'It's what I'm here for. Now, I'd better go down the canal, check everyone else is sorted. I'll be back as soon as I can.'

'Don't rush. Honestly, it's fine.'

He squeezed her hand once more, before jumping back on to the towpath and towards the lock, leaving Daisy alone on the *September Rose*.

Had it not been for the dog walkers beginning their very early-morning strolls and Daisy not wanting to be seen in the full glory of her pyjamas, she probably would have stayed outside a lot longer, but, after a brief deliberation and a deep breath in, she stepped back inside her home.

There may not have been a branch in her living room any more, but there was still an awful lot of tree. Splinters and twigs littered the floor, so much so you could barely see the blue rug under the coffee table. There was also a distinct scattering of leaves that had somehow made their way into her bedroom and bathroom, not to mention an unfeasible amount of mud.

Any hope she'd had of doing a quick sweep around, and maybe opening the coffee shop mid-morning, was gone. This place needed a proper clean.

Daisy, however, needed coffee.

She headed through to the kitchen and switched on the coffee machine. She might not be opening for business, but that didn't mean she couldn't fix herself a proper drink. With the whipped cream in hand, the double shot of coffee was still dripping through the filter when her phone rang.

'Daisy. Thank goodness. Is everything okay?' Her mother was almost breathless with panic on the other end.

'Not really, Mum.'

'Oh, darling. How bad is it? Is there much damage to the boat?'

'More than I can deal with. It got a branch through the window and— hold on?' Daisy paused, feeling like she'd skipped part of the conversation somehow. 'How did you know something had happened to the boat? I was going to ring you after I had a coffee.'

'Well, I... I mean you...' Her mother's voice cracked down the end of the line. 'I mean, I just figured you would ring as soon as you got up, you know, before you opened the coffee shop, in case you needed any cakes and things, and when you didn't... I just... It just...' Her mum was babbling, and for a split second, Daisy wondered if it was ever going to stop, when she finally seemed to find her focus again. 'What about the hatch?' She spoke more definitively now. 'The coffee shop, your machine? Is that okay?'

Daisy was slightly grateful her mother had thought to mention it. It was, after all, a positive.

'Thankfully. I'm just making myself a cup of coffee now.'

'Good. You deserve it. Have a slice of cake too. Screw it, have the entire thing. You probably need it.'

'Thanks, Mum.'

Daisy paused. Ringing her mother had been on her list of things to do, but she hadn't expected her mother to get there first. Certainly not before her coffee.

'I better get to work tidying this place up, Mum. It's a state.'

'Well, let me know if I can do anything to help, love. I can always come down, if it will help you.'

There was an undoubted quiver to her mother's voice. An implication that she really didn't want to come and help fix up the *September Rose*, but she would do it for Daisy, if she needed to, because that was what mums did.

A pang of gratitude struck her.

'It's fine, Mum. I'll be fine. Theo will help me sort everything.'

'You've got a good one there, haven't you?'

'He's just a friend, Mum.'

'So you keep saying. And I'm saying he's a friend that you should probably keep.'

'Thanks, Mum. I'll bear that in mind.'

With that, she bid her mother farewell, and finished making herself a drink.

Tidying was a slow process. It started with her picking up the branches that were too big to be swept up and stacking them on the roof of the *September Rose*. Had it been a different time of year, she would have kept them in the boat for the wood burner, but given how hot the last couple of days had been, she didn't imagine herself needing any more soon. Still, she didn't want decent wood to go to waste and was sure if she left it there, someone would find a use for it.

She had just finished that first part of the clean-up when Theo returned.

'You're back quicker than I thought. How's everyone else doing?'

'Honestly? It looks like you got the worst deal. I don't know if that makes you feel better or worse?'

Daisy didn't know either. On the one hand, it was great that other people's homes hadn't suffered too much damage. On the other hand, she was the only one who had started a business out of hers and really needed it to be up and running. So, she did the obvious thing and stayed silent, letting Theo continue.

'So, for some good news, my buddy can make it this morning. He should be able to get the repairs done later too once he's measured up, which means you might be able to open up in the afternoon if that's what you want? Or tomorrow morning at the latest. Also, the police have arrived. They're dealing with last night's jokers. So that's something.'

'The police?' Daisy hadn't really thought about how they would deal with the stag do, but it made sense. After all, they could have done some serious damage, not only to the boats, but the people who lived on them. Still, it didn't feel great. She thought about that cheery group of young men who had given her a large tip only the day before. This was a less-than-ideal way to end a stag do. For a moment, she felt a flicker of sympathy towards them, before she remembered the state of the *September Rose*.

'I was going to head out today, take the *Escape* for a drive while the sun's out, but I can stay and help you if you'd rather?'

The way Theo looked at her made it feel as if he wanted to be asked to stay. But her mother's voice was still ringing through her head. It was hard to pretend they were nothing more than friends when she relied on him more than she ever had a boyfriend.

She shook her head. 'Thank you, but I'm fine by myself.'

## 12

Daisy was still on her hands and knees, cleaning up leaves and twigs, when there was a knock on the door. Considering how it had only been half an hour since Theo left, she thought it miraculous that the window repairman would make it over so fast, but it was good news. The sooner he came, the sooner she could open the shop.

But when she opened the door, a familiar face was standing there. A familiar face with a shock of pink hair.

'Daisy, I'm so sorry.' Yvonne peered over Daisy's shoulder to get a better view of the damaged living room. 'What a nightmare. These fools. I'd put them behind bars if it was up to me. Every one of them.'

Daisy wasn't sure whether imprisonment was quite the right punishment, but as Theo said, the branch could just have easily gone through her bedroom window. Broken bones would have been a lot harder to fix than broken glass.

'Do you want to come in? I can make you a coffee? The machine is still in one piece, thank goodness.'

Yvonne shook her head. Then immediately changed her mind.

'That would be lovely, thank you. Though is there any chance you have herbal tea?'

'I do, but I'm not sure I recommend sitting down anywhere. It's almost impossible to see all the bits of glass. I've hoovered the seats, but I think I'm going to have to re-cover them.'

Yvonne looked at said seats with a pang of sympathy.

'Not to worry. Not to worry, love. I'm fine standing. It'll be nice to have a chat. And there was something I wanted to ask you.'

'Oh, okay. Ask away.'

So far, Daisy and Yvonne's relationship had been very one way, with Daisy asking questions about her father and her past on Wildflower Lock, and Yvonne showing her photos. Daisy couldn't think of a time when Yvonne had ever asked her anything.

'I heard your mum visited.'

It wasn't exactly a question, but Daisy paused from where she was pouring water into the kettle and turned to face her.

'She did. Just to come and wish me luck. And drop off some scones she'd made for me to sell.'

'That's good. Did she come onboard the boat?'

Daisy shook her head. 'No.'

Yvonne pressed her lips together as she nodded. 'I suppose that's not a surprise, really. I suspect it's hard for her, coming down here. You know, she used to think we didn't like her. I know she did. Johnny told me as much, but that wasn't true. It wasn't. She was just a bit closed off, you know? A bit timid. But I'd like a chance to speak to her if she comes back. Would you tell her that? I'd like to see her.'

As Daisy looked at the old woman with her pink hair and deeply creased eyes, she couldn't help but feel a pang of jealousy.

After all, Yvonne would know a side of her mother and father that would forever be hidden to her. But wasn't that the way with everyone?

'I can tell her that.' She reached up to the cupboard to grab the tea bags, but Yvonne stepped forward.

'Don't worry about that, my love. I should head back. And you've got too much on your plate to stop and natter to me. Come over and visit soon, though. Please.'

'I will do.'

If nothing else, Daisy was grateful it was summer. The breeze that blew in through the broken window was surprisingly refreshing and offered her a different view from which to see the world outside. A different view which she had every intention of painting. Not that she was going to do that yet. When the window was fixed, she would have the quickest shower in the history of showers before opening the coffee shop, even if it was only for thirty minutes. That was the plan, at least.

It was just gone midday when Daisy got another visitor. Abandoning her cleaning, she opened the door to find a short, stocky man with an immense beard standing there.

'Theo's girl?'

'Sorry?' The abrupt introduction caught Daisy by surprise.

'You're Theo's girl, right? With the broken window.'

'Theo's my neighbour. I'm not – we're not —'

'Do you need your window fixing?' He lifted the toolbox by his side.

'Oh, yes. Yes.' She could feel the flush in her cheeks as she stepped back and let the man in. 'It's that one there,' she said, pointing to the large, plastic covered hole in the side of her boat.

For several minutes, the man umm'd and ahh'd as he plodded around the window frame, pulling loose shards of glass out from the wood.

'Well, you're lucky it went through this one,' he said eventually. 'Any of the others would be a lot fiddlier, with their latches and everything. You could keep the frame, but I'm not sure I'd recommended it. Got some damp around here. Bits breaking off.' To prove his point, he pinched an edge of the window frame and pulled it away with his fingers. Daisy grimaced. She had assumed the person coming to fix her window would mend things, and not destroy more.

'But you can fix it?' she pressed, with too much stress in her body to consider smiling. 'Can you fix it today?'

'Aye. I'll have to go back to the workshop, cut the glass up to measure. And like I said, better put a new frame on there, too.'

'But you'll do it today?'

'Couple of hours. That's all.'

That was one element of relief, though there was still an added moment of fear to come. With a deep breath, she took the plunge.

'And how much is it going to cost?' She tried to sound neutral, but knew she'd failed horribly.

The man tilted his head from side to side, before taking another step back and eying the broken window yet again. Although what more he needed to know, Daisy couldn't say.

'You're a mate of Theo's and Theo's good folk, so I'll do it for you for four hundred.'

'Four hundred pounds?'

'Should be about five, but I owe him a favour or two.'

Daisy took another deep breath in. There was nothing she could do. If it cost four hundred pounds to get the window fixed, then that was what she was going to have to pay. She only hoped her credit card didn't melt in the process.

By four-thirty in the afternoon, Daisy had a new window, a clean-ish floor, and had finally opened the hatch to serve her first customers of the day. It wasn't a complete bust. She had several people wanting cake and drinks, and a crowd of kayakers purchased a mass quantity of crisps and soft drinks, but the early and distressing morning had left her exhausted. So at six o'clock, she closed up again, with sixty pounds in the kitty; she was going to need to do this this several times more just to cover her new bills.

She had opened her fridge and was debating whether the jam in a Victoria sponge could count towards her five a day when Theo opened the door and let himself in.

'Hey. I got takeaway. Figured you could do with it after the day you've had.'

A deep and heartfelt groan left Daisy's lips. She might not be dating Theo, but he was the best non-boyfriend she'd ever had.

'Takeaway is exactly what I need.'

'Good. And I wasn't sure what you'd like, so I ordered a mix of things. Do you want to eat here, or at mine?'

Daisy double checked the fridge was closed, before looking back at Theo and the plastic carrier bag in his hand, which was wafting scents of deliciously deep-fried food into the boat.

'Any chance we can eat at yours? I'm pretty sure there's half a bird's nest under my sofa that I can't reach. Not to mention a thousand hidden glass splinters.'

'No problem. I'll go back and dish it up now.'

Less than five minutes later, Daisy was sitting on Theo's sofa, with a large plate of fried rice and sweet and sour chicken balls.

'I'm just terrified that the whole bad luck comes in threes is going to make an appearance here. I'm not sure I can deal with any more. A freak storm on opening day, a tree smashing through the window. I don't even want to know what else might come up.'

'You've forgotten the broken propellor. That makes your three things.'

'It does!' Daisy spoke with surprising joy on remembering she had to pay for yet another repair, but if it meant the string of bad luck was over, then that was what mattered.

'Tomorrow is going to be bright and sunny, and it's going to be your best day yet. I can feel it.'

Daisy grabbed another prawn cracker from the bag. 'I don't mean to be rude or anything, but I don't really trust your feelings any more.'

'Fair enough.' He let out a light chuckle before finishing the last spring roll on his plate. 'You want seconds?'

'No, I'm good. This is plenty for me.'

Theo stood up and took his plate over to the kitchen.

'There's loads left. I'll put some in a box for you to take home. You can heat it up tomorrow.'

'It's fine. Leave it here. You can take what you want for lunch, then if there's any left, I'll come and share it with you in the evening.'

She expected Theo to be fine with the suggestion. After all, she was hardly going to take any more of the food when he was the one who'd paid for it. But instead of agreeing, he frowned.

'What? What's up?'

There was a shift in the air, as if an unexpected tension was rising around her.

'This.' Theo gestured to them both. 'What we're doing – it's a relationship. You know that, don't you?'

Daisy flinched, before tipping her head back and laughing. 'No, it's not. It's a friendship.'

'Really, how many of your friends' houses do you walk into and help yourself to food?'

'Most of them,' Daisy replied truthfully, though she only considered herself to have two close friends.

'And call at whatever hour you want? And sit with your feet up on their coffee table?'

Daisy noted her feet and hurriedly lowered them back on to the ground.

'If you have a problem with me coming over here so much, you should have said. We could have eaten at mine.'

'I don't have a problem with you being here. You know I don't. I just find it ridiculous that you are so hung up on me not being ready to date that you don't see what's actually happening here is a relationship.'

The calm that Daisy had been feeling only moments ago was gone.

'My mistake. I just thought you were a friend I could rely on, but if my presence here is making you that uncomfortable, I'll go.'

'That's not what I said. I actually think I said the exact opposite of that.'

Daisy was already on her feet, but Theo grabbed her by the hand. 'Daisy, please.'

She turned and looked straight at him.

'Theo, today I've had to keep my coffee shop closed for almost an entire day, again, after only two days. I've had to pay out money I don't have, and even now, I don't have a boat that can actually go anywhere. I can't think about anything more. I can't. I'm sorry. And if you can't wait, then that's on you. It just confirms what I already knew. You're not ready for this.'

## 13

Theo sent her several apology text messages that night, all of which Daisy ignored. After the day she'd had, she couldn't believe he'd picked that evening to have a go at her. And what right did he have to speak to her that way? She was being cautious. Protecting her heart. That was all.

Her anger at Theo kept her awake far longer than she would have liked, and even when she finally fell asleep, she found herself jolting awake at every slight sound or movement the boat made. So when her alarm blared out at six-thirty, she instinctively rolled to switch it to snooze, only to remember she now had a business to run, and missing vital hours of weekend trade was bad enough, but missing two – just because she wanted a couple of extra hours sleep – was unacceptable. So, with her mind still groggy, she dragged herself up and out of bed.

A hot shower and strong coffee did admirable jobs, though it was the sound of voices on the canal that spurred her into action. People on the canal meant potential customers, and she wanted to serve them all. This time, she barely had the hatch open when her first person was there, wanting a cappuccino. As Daisy made the drink, she couldn't help but think this woman, with bags under her eyes and smudged mascara, needed more than just caffeine to keep up with the three spaniels that were currently tugging on their leads.

After that, there was a brief respite before the customers started arriving in droves. For over an hour, Daisy barely paused for a breath, as she steamed milk and pressed coffee grinds into the filter, fetching cold drinks from the fridge and trying to keep the basket of crisps and chocolates fully stocked.

'A slice of humble pie, please?'

Daisy turned back to the hatch, a washcloth in her hand, ready to wipe up a previous customer's spillage, when she stopped and frowned. She had been too absorbed in serving to even notice Theo was standing there. The sight of him caused an unprecedented tension to wriggle down her spine.

'Unless you want something real, I'm very busy,' she said, wiping the surface, only to notice that Theo was currently the only customer. After finishing clearing up. She turned her back to him and began to wash out the milk jugs, though she knew that wouldn't be enough to get rid of him.

'I wanted to apologise. It appears my text messages aren't getting through, and I needed to say I was out of line.'

'You were.'

'But I'm crazy about you.'

Daisy pursed her lips, pausing as she considered her next response. With her hands now empty, she turned back to face him.

'Theo, I don't have time for this right now. You know that. With everything that's going on, I can't deal with any more drama.'

'I understand. And I respect that. So I will not bring up anything about our dates and relationship status until you think I'm ready. However ridiculous that is. I'll pinkie promise on it?'

It was hard not to smile when he was looking at her with those big, puppy-dog eyes and half-smirk.

'Fine. Now, unless you want something, I really am busy.'

Theo went to speak, when a shriek from further up the canal caused him to turn his head. A sly smile curled on the corner of his lips.

'If it's being distracted you're worried about, I think I'm the least of your concerns.'

This time, when the second shriek came, it sounded almost like her name. That was when she recognised the voice. Or rather, voices.

'Want me to cover the coffee shop for ten minutes?' Theo's eyes were bright.

'Would you mind?'

'It's fine.'

As Daisy rushed out of the boat, she crossed Theo on the stern and threw him another thank you as she jumped onto the towpath.

'Daisy!' Her friends' voices were a chorus as they ran towards her. Bex was dressed in her usual crazily coloured array of clothing, while Claire was in a far more subdued jeans and jumper combo. However, both of them were holding large overnight bags.

When Daisy reached them, they squeezed in a large group hug, before she hugged them again individually.

'Now where's our coffee?' Bex said immediately, before spying Theo behind the hatch. 'You have staff? Excellent choice.'

Ignoring the comments, Daisy gestured to the large bags in their hands.

'What are those for? Are you guys going somewhere?'

'Yes, here,' Claire replied. 'We thought we'd have a sleepover.'

'Seriously?'

'Yup, Ian is having a Daddy-date night with Amelia. We probably can't have a crazy one, as we all have work tomorrow, but I thought we could put on a film and get a pizza or something. Is that okay?'

Daisy's instinct was to say it was perfect. Some quality time with her best friends felt like exactly what she needed after all the stress of the last few days. It would also help to get an unbiased opinion about things with Theo, but it wasn't even midday. She still had the busiest hours of the coffee shop to get through.

'It's a really lovely offer, but you know I have to work, right? I won't be able to close up early or anything. And Theo's only covering now so I can speak to you guys. I really should get back and let him go.'

She expected the girls to look disappointed, given that they'd brought all their things for a sleepover. Instead, they exchanged a look and their faces simultaneously broke into even wider smiles.

'Sorry, we obviously didn't explain ourselves properly. We're here to help. To work in the coffee shop with you. If that's okay?'

For a second, Daisy wondered if they were winding her up, but she knew her friends well enough to know they were deadly serious. A warmth she only felt when amongst the girls flooded through her.

'I guess I better show you the ropes, then.'

\* \* \*

It was by far the most fun she had had since opening the coffee shop. Not only was there a steady stream of customers, but Daisy got to work with her best friends. Given that there wasn't that much room by the hatch, Bex was in charge of taking orders and money, while Daisy made the drinks. With no space for Claire, she sat in on one of the small cabin bunks, reading her book, making the most of a child-free afternoon, while continually checking if either of them wanted to swap.

'I was thinking.' Bex turned to Daisy after handing a customer her change. 'Have you thought about displaying your paintings? You have a space now. You could put some up on the wall here. I'd bet you'd get some sales.'

It was hard not to laugh.

'Theo said exactly the same thing. Well, he nagged me until I agreed, actually.'

'That's because we're both intelligent people.'

'Well, the one I put up sort of sold.'

Given how hectic yesterday had been, Daisy had forgotten all about the woman and the painting she was going to come back to collect. For a second, she'd worried that perhaps the woman had come past and seen the coffee shop was closed, but Daisy quickly dismissed that idea. She had been in the boat all day. It would only have taken a knock on the door or window. It was far more likely that she had simply changed her mind and decided the painting wasn't worth the money after all.

'Sort of sold? What does that mean?'

'It means she said she was going to come back when she had the money, but hasn't. It's fine, though.' Daisy felt far less despondent than she had expected to. At least it meant she didn't have to go on that date with Theo.

'That's brilliant news.' Bex replied with far more enthusiasm than Daisy thought the comment warranted. 'You had someone interested in your art. Even if they didn't end up buying it, that's still great. Really great.'

'Yeah, I suppose.' A small amount of Bex's enthusiasm filtered through to her. 'I should probably put it back up now.'

Daisy looked over the room to see where she had placed it. In the mayhem of the broken window, she'd moved everything, but there was no rush. She could find it later and put it up. Or perhaps choose a different one to display this time.

She was about to ask Claire whether she fancied a turn on the coffee machine when a woman strode up to the counter.

The woman's crisp shirt and tailored trousers were a stark contrast to the majority of people on the canal, who were wearing summer dresses or shorts, and Daisy's first instinct was to assume she was a broker, here to make a deal on one of the many boats on the lock. It hardly seemed fair, having to work in a place like this, when the sun was shining and everyone else was enjoying themselves, but Daisy had met her broker here on the weekend too. That meeting hadn't gone to plan for him, as she had decided to hold onto the *September Rose* rather than selling it. While Bex got to serving her, Daisy retrieved a bottle of fresh milk from the fridge.

'Good morning.' Bex's charm offensive was second to none. 'What can I get you?'

'Are you the owner?' the woman responded, piquing Daisy's attention as she stood up with the milk.

'No, I'm the owner.' Daisy tried to match Bex's smile, but there was something about the woman that was making her nervous, and she couldn't think why. 'What can I get you? We have cold drinks as well as hot ones.'

'Oh, no. I'm not here for a drink.' The woman scanned the kitchenette from Daisy to the counter and back again. 'I'm here to see your licence.'

# 14

Daisy shook her head. This was the last thing she needed. Still, hopefully it wouldn't take too long to sort out.

Bex took a large sidestep out of the way, leaving Daisy room to stand next to the counter, but she didn't want to move. Her throat had turned too dry to swallow and beads of sweat were pooling in her palms. It didn't help that the woman was staring at her so intently, she could practically feel the heat of her gaze. Still, Daisy had read up on the rules. Even she wasn't so naïve in the world of business not to think about things like licences before she opened.

'I studied the details quite extensively,' Daisy said, trying to keep her voice as amiable and pleasant as possible. Just because the inspector was in the wrong, it didn't mean she couldn't make life difficult for Daisy. 'And I believe I don't need a licence. Because it's not a fixed mooring. I can move the boat. And therefore the coffee shop. I emailed someone about it too.' She pulled out her phone, ready to share the contents of her messages.

The woman shook her head and a smile flashed in her eyes which brought Daisy the slightest glimmer of relief.

'That's fine. I can tell you've done your research. I just need to do a few questions so that you don't get bothered in the future, and then I'll be on my way. Does that sound okay?'

'That sounds great,' Daisy said, unable to stop the sigh of relief leaving her lungs.

'Is this your permanent mooring?' the woman asked, retrieving a tablet from her bag. The way she posed the question made Daisy think that there was definitely a right or wrong answer to this, but she had no idea which one that was. Besides, there was only one truthful answer she could give.

'Yes, it was my grandad's boat. His mooring. Well, he rented the mooring, but it's been passed to me now.'

The woman nodded and jotted something down on her tablet. Daisy's heart inched higher up her throat.

'That's a lovely inheritance. And tell me, do you leave this mooring, or keep the boat fixed here permanently?'

Again with the questions, though Daisy could barely focus on what the woman was saying. Instead, the word *licence* played on repeat in her head. When she didn't answer, the woman asked again, this time rewording her question. 'Is this a working narrow boat? Can you move its moorings?'

'Yes, yes,' Daisy replied, only to realise that wasn't quite true. Feeling like she was on trial for a crime she didn't know she'd committed, she back tracked. 'At least, it was until yesterday. There was a stag do, you see, and they untied all the moorings, and the *September Rose* – that's the name of this boat – she was set adrift. The propeller was broken. So I had to be towed here.'

'So, you will be trading from this location only?'

Daisy wished she knew the right thing to say, but the panic that was coursing through her veins made it impossible to think. Besides, the last thing she wanted to do was lie and get into trouble for that.

'Yes. For now. For the summer, this is where I plan on being.'

The woman nodded, and scribbled something else on her tablet, before lifting her head up and looking back at Daisy.

'You are trading on a public towpath in a fixed mooring, with a boat that can't leave. I'm afraid in this situation, you do need a licence.'

'But it was the stag do. Yesterday, the boat drove. I promise you. You can ask anyone here.'

'I really do sympathise. Is there any chance of you being able to get the boat fixed immediately. Today? I could come back this afternoon?'

Daisy felt nauseous. No, she wanted to scream. Of course she couldn't. Because getting a propeller fixed cost money she didn't have. And money she wouldn't be able to earn unless the coffee shop was open. As tears welled in her eyes, the inspector nodded. Daisy's lack of response had answered her question clearly enough.

'The good news is, the licence is very easy to obtain.' The woman's voice still managed to maintain an air of positivity, despite how hopeless Daisy currently felt. 'All you need to do is fill out the forms online. I doubt it will even take the afternoon to do.'

'Thank you.' For a split second, Daisy felt a pinch of sympathy for the woman. After all, hers couldn't be the most pleasant of jobs to do. Especially not on a sunny Sunday, when the rest of the visitors at the canal were there to enjoy the sunshine and water while she was having to walk around in a suit and interrogate people. 'I will do it now. I will get on it now.'

'I'm already filling in the form!' Bex yelled from the kitchen.

The inspector smiled.

'Fantastic. I'm glad that's all sorted. Obviously, you'll need to close the shop until the point that the licence is granted.'

'Oh, yes. Of course.'

Daisy looked past the woman to the mass of people that was forming behind her. She suspected one or two were just listening in to the conversation, but there were bound to be some who were after drinks. Drinks she wasn't allowed to sell them.

A heavy weight pushed down on her chest. 'I'll close up the shop now.'

With the inspector still watching, Daisy removed the chalk board sign, while Claire helped her put away the cakes.

'I am truly sorry about this,' the inspector said, just before Daisy closed the hatch. 'I hope when I come back, it'll be under more pleasant circumstances.'

'Thank you.' Daisy forced herself to smile, knowing it didn't do any good to get on the wrong side of an inspector, even if she'd done everything she asked.

As the hatch doors clicked closed, she felt the prick of tears behind her eyes.

'So, that wasn't the day we had planned.'

Claire was ready with a hug, squeezing Daisy into her shoulders.

Bex remained exactly where she was at the kitchen counter, typing on her phone.

'Do you want the good news or the bad news first?' she said.

As a strict rule, Daisy always went for the bad news first, but at that moment, she didn't think she could take another blow.

'Good news.'

'Okay, well, the good news is, the licence seems really easy to get. I've already filled in the first page. I just need you to do a few more details.'

'So, what's the bad news?' Daisy closed her eyes, hoping to soften the blow of whatever was going to come next.

'The bad news is, it's going to cost you.'

# 15

They went to the pub. It probably wasn't the most sensible idea financially, given that Daisy needed to find another seventeen hundred pounds for the licence for the coffee shop, on top of whatever was required to fix the propeller, but she needed a drink. And to get away from the canal.

Whatever worst-case scenarios she had envisioned about opening The Coffee Shop on the Canal, she had surpassed them all. She was only three days into running her business and already her outgoings exceeded her income by many multiples. And right now, unable to open up, she had no way of clawing that money back.

When the inspector left, Daisy had needed to get out of the boat and had hoped a change of scenery might make her think a bit clearer, but so far, that hadn't happened. All that she'd done was sink further into her pit of despair.

'Seventeen hundred pounds isn't as bad as I thought it was going to be,' Bex said, stealing a chip from Daisy's plate and dipping it in her ketchup. 'And the licence says it'll only take five days to come through.'

Daisy had insisted that her friends take their bags back with them. There was no way she was going to be good enough company to have them over for the evening, and the last thing she wanted was to inflict her misery on them. Besides, knowing her current luck, one of them would sit on the sofa and end up with a piece of glass she'd missed impaled in their thigh. A trip to A&E would really be the icing on the cake.

'Five working days.' Daisy corrected Bex's statement about the licence time. 'This is the weekend. The application won't go in until tomorrow, which means I might not be able to trade until next Monday. That's a full week, right at the beginning of summer. And all of that's a moot point, anyway, because I don't have seventeen hundred pounds.'

That was the crux of everything. She did not have seventeen hundred pounds. She'd avoided looking at her bank balance ever since purchasing the coffee machine, knowing that her credit card limit had reached its max, just like both her overdrafts, the last of which had been cleared out by the trip to the cash and carry. And she still had the mooring fees, which would need paying at the end of the summer. It didn't matter what the sum was. She didn't have it.

'Maybe I could shut up shop and rent the boat out for a couple of weeks?' She verbalised her ideas as they came. 'At least that way, I'll be guaranteed an income. I could crash at Mum's. Take a temping job at the same time. She'd probably like a chance to have me back home. Then I can start looking for a more permanent position near the lock.'

'Do you really want to hire out your boat, after what the stag do did? With the way they played havoc with everyone else's boats, I can't imagine what they did to the one they were staying in.'

'I agree,' Claire said, joining in. 'That doesn't seem like a great idea, not given all the time and money you've spent on it.'

'And there's the fact that she doesn't currently move. But I don't know what other options I have. Maybe I just have to rent her out cheaply. It's either that or I sell up.'

Daisy didn't want to sound exasperated, but she was. Since opening the coffee shop, she had been hit with one disaster, then another. So much for Theo's belief that she had already suffered her three bad things. If that was the case, she was already on for another run of them, and she wasn't sure she could take that. What she wouldn't give to go back to the type of job where you walked in, sat down, followed instructions for eight hours, then headed home.

'How about I lend you the money?' Bex's voice broke the silence. 'My work bonus is still sitting in my bank account from Christmas. And they'll give me a summer bonus too. I was going to go on holiday, but Newton can't get the time off work, so we're going to have to wait until the autumn anyway. There's more than enough there to cover it.'

'That's a really sweet offer, but I have no idea when I'll be able to pay you back. Or if I'd be able to pay you back.'

'We could work something out.'

Daisy shook her head. It had been such a romantic idea to open a coffee shop in the narrowboat. A way to connect with her father now he was gone, in a manner she had never managed while he was alive. But now the romance had faded and a very bitter taste was taking its place.

'Why don't you come back to mine tonight?' Claire offered, trying to lighten the mood. 'Amelia would love to see you. And I'll make her promise not to practise the violin in front of you.'

Daisy let out a small, obligatory laugh.

'Or you could stay at mine?' Bex suggested. 'You could both

stay at mine. We can have the pizza and film night, just liked we planned.'

Tears pricked Daisy's eyes. Though not because she was upset. She was lucky that she had been blessed with such amazing friends, and times like this reminded her of that.

'Thank you, guys, but honestly, I think I need to spend tonight by myself. Try to get my head straight. You don't mind, do you?'

The two women exchanged a look.

'Only if you're sure,' Claire said eventually.

'I'm sure. Are you okay to drop me back at the lock? I'll give you a ring later, when I'm feeling better.'

'As long as that's what you really want.'

'It is.'

They didn't speak on the car journey back. Daisy's thoughts were on her failures. How could she have thought she could run a business with zero experience? The truth, plain and simple, was that she was a mess.

When they reached the car park, she kissed the girls goodbye and headed back to the *September Rose*. To make the pain of closing up the coffee shop even worse, the canal was packed. Families and friends blocked the towpath as they laughed and chattered. She watched one group point to a family of swans, the cygnets now as tall as their parents but entirely grey.

Daisy tried to cheer herself up. If even 10 per cent of the people here bought a coffee from her, she could pay off a chunk of her debts; it was a humbling thought.

For a split second, she considered opening the coffee shop, despite the inspector's warnings. It was unlikely that she'd come all the way back, just to check Daisy hadn't done something silly like start trading again. She'd never need to know. That way, Daisy might be able to get a few more pounds in the till.

No sooner than the thought had entered her head, she

hurried to quash it. The last thing she needed was a fine on top of the licensing fee. No, she needed to go through all her finances, to the very last penny, and decide on a course of action.

She was just by the bow of the *Narrow Escape* when she spotted a man pacing up and down the towpath.

At first, Daisy feared it was another inspector. Despite the heat, he was wearing a pale-blue shirt, although the top button was undone. His shoes were patent lace-ups and though he couldn't have been much older than Daisy, his rolled-up sleeves displayed a watch which indicated he had more than enough money to pay a boat licence fee several times over.

There was something about his look of confusion that gave Daisy the need to check he was okay.

'Is everything all right?' She took a step towards him, still fearful he was going to end up demanding she paid yet another fee. 'You look a little lost. Can I help you?'

When he turned to face her, Daisy got her first proper look at his deep brown eyes, which were currently crinkled in confusion.

'Possibly. It's my mother, I think she's sent me on a fool's errand. Apparently, there was a coffee shop here earlier in the week selling paintings. And the woman who painted them put one aside for her. But I can't find the place.'

'Your mother? Of course.' Now he had mentioned it, Daisy could see the resemblance between the pair. The same dark skin and darker eyes. Though he was broad shouldered and at least a foot taller than the woman had been.

'You know what I'm talking about?'

'Yes, yes. Sorry. It's me. I'm the coffee shop. I mean, I run the coffee shop.'

Whether it was midday drinks, being caught unaware, or simply the fact that this man looked like he belonged at a polo club, clinking champagne glasses rather than on a towpath next to her boat, Daisy found herself unusually tongue-tied.

Swallowing back the heat that was flooding her cheeks, she tried again.

'Why don't you come in?' she said.

# 16

The man was looking straight at her, with dark-brown eyes so deep, it was almost impossible to see his pupils from his irises, although it was only when he coughed that Daisy realised she'd been staring directly at them for far longer than was socially acceptable.

'Sorry. Yes, the painting. My painting.'

'I'm glad you turned up when you did.' He smiled broadly as he spoke. 'I thought I was going to be here for hours.'

'It's just inside.' Daisy took out her keys and opened up the door to the *September Rose*. 'But I haven't wrapped it up yet. Sorry, are you okay to wait for a minute?'

It wasn't just a case of not having wrapped it. With all the business of the last twenty-four hours, she didn't even know where it was. But she wasn't going to say that.

'Did you want to come inside? I can fix you a cup of coffee while I sort out the painting. Or a cold drink?'

'If you're sure that's not too much trouble. A glass of water would be appreciated. I have to say, I didn't anticipate such a heat wave. It's left me rather parched.'

She couldn't remember the last time – if ever – that she had heard a man say he was parched, but there was something endearing about it.

'Great, well, this is me.'

She led the way onto the *September Rose*, noting how the man ducked as he entered. She had seen plenty of tall people on narrow boats before, but thought what a pain it must be for them to constantly have to bend to get into their home. At least that was one advantage of being short. As impolite as it was, she couldn't help but watch him as he surveyed the inside of the boat. Other than herself, only four people – Claire, Bex, Theo and Yvonne – had been aboard since she'd renovated, and she was keen to see his reaction to the space.

Had Daisy had an unlimited budget, there were things she probably would've changed about the set-up, not to mention the furniture, which had either been crammed in from her flat or bought on the cheap second-hand. But her artistic flair had prevailed in the motifs she had painted on the walls, and in the manner she had arranged dried wildflowers in vases on the tables and shelves.

She stayed there for a minute, watching as the man took it all in, before realising that she was, once again, staring.

'Let me fetch you some water, then I'll get the painting sorted.'

As she filled a glass from the tap, she couldn't help but note the change in her heart rate. What was wrong with her? Yes, this man was clearly attractive, but she had been in enclosed spaces with attractive men before. This had to be something to do with the drink at lunchtime. Or the shock of the day finally sinking in. Yes, there was definitely the stress of the day still evident in the skipping of her heart.

'Here.' She handed him the glass of water before walking across to the living area to start the search for the painting.

'So, this is your place?' he asked, following her into the living space. 'How long have you had it?'

'Not long at all. I inherited the boat at the beginning of spring and I've spent the last couple of months doing it up.'

'I'm sorry for your loss.'

It took Daisy a minute to realise where his comment had come from.

'Oh, it's okay. I didn't know him, actually.'

'That sounds like a story.'

Daisy moved various art supplies to the side, still searching for the painting. Given that it was framed and sizable, it really shouldn't have been that hard to find, but everything had become so disorganised after the crash nothing was in the right place.

'It's not a very interesting story, really,' Daisy said, not wanting to get into the intricacies of her broken family. 'Ahh, here it is.'

She picked up the painting with one hand, and a roll of brown wrapping paper with the other, yet before she could move to the dining room, he had stepped across and blocked her route.

'Don't wrap it up yet. I'd love to have a look first.'

Daisy froze. She knew she was the one who had invited the man in, rather than suggesting he stay outside and wait, but showing him her work, with him standing so close to her, made her unduly nervous.

Though it wasn't like she could refuse. She held the painting by the edge of the frame, giving the man enough space to look at it.

'You painted this?' His voice sounded almost as though he were in awe. 'You have a talent.'

'It's just a hobby, really. I mean, I love it. I'd love for it to be more. But I'm not quite good enough for that.'

'This is definitely more than just a hobby.'

At any other time, Daisy would have basked in the compliment. It was clearly just misplaced flattery, but hearing something remotely good after the day she'd had didn't make her feel any better. Somehow, it made her feel worse.

'Trust me, apparently this kind of "derivative work" doesn't have a market.'

At this, the man tilted his head.

'I'm sorry, I'm going to disagree with you. I've seen far less talented works of art on display. Trust me, if you wanted to sell these, all you'll need is a bit of marketing.'

'Yes, but marketing requires money and that's something I do not have at the minute.' She realised how curt she sounded, but it was how she felt and now the rant had started, it proved difficult to stop. 'Besides, if I had any money at all, I would use it to keep this coffee shop running, or fix up the boat – not following a dream I know is destined to fail.'

'I sense I've hit a nerve.'

'Sorry.' She dipped her head as she cursed her own rudeness. 'Let's just say it's been one of those days.'

'In that case, I shall let you get on with the wrapping. Mother said it was thirty pounds. Is that right?'

'Yes, thank you. And sorry again.'

'Don't apologise. We've all been there.'

It was remarkable how genuine he sounded, which was the last thing she expected from someone whose watch probably cost more than she earned in a month. In her opinion, people didn't make their money by being nice. She turned to the wrapping paper, not really noticing as the man moved over to the sofa.

At least the sale was something, she thought, though she was going to need to shift a hundred more to cover her costs, and she didn't have anything near that many.

The painting was flat on the table in front of her, ready to be slipped into a cellophane sleeve, when the man let out a howl.

'There's glass in my hand!'

## 17

Daisy dashed across to the other side of the boat. The man was cupping his hand, a slight trickle of blood running down towards his wrist from where a short shard of glass was sticking up out of the heel of his hand.

'Oh, my God. I'm so sorry.'

'It is glass, isn't it?'

'I think so. Yes. Yes, but it's just a small piece.' Daisy felt nauseous, not from the sight of blood that was pooling, but from the fact that she had caused this man an injury. 'The window broke. I should have... I... I...'

'I'm so sorry. I'm going to bleed on your floor.'

His Adam's apple bobbed up and down as the colour drained from his cheeks. Was he having some sort of allergic reaction? Daisy had never seen anyone respond that way to a cut, other than a toddler, but maybe it was deeper than she thought.

'You really do not need to apologise,' she said. 'And it's not bleeding that much. So don't worry about that.'

'Can you pull it out?' The man's eyes were half closed, as he offered his hand only the slightest sideways glance. 'Is it deep?'

Daisy lifted his hand in hers, wondering how she had missed such a large piece of glass. It was nearly a centimetre long and sizeably thick, too. It was probably the thickness that had saved it from going in too deep. From what she could tell, it had only really pierced the surface.

'I think I can get it out. If you're okay with me doing that?'

The man glanced down at his hand, only to pale again, becoming another tone lighter.

'I'm sorry, I'm being ridiculous. I'm just not good with blood or injuries. I'm not sure why. I never have been. Injections too. I can't stand injections. It's humiliating, really.'

'Do you want to pull it out yourself?' Daisy suggested, thinking that was what she would do in the same situation. 'It doesn't look very deep. I don't think it would be too difficult.'

'No!' The sudden loudness caused her to jolt in surprise, though when the man spoke again, he was far quieter. 'I'm so sorry. Honestly, I'm an idiot. I don't know how I'll ever cope when I have children of my own. Hopefully, their mother will be better at dealing with this type of thing than I am. I'm a grown man whose kryptonite is a splinter. Jeez, you don't get more embarrassing than that.'

It was such a sweet display of vulnerability; Daisy couldn't help but smile.

'Okay, well, I'm sure I can get it out if you want me to?'

'Yes. Yes, please. God, you must think me such an idiot.'

'I think the only idiot here is the one with glass on their sofa.' Then, realising she had been holding the man's hand for quite a while already, she said, 'I'm Daisy, by the way.'

'Christian.' His eyes were still squinting as he spoke.

'Okay, Christian. Let me just wash my hands.'

Trying to stay calm, she darted into the bathroom, where she soaped her hands with warm water, before drying them thoroughly. Her heart drummed. Could someone sue her for getting a piece of glass in their hand from her sofa? She was technically trying to run a business out of the boat too. Maybe he would be able to shut her down for good. If it was possible, then she could almost guarantee it was going to happen to her with the week she was having. But that didn't change the fact that the glass had to come out of the man's hand, and it didn't look like he was going to be the one to pull it out. For a second, she debated whether she should use tweezers, only to change her mind. From what she had seen, the piece was big enough to pinch between her fingers, and the last thing she wanted was to squeeze too hard with tweezers and end up cracking the glass. Then she was sure there'd be a lawsuit on her hands.

When she returned to the living room, Christian was holding his hand out at arm's length, his eyes still scrunched shut.

'Okay, are you ready?'

He opened his eyes by a sliver to look at her again, only to close them almost immediately. 'As ready as I'm going to be.'

Stepping forwards, Daisy took another look at the glass. The fact he hadn't touched it at all meant it was still sticking out at the same angle, and just as she thought, it was definitely big enough to take a hold of.

'Do you want me to count down, or do you want me to pull it out without warning?'

'Without warning. No.' He changed his mind. 'Count down. I think a countdown would be best. Shall I do it or will— Ow!'

'I went with your first answer.' Daisy smirked, holding the splinter of glass between her fingers.

Christian opened his eyes wide in disbelief.

'You got it?'

'I did.'

The sigh of relief expressed from his lungs was so great, Daisy thought he was about to fall back onto the sofa, and she was ready to grab him before he did so, but thankfully, he stayed upright, staring at the hand that only a few seconds ago he had been unable to look at.

'You should probably give it a clean?' She gestured to the sink.

After nodding in agreement, he finally lowered his hand and moved towards the kitchen. 'I'm so sorry for causing you so much fuss.'

'Honestly, you have to stop apologising. This was not your fault.'

'The glass, no, but the behaving like a baby was definitely all me. Honestly, it's a good job I work in an office. I don't think I'd be able to last one day out here like you.'

'It's a boat. It's hardly the wilderness.'

'No, of course. You're right.'

The glass may have been out of his hand, but he still looked decidedly peaky.

'Do you want a cup of tea?' Perhaps some sugar would make him slightly steadier on his feet.

'Only if you don't mind. I don't want to cause you any more trouble.'

'You're really not. I'm the one who had the glass on the sofa, remember? But maybe we should sit outside to drink it.'

Five minutes later, the painting now wrapped, the pair were sitting out on the stern of the boat with very sugary cups of tea and a fruit scone each. While Daisy was still suffering from the embarrassment of someone getting injured in her home, Christian was still apologising for his response.

'I think I'm going to try hypnotism for it,' he said, as he broke off a piece of scone to eat. 'I know exactly why I'm like it. It was an incident in my early teens, involving a large wooden splinter and a needle which broke.'

'That sounds painful.'

'It was, incredibly. But it was years ago. It's ridiculous that I still can't pull out my own splinters.'

'You weren't that bad,' Daisy said, trying to make him feel better.

'Yes, I was.'

'Yes, you were.'

His eyes met hers, and in that moment, something passed between them. Something that was shared and private, yet at the same time so utterly ludicrous that the pair burst out in laughter. It wasn't a subdued laughter either. It was the full belly-shaking, diaphragm-aching type that caused their eyes to fill with tears. Daisy was unable to stop the stream, as each breath caused another cascade to follow and then another. And when a minute passed, and Christian had finally gathered himself, she realised she wasn't crying with laughter any more. She was just crying.

'Daisy? Daisy, are you okay?'

But she couldn't stop. And she couldn't answer, because she wasn't okay. She wasn't okay at all.

## 18

Daisy didn't know how long she sat on the stern of the boat crying, but it was long enough for Christian to ask several times whether she was all right. And then, after failing to receive an intelligible answer, he'd headed back into the boat, found her bathroom, and brought out a roll of toilet paper for her to blow her nose on. When she had finally steadied her breath enough to speak, her eyes were red-raw and stinging and her throat scratched as if she had swallowed a pinecone.

'I'm so sorry,' she said, still snivelling into a piece of tissue.

'Now who's apologising unnecessarily?' Christian was crouching down, looking up at Daisy with concern etched in his brow. He really was an obscenely perfectly constructed man, facially at least. His eyes and eyebrows were perfectly symmetrical, as were his wonderfully chiselled cheek bones. Even his frown lines spread out equidistant from the centre of his forehead. 'You don't have to tell me what's up. I'm a complete stranger, I get it. But it might help to tell me. You know that old saying, a problem shared?'

'Thank you, but I'm not sure that works in this case.' Daisy dropped the tissues onto the table between them before rubbing her temples with her thumbs. 'And I wish it was one thing. You getting stabbed with glass is the last in a very long list of disasters. It's been one thing after another since I tried to open the coffee shop, from a broken window and a damaged propeller to an inspector and a licence fee I have no way of paying. Honestly, I don't know why I'm even trying to keep this business afloat – excuse the pun – I can't see a way out of this hole.' She took a deep breath in, before looking back down and seeing Christian still crouched there, with the same concerned expression. 'I'm sorry, you don't want to hear this. You just wanted to pick up the painting for your mum.'

'I know.' He stood back up. 'Here was me thinking I was going to have an uneventful afternoon. It's certainly taken a turn.'

'I'm sorry.'

'How about we both just agree to stop apologising? Would that work?'

He had an incredible smile, Daisy noticed. The way his mouth curved, entirely symmetrical, to reveal perfectly straight, white teeth was more than enough for her to feel even more conspicuous about the red blotches on her face that were bound to have followed her bout of crying. She rubbed her eyes and sniffed again.

'I'm— Yes. Yes, that would work.'

A paused filled the air and Daisy noticed how Christian had finished his tea. No doubt he was waiting to find the right time to leave, but rather than making his apologies, he spoke again.

'You can tell me to butt out if you want, but if it's money issues that are causing all this stress, why don't you sell more of your paintings? I saw dozens in there. I'm sure if you were willing to let go of a couple of those, it would have to go some way to footing the bills.'

Daisy couldn't help but laugh. Willing to let them go? She would throw them at people if it would help her cause. What was it with people recently suggesting she sell her art? Didn't they think if it was that simple, she would have done it by now?

'I would love to sell them. Believe me. But even if I sold them all, it wouldn't be enough to cover all these bills.'

'It would if you charged people properly. Thirty pounds can hardly cover your materials.'

Her back teeth ground together. It was bad enough taking this advice from Bex and Theo, who actually knew her, but she wasn't going to from a man who cried like a baby over a splinter. She drew in a long breath and picked up the now-wrapped painting from where it was propped up on the side of the boat.

'I should let you get on.' She handed the painting to him. 'I hope your mother likes it. And I'm sorry again about the glass.'

Understanding the less than subtle hint, Christian stood up. 'What did we say about apologising? I'll see you again, Daisy. Soon, I hope.'

And with that, he stepped off the boat and headed back towards the car park.

\* \* \*

The rest of the evening was spent filling in the licensing form. It seemed like the right thing to do, even if she couldn't afford it. Hopefully, with the details all in place, she could send it on the off chance a two-grand miracle might land in her lap. Though where that would come from, she had no idea. Several messages buzzed on her phone, from Bex and Claire, and her mother too, who had somehow heard the news, but for now, she ignored them. Her friends, just like her problems, would still be there in a morning.

When the form was complete, she sat on her bed and began to look up the prices of second-hand sofas. Again, another expense she couldn't afford. Perhaps, she thought, she would just give up hope of ever using her living room again. Or opt for that style they used in parts of Asia, where people sat on cushions on the floor – although at the minute, even cushions were out of her budget.

'Daisy, are you in?'

Theo's voice caused a tension to grip her. He knocked once before she heard the familiar twist of the door handle. She held her breath, praying he wouldn't use his key to let himself in.

While she hadn't told Theo about the incident with the inspector, the canal gossip train was faster than fibre optic, and he had already sent her a message saying he'd heard what had happened. But just like with Bex and Claire, she wasn't in the frame of mind to talk about it yet. Besides, he'd supported her so much in getting the business up and running, she wasn't sure she could deal with the humiliation of telling him about this whole licence mess. And so she remained where she was, her heart hammering against her chest, as he knocked on the door.

Finally, the knocking stopped. With a sigh of relief, she dropped on the bed. The day had been one of twists and turns and it had left her mentally exhausted. So many parts of her brain hurt. It would have been easy to stay there and fall asleep. To not even bother with a shower. But then, she decided, perhaps she would watch a horror movie in bed instead. After all, it wasn't like she needed an early night when there was nothing to get up for.

# 19

As much as Daisy wanted to sleep in, her body clock, or just pure bad luck, wouldn't let her, and by eight-fifteen, she was lying wide awake, with her eyes open, wishing another freak storm would strike. A once in a lifetime June snowstorm, or sudden plummeting temperatures would do. Anything that meant she was justified in staying under the duvet for the entire day. Yet she could already hear the birds chirping away, and a sliver of light creeping in from beneath the curtain.

A sunny day on the canal would normally fill her with optimism, especially at the start of the week. But that morning, it only reminded her how much trade she was missing out on. The Coffee Shop on the Canal was closed, and there was nothing she could do about it.

With no need to set up the hatch, or start the coffee machine up, she skulked out of the bedroom still in her dressing gown. At least she didn't need to think about what she was going to have for breakfast: there were still a dozen scones left that would go stale if she didn't eat them. After dropping one onto a plate, she moved over to the dining table, eyeing her painting kit.

At least that would keep her busy.

After selling the heron, she had set her sights on more birds, and the night before, she had sketched out an image of a kingfisher. That morning was all about the painting. The bird was in full focus in front of a blurry canal that was set with spring colours. It was one of her more characterful paintings, and the bird wore a golden crown perched atop his head. She could easily imagine him as the ruler of the river folk, commanding frogs and fish to do his bidding, and she jotted down some ideas for other characters that could go with him, such as the jester newt, or chamber-maid moorhen. Perhaps these, she thought, could form the basis of the children's book she had promised herself she would complete one day.

Her focus was still on the kingfisher and his brightly coloured plumage when there was a knock on the door.

After finishing the stroke she was on, she placed her brush back into the water and went to stand, only to stop.

Given how many people visited her, she was almost certain it was Theo standing outside her front door, waiting to load her with sympathy, the same way he had tried to do the night before. And while she was grateful that he was here, supporting her, the last thing she wanted to do was talk about the coffee shop. Especially to him. Still, she should probably say as much to him herself, so after checking her water pot was well away from her painting, she stood up and opened the door.

'Daisy?'

The man's voice wasn't Theo's, that was one thing she knew, though that was all she could make out about this stranger. Despite him being only two feet away from her, she couldn't have told you the height, hair colour or any other discernible features of this man standing on her doorstep, as his entire head was obscured by an enormous bunch of flowers. It was without doubt the biggest bouquet she had ever seen and rather than the normal combinations of carnations or lilies, this one was chockful of wildflowers. Every variety of colour, from deep purples to blush pinks, and bright yellow, was displayed in the string-tied extravagance; there were dog roses and wood anemones, fox gloves and forget-me-nots. It was like all the best bits of nature, in one enormous package.

'Are you Daisy the painter?' There was a definite sense of confusion in the man's voice. 'There isn't a proper surname given. Unless your surname is The Painter?'

Daisy was still awestruck by the sight in front of her and it took a moment before she finally realised what had been said.

'Um, yes. Yes, that's me. I think. Yes.'

'Great, then these are for you.'

He thrust the flowers outward for her to take, though it took a second to work out how she could take hold of them and bring them into the boat without knocking half the flowers off.

'Just hold there for a sec,' the man said. 'I need to get a photo for proof of delivery.'

Her arms dropped with the sudden weight as she continued to stand, wondering what his next move was going to be. There was still no way of seeing the man, but the footsteps that rattled on the stern of her boat told her that he had got his photo and was off for the next delivery. She cursed internally at the fact she hadn't asked him for some help in getting the bouquet inside.

With her arms already feeling the burn, she stepped carefully back, twisting the flowers slightly to the side and bending her knees to avoid clipping them on the doorframe. Once she was inside, she inched her way over to the table and placed them down. There, in the centre, was a small envelope. She plucked it out from between the flowers and opened it up.

These are to buy your silence after my hugely embarrassing display. Hope it's comfy. Also, I have an idea to help you raise some funds. Call me. C x

Underneath was a telephone number.

Daisy re-read the note. Comfy? It was a typed message, and she assumed there must have been some confusion. Colourful felt like a much better fit to describe the flowers. Like a burst of springtime now inside her home.

'Excuse me?'

Daisy turned her head back to the doorway, where the delivery man had reappeared. She had assumed, given how he had his proof of delivery, that he was done, and yet he was still standing there, looking at her expectantly.

'Do you need me to sign for something?'

'I will in a minute. But first, what do you want us to do about this?'

He glanced to his side, though Daisy couldn't see what he was looking at.

Abandoning the flowers and the note, she headed out of the boat and looked to the towpath, where three large men were standing and waiting, a bright-blue sofa in their arms.

## 20

---

'I cannot accept this,' Daisy said the moment Christian picked up the phone.

'The flowers?' His amusement rattled down the line. This was a far more confident Christian than the one she'd met yesterday. Or at least the one with a splinter of glass in his hand.

'No, not the flowers. The sofa. You have sent me a sofa. Who does that?'

'Someone who is worried you're going to impale yourself on glass each time you sit down. Honestly, it's not that big a deal. Besides, it's non-refundable, and it wouldn't go with my decor. And don't worry, the men will take away the old one. I told them to bring gloves.'

Daisy felt like she was still dreaming. She didn't even know this man, and yet here he was, sending her a sofa. It didn't make sense.

'No rush or anything, love, but we have got other jobs to get on with.' The delivery man's voice was loud enough that even Christian heard him speaking.

'Sounds like you're busy. And I've got a meeting. But message me about the paintings, okay? Perhaps while you're sitting on your new, glass-free sofa?'

Before Daisy could reply, he had hung up the phone.

It took the four men twenty minutes to get the old sofa out of the boat, while Daisy repeatedly reminded them to watch their hands for broken glass. The new one slotted perfectly into the space. It was a stunning cornflower blue, not dissimilar to the old one, only there were no faded or worn patches. No strains or tears, or broken springs. When the men finally left, she sat down and sank into the soft cushions and closed her eyes. This wasn't a discount, bargain-basement purchase. This was a top-of-the-line sofa. The perfect place to relax after a busy day at the coffee shop. The thought was enough to make her eyes ping open again.

She couldn't stay here right now. Not after the mess of yesterday, and the ridiculousness of Christian. She needed a change of scenery, not to mention someone to talk to. So, as she used to do when she worked in London, she messaged Bex to see if she fancied meeting in a park for lunch. And just like always, Bex was more than happy to oblige.

Thirty minutes later, Daisy was on the train with a homemade sandwich and yet more slices of Victoria sponge for their impromptu picnic.

When she arrived, Bex had already bagged a spot under the shade of a large cedar tree, a decent distance away from where a group of middle-aged men were involved in a very heated game of football.

'I might have to take a phone call in half an hour,' Bex said as she sat down next to her. 'But other than that, I don't need to head back to the office for at least an hour.'

'Sounds good.'

As she opened her bag and pulled out the cake and sandwiches, she could feel Bex's eyes staring at her.

'So, you wanted to chat. I don't suppose that means you're accepting my offer to lend you the money?'

Daisy pursed her lips.

'No. I asked you to meet me for lunch because I needed to get off the boat and stop thinking about what a horrendous state my finances are in. And...'

'And?' A short pause followed, in which Daisy took a deep breath and prepared herself to tell Bex about Christian and the sofa, but before she could, Bex was talking again.

'So, what's the low-down on you and Theo? He was quick to step in and help you run the coffee shop. Almost like a boyfriend would.'

'Theo?' Daisy found herself confused by the direction the conversation had taken. 'He was just being a good neighbour. A good friend. That's all. And he knows how to work the coffee machine.'

'Yes, that's definitely all it was. All neighbours help like that. You know, I wish you'd hurry up and get together. I've been telling Newton for ages now that we're going to do a double date.'

Daisy resisted the urge to respond curtly. That was what Bex wanted. There was nothing her best friend loved more than a bit of relationship drama, though usually it was her own.

'Theo and I aren't rushing into anything. Why not go out with Claire and Ian if you're desperate to double date?'

'Because Claire and Ian are a scary couple. You know what they're like with all their hand holding and sweet little giggles and whispers and secret language that no one else can speak. Newton will be terrified. I figure you and Theo would be a much more relaxed couple to introduce him to.'

'Only, Theo and I aren't a couple yet.'

She hadn't meant to lean on the word *yet* at all. She had

meant it to be a throwaway comment, but the sentence had barely left her lips when Bex pounced.

'Something has happened, hasn't it?' Her eyes widened with glee. 'Was it yesterday? What was it? You know I can tell something has changed.'

'No, it hasn't.'

'It has. You can't lie to me.'

'I'm not.'

'You are.'

'Did you nearly kiss him again? Or actually kiss him? You actually kissed him, didn't you?'

She was bouncing on her knees as she spoke.

'No, no kisses. But—'

'There's a but! I knew there was a but. What is it? Let me guess, he invited you to meet his family? He wants to go on holiday with you? He confessed his undying love?'

'What? No. We've decided we might look at being more than friends in the future.'

The shriek, which resounded in the air, was undoubtably too dramatic for the reality of the situation and in some ways, Daisy wished she'd arranged a date, just so Bex wasn't disappointed, but Daisy knew she had to break reality to her.

'Before you get too carried away, it's not going to happen yet. Not for a while.'

'What?' Bex's eyes bugged from her face. 'What does that mean?'

'I just need time to be sure.'

'Why do you need that? You know you're crazy about him.'

'But I need to make sure he feels the same way about me, too.'

Bex replied with a look that shot daggers. 'You have to be joking. The guy practically renovated your boat for you. He cooks you dinner nearly every night. You cannot possibly have doubts?'

'But who's to say he doesn't do that because he needs a distraction to stop him from thinking about Heather? Who's to say this time they are having apart isn't just what he needs for him to realise she's the one he wants to be with? Our lives have gone through some pretty big changes in the last few months. I think we both need to make sure that us getting together isn't just a knee-jerk reaction to that.' In need of a change of subject, Daisy redirected the conversation to something she needed to discuss far more urgently. 'Moving on from Theo, I meant to tell you, the lady who wanted to buy the painting came back. Well, she didn't come back. She sent her son to come and get it.'

'And was her son young, single and eligible?'

Without meaning to, Daisy found herself momentarily considering how dark Christian's brown eyes were. And the bunch of flowers, and the ridiculous gift of a sofa. And the way he had had to duck to get into the boat. In her mind, the thought was a split second long. But it was evidently long enough for Bex to notice.

Bex pounced. 'He was, wasn't he? You had a hot guy in your boat, after kissing another hot guy!'

'Theo and I did not kiss. And yes, Christian was more than averagely attractive. But he was there to pick up a painting for his mum. Besides, he's well out of my league.'

'What's that supposed to mean?'

'You know what that's supposed to mean. I'm a good catch and everything, I get that, but I'm not the best catch out there. Somehow, I got the impression that this guy can get whatever catch he wants.'

Bex frowned.

'Do you know how many times you said catch just then? It was weird. And anyway, it's nonsense. Any man in the world would be lucky to have you, and I mean it. And if you're not going on a date with Theo for another five months, maybe you should see if this guy's free.'

For a second, Daisy considered telling Bex about the bunch of flowers and the sofa, but she knew she'd read more into it.

'Anyway, I don't know what his job is exactly, but he says he does marketing. And that he could help me sell the paintings.' She paused, thinking that Bex might say something, but when the silence began to spread between the two, she had to push a little harder for a response. 'So?'

'So what? You're asking if I think this is a good idea? You know I think it's a good idea. I think your paintings are amazing.'

'I know you think they are, but you have to admit you're biased. Besides, he might end up wanting a fee.'

Bex's smile disappeared into a tight line. Daisy knew the expression well. It meant she wanted to say something she probably wasn't going to like. It only took a minute to discover what that was.

'This guy? What does he look like?'

'Bit older than us, early thirties, I guess. Dark hair, dark skin, dark-brown eyes, taller than average. And he dressed nicely, an expensive shirt, and shoes. Flashy watch, that type of thing.'

'Not that you paid much attention?'

'I already told you he was attractive. That's not what we're talking about here. I want to know whether you think I should take him up on the offer to help me with marketing my paintings.'

'Sorry, you're asking whether you should accept the help of an attractive – probably single – man who might know how to solve your financial problems?'

Daisy rolled her eyes. 'I don't know if he's single, and I don't even care. I just want your opinion on what you think I should do.'

'Well, are you going to take me up on my offer to loan you the money for the licence?'

Daisy's response was a reflex.

'You know I can't do that.'

'But you don't want to lose The Coffee Shop on the Canal. Which means you need to make money. If this guy is serious about what he does and thinks he can sell your paintings, then honestly, you'd be a fool not to at least give him a text and see what he says. Assuming you have his number?'

Daisy didn't reply. Instead, Bex's words had lodged in her thoughts. Like giving up on things, being a fool seemed to be a recurring theme in Daisy's life. She had been a fool to believe she'd found her happy-ever-after in her childhood sweetheart. A fool for dropping out of art college when things got a little tough. A fool for thinking she could run a coffee shop with no prior experience. Being a fool was getting somewhat tiresome.

What if this really was a good opportunity, and it was only her pride that was stopping her from selling her paintings? But then again, would she be able to live with being a fool again?

'Fine,' she said, picking up her sandwich and taking a bite. 'I'll message him.'

## 21

Daisy had decided to message Christian before she had even eaten her lunch, although it wasn't until she was on the train, heading back to the canal, that she finally plucked up the courage to text him. Despite having spoken to him that morning, finding the right words proved substantially harder and it took several attempts before she was finally satisfied with what she had.

Thank you for the flowers. Your secret is safe with me.

She sent the first one and watched until it had said it had sent, before she typed a second message. The one where she admitted needed help.

I'd be grateful for any advice with the paintings, too. If you're sure you don't mind?

She held her breath, closed her eyes, and clicked the send button. Then, after checking that she hadn't pressed delete by mistake, tucked her phone back into her bag. Deep down, she expected him to reply straight away. After all, he had picked up the phone immediately that morning when she'd messaged about the sofa. As such, when she got off the train and checked her phone, she was somewhat disappointed to see there was no reply. Even when she reached the boat, her phone remained unusually quiet.

Perhaps the texts hadn't sent, she considered, only to check her phone and see that not only had they been delivered, but read too. Why would he leave her on read for so long unless he hadn't actually wanted to hear from her?

Finally, after a very unexciting dinner of beans on toast and two true-crime episodes, a message came through.

How does brunch sound? Tomorrow?

* * *

A fair amount of thought went into Daisy's outfit for brunch. Not because, as Bex had insinuated, she found Christian attractive – although he was undeniably good-looking – but because she didn't know how she was meant to dress for a marketing meeting. Marketing implied business-minded, for which some of her old work clothes would have been suitable. Only she didn't have that many of those left. When she had downsized to the *September Rose*, she had given away a lot to Claire and charity shops, but she still had a smart skirt and jacket that would convey a professional vibe. Or should she go for a more artistic feeling? After all, that was what she intended to market herself as. An artist. Would she be better in a pair of dungarees, as a sign of how passionate she was about her craft? But then the only dungarees she had were the paint-stained ones she'd used to do the boat up in, and they didn't really seem suitable for a brunch meeting. And so the debate went on and on in her mind, until in the end, she settled on a pair of jeans and a black top which she hoped conveyed somewhere between professional and artistic.

Christian had suggested they meet at the Westfield shopping centre, just outside of Stratford station. She guessed he worked and lived in London, choosing something on the east side to benefit her as well, for which she was grateful. All this travelling in and out of London to see Bex and her mum was eating away at money she did not have. She just hoped that wherever he had chosen for brunch she could pay for with the remaining shrapnel of coins in her purse.

As per Christian's instructions, she made her way through the shopping centre to a small, Malaysian restaurant on the ground floor. It had been her plan to arrive at least ten minutes early, but she'd never parked here before and it took two attempts around the roundabout to even get into the car park. Then she had to find a space. By the time she arrived at the restaurant, she was five minutes late. And more than a little agitated.

As she suspected, Christian was already there, sitting and waiting. He stood up when he saw her enter.

'I'm so sorry,' she said as she slid out one of the small, wooden chairs. 'I thought I'd left plenty of time.'

'Really, it's not a problem. I've just got here myself.'

She smiled, only to notice the empty coffee cup in front of him. Obviously, he'd been here long enough to enjoy a drink.

'You don't mind meeting here, do you?' he asked. 'I love this place. It does the best roti canai. Are you a fan of Malaysian food?'

'What I've had of it, I've loved,' Daisy said truthfully. 'My mum's a chef, and she's made some Malaysian curries in the past, but I don't know how authentic they were, if I'm honest.'

'Well, if you haven't tried it before, the roti is my favourite. I definitely recommend it.'

The waitress appeared to serve them, a petite woman with deep brown eyes and one of those faces that immediately put Daisy at ease. It probably helped her on the tips front too, she thought.

'Are you ready to order? Although I already know what you'll be having.' She threw a mega-watt smile at Christian before turning her attention to Daisy. 'What about you? Have you decided what you'd like?'

Daisy glanced down at the menu. She hadn't even had a chance to scan through it yet, let alone decide what she wanted.

'I'll have whatever it was he suggested.' She nodded to Christian. 'The roti—'

'Canai?' the woman finished for her.

'That sounds perfect.' Daisy hoped she'd smiled confidently enough to look like she knew what she was talking about. She had had roti – flat, brown bread – often enough, but it was the canai part she wasn't sure about.

'So, I take it you come here often?' she asked Christian as the waitress headed back towards the kitchen.

'I'll be honest, I find any excuse I can to come over this way. My grandmother's Malaysian, so I'll do anything to get a taste of that cooking, and here is one of the best I've found.'

Daisy smiled. There was something incredibly easy going about Christian once you got past how ludicrously good-looking he was.

'Well, now I'm excited to try it. The food here smells delicious.'

'It does. But we didn't come here to talk about food. I want to know about you. How come you're selling paintings at the back of a canal boat, not in some great exhibition in London?'

'I don't think my paintings are good enough for that.'

'Trust me, I've seen a lot of paintings in my time. I own a fair bit of art too. I'm guessing you trained. Art college?'

'Only for a very short time.' Daisy didn't want to get into that story, so evaded it the best she can. 'I started, but then life took some twists and turns. Last year, it took an even bigger one, and I ended up both redundant and inheriting a houseboat.'

'Now there has to be far more to that story.'

'There is, but I'm sure you don't want to know it.'

'Trust me, I do. Besides, the longer you and I talk, the more I can justify ordering extra food.'

That smile struck again. That same ineffability that probably made everyone spill all their secrets to him without a second thought. But Daisy didn't want to expose that side of herself, because talking about the inheritance meant talking about her father, and that was something she wasn't comfortable doing with a man she'd barely met. At least, not sober. Besides, this was a business meeting.

With a tight smile, she steered the conversation back in the direction she wanted.

'The thing is, I love painting, but for the last four years or so I've never seen it as more than a hobby. And I never considered myself living on the water, but I've fallen for it way more than I expected. I should probably confess I've not been there that long, not full time at least, and I know everyone says that winter is the true test, but I can't imagine living anywhere else. Or at least, wanting to live anywhere else. The thing is, unless I can raise this money for the licence, I can't run the coffee shop at my mooring, and I can't change moorings because my propeller got wrecked because of an idiot stag do. And if I can't get the coffee shop up and running, then everything I've put into it already has been a complete waste.'

'Wow, that's quite a lot to take in one go.' Christian's eyes twinkled as he spoke, and Daisy felt a flush of embarrassment colour her cheeks. 'Don't take this the wrong way, but I'm guessing this is your first venture into business.'

Her embarrassment deepened. 'Is it that obvious?'

'To someone who's been in business for a long time, yes.'

There was something about the way he said *a long time*, like he was a retiree who'd just sold his third Fortune 100 business, that prickled slightly.

'You hardly look old enough to have had that many businesses.'

Christian sat back in his chair and pursed his lips before he spoke.

'I set up my first business when I was seventeen: landscaping and gardening. It was really just mowing lawns, but I was earning enough that I was paying taxes and could afford to take a gap year before I went to university.'

'Impressive,' Daisy said, and she meant it. It was hard to imagine how many lawns he'd had to mow to fund a year of travelling.

But Christian wasn't done yet.

'As it happened, university and I didn't click. I left after the first term and set up a business, partnering with local establishments and selling discount cards to students. The business started in one town, but then it went national, at which point I sold it for far more than I'd expected. Realising I'd got an eye for seeing what people want, I started my marketing business six months later with a friend, but that ended abruptly. Nearly five years ago.'

'Why, what happened?'

'Nothing that's worth bringing into our conversation now. And it was definitely for the best, though it didn't feel like it at the time. I set up on my own marketing company again and my turnover's already doubled what it was at the previous business. I've got a couple of side projects on the go, too. I find it helps to have fingers in different pies, you know, just to keep your eye on the economy and that sort of thing. But yeah, I've got a bit of experience in this area.'

He had put Daisy firmly in her place, and he knew it. Despite that, she couldn't help but feel herself smile.

'Okay then, Mr Businessman, what would you do in my situation?'

'In your situation, I'd probably stop talking shop for a minute so I could enjoy the roti.'

His smile twisted and he looked to his side. Daisy followed his gaze to see the waitress returning, holding two large, silver trays, the smell of which was enough to make her salivate.

'Fine then. But I'll be talking shop again soon.'

## 22

Just as Christian had said, the food was delicious. The rotis were simultaneously flaky and crisp, while soft and moreish. Daisy could happily have eaten the dahl with just a spoon, rather than as a condiment to dip the bread into. However, it didn't take long for them to start talking business again.

'I'm in a catch-22,' she admitted, leaning back from her plate to avoid finishing it embarrassingly quickly. 'I need to earn money to buy the licence for the fixed mooring, but the coffee shop was my way of earning money. Alternatively, if I could move the coffee shop around every couple of days, I wouldn't need that licence. But the propeller is broken, so—'

'So you can't move the coffee shop around until you have the money for the propeller? I get what you're saying.' Christian dunked a piece of roti into his curry. 'So, what can you do?'

It was a valid question. Daisy already knew the answer but didn't want to say it aloud, as doing so felt like admitting failure in some ridiculous way.

'I could go back into **London** and **get** a temp job for a couple of months. It's probably my best option, but by that point, I'll have missed all the summer trade. That means I won't have enough to get me through the winter, so I'll be back in a temping job again, with the bonus of probably having to drive between London and Wildflower Lock the whole time. Consequently, I still won't be able to save up the money for the licence. Not unless I starve myself.'

Christian nodded as he considered her situation. 'Okay, well, we're not going to let that happen, but we need to find ways of getting you that money for the licence or propeller as quickly as possible. Which would it be? Which would you rather do?'

Daisy thought about it, though it didn't take long.

'I think the licence would be the best bet. The propeller is a complete unknown. I might need to take it out of the water to fix, which will incur a whole other set of costs. Besides, I don't know where else I would want the coffee shop to be. Wildflower Lock is the perfect place.'

'Okay, so the licence it is. Let's think of the easiest route first. Is there anyone who would lend you the money? A relative or friend?'

It wasn't the business proposition Daisy had expected Christian to suggest, and given how uncomfortable she had felt with Bex's offer, she didn't really want to mention it, but he clearly knew what he was doing.

'My friend has already offered to give me a loan. But I can't take it.'

'Why not?'

'I can't. I don't feel comfortable with it.'

'But why not?' He was pushing her, and she didn't like it; she wanted to defend herself.

'Because it would be taking her money. And that doesn't feel right. She might need it.'

Christian pressed his lips tightly together.

'Look, I'm not saying this to wind you up. I'm not. I'm trying to get you to think of it from a business mindset. Firstly, would your friend have offered you the money if they couldn't afford it?'

Daisy chose not to respond. Bex had always been the most financially shrewd of them, and there was no chance she'd risk leaving herself short, but Daisy didn't say that.

When her lack of reply stretched out, Christian tried another way.

'Okay, can you tell me this?' He had abandoned his meal altogether now. Unlike Daisy, who was still picking at hers, although that was partially to avoid speaking. 'If the bank offered you a loan for the licence, would you take it?'

Daisy couldn't help but laugh.

'Believe me. No bank would give me a loan right now. I don't have a job. I had to take out credit cards to buy the coffee machine, and mooring fees are due in a matter of months. I'm a disaster in the making.'

'But I didn't ask you whether the bank would give you a loan. What I asked was, would you take one from them? If they offered?'

Daisy thought about the question. 'If it was possible, I don't know, maybe.' The certainty fixed itself in her. 'Yes, of course I would. If I could get a bank loan, then I could be back trading in a week.'

'Right. So let me ask you another question. Do you believe in The Coffee Shop on the Canal? Do you believe in your business?'

This time, she didn't hesitate to answer. She could remember the moment the idea of the coffee shop had struck, and the way she and Theo had looked at each other. In that moment, it felt like a bolt of energy had flooded through her. From that second on, she had known it would work. If she could just get it open.

'Yes. Yes, I do. You couldn't imagine the number of times I've heard people asking for exactly this. And on the days when I was open, we practically sold out of everything. We even ran out of cups on the first day.'

Christian's smile was small, yet it glimmered with the reflection of her excitement.

'Okay, so if you believe in this project, and you believe it will work – scrap that, we know it works – so why not take the money from your friend if they're offering it to you? Hell, I would offer to lend you it if I thought you'd take it.'

Daisy smirked.

'As payment for keeping quiet about your splinter phobia?'

Christian offered a mock glare in response, though it quickly faded.

'You know you can make this work. And you have backed yourself this far. Why not let other people back you for a bit, too?'

It was crazy, having this man, an almost complete stranger, believing so fiercely in her idea. And she had thought she was coming to talk to him about the paintings, not the coffee shop. Still, it was all about business, and it was hard to deny that he'd raised a valid point.

'I guess I don't like the fact I might not be able to pay her back straight away. By the time I've got my costs covered, I might have to give it back to her in dribs and drabs, and that doesn't feel right. I don't like the idea of this debt hanging over us. It could take months for me to pay her back.'

'But what if it didn't take months? What if it only took a couple of months? Or maybe even a couple of weeks?'

'I don't see how that could happen, though.'

Christian was looking straight at her, and there was something about the way his smile twisted at the corner of his lips that made Daisy inexplicably excited. She waited for him to reply, her plate now empty, a hint of butterflies forming within her.

'I've got an idea,' he said, that smile now breaking wide of his face. 'And I think it'll work. We're going to shift your paintings and make you some money. Big time.'

## 23

By the time they had finished their conversation, Daisy was on cloud nine.

'And you're sure this idea will work? I don't want to put you to loads of effort and waste your time.'

'I've got a feeling that helping you will never be a waste of my time.'

As he spoke, his eyes met hers, and an unexpected tingling fluttered through her. Trying to ignore it, she reached down and picked her bag up from the floor.

'I should let you get back to work. I've taken enough of your morning already.'

'Trust me, I would much rather spend my time with you. But you're right, I should probably head back to the office. We'll speak again soon. You sort out the loan with your friend, and I'll do my part with the painting. Deal?'

'Deal.'

Back at Wildflower Lock, her excitement had yet to fade. There was something about the way Christian had spoken that made her feel like she could do anything, and it was a long time since she could remember feeling that way. Especially about her art.

As she headed through the gate to the canal, she spotted Nicholas Granger, once again tending his plants. Given how pleased he had been to see Pippa the previous week, Daisy thought that he might have softened to her too, and she lifted her hand optimistically.

'Afternoon, Nicholas.' She had barely got the first syllable of his name out before he ducked out of view behind his perennials. 'Nice to see you,' she added, partly for emphasis, partly because she refused to let anything dampen her mood. Besides, it didn't matter what Nicholas Granger thought of her, because at that moment, there was only one person on the lock she wanted to speak to.

He opened the door to his boat before she had even knocked on it.

'That was good timing,' she said, about to step inside.

She stopped. Theo was looking straight at her, but there was something different about him. Something she couldn't quite place.

'I saw you coming. And you were smiling. Which I took to mean you were going to come and bug me about some good news.'

'Well, if you don't want me to tell you.' She turned to go, but Theo grabbed her hand.

'Of course I do. Is this a coffee type conversation? Or should I grab us a beer?'

'Beer, definitely.'

While Daisy took a seat on his sofa, Theo went to the kitchen to fetch their drinks, at which point she realised what it was that had been bugging her about his appearance. For the first time since they'd become friends, his long hair was out of the man-bun and loose, falling in waves down well past his shoulders.

Other than their initial meeting, where she had walked in on Theo in his bathroom, Daisy couldn't recall seeing him with his hair down like this. There had been occasions when he had let it out of its bun and removed the elastic band just to tighten it back up again, but even those moments had been brief and he'd usually scraped it back behind his head before Daisy could fully appreciate how long it was. Not to mention thick and wavy.

'You okay?' Theo was walking back towards her with the beers in his hand, looking at her intently. She cleared her throat, praying she hadn't been staring for that long.

'Sorry, yes. Yes, just a lot going on, that's all.'

'I heard.' He handed her a beer and took a seat. 'A licensing officer, right? I'm sorry. Did you tell her about the email you sent checking if you needed one?'

'I did. And she was sympathetic, but her hands were tied. The boat doesn't move so I have to have a licence to run a coffee shop from it.'

'I'm so sorry. I tried coming over,' he said. 'But I guessed you needed space.'

'Sorry, I know. I heard you knocking. I just couldn't deal with people straight away. You understand, don't you?'

'Of course I do.' He took a long swig from his beer. 'So what about now? How are you feeling? Have they shut you down for good?'

'No, I just didn't have the licence. But I think I've found a solution. And it's to do with my paintings.'

'Your paintings.' His smile widened, and a wave of warmth washed over her. There was something about making Theo smile that made everything else feel better. Not that today hadn't been a good day already. 'You sold one, didn't you? I told you you would. You're amazing.'

'I might have sold one.'

In a single sweep, he placed his beer down on the table, twisted around and wrapped her tightly in a hug. For a second, the pair remained squeezed together, her head tight against his cheek. Theo pulled back apart, but it was only by a fraction.

'I really want to kiss you right now,' he said quietly.

The same thought ran through Daisy's mind. It would be so easy to tilt her head forward and plant her lips on his. But then what? It might be easy to kiss him, but what followed was likely to be anything but. Five months, wasn't that how long they'd said? That seemed a reasonable amount of time to make sure he was actually over Heather and Daisy wasn't going to end up broken hearted. If they both still felt the same way in five months' time, then she would let herself kiss him. And if these feelings were as genuine as they both believed, then what was five months in the grand scheme of things? Her heart drummed in her chest as she slipped back away, picked up his beer and handed it to him.

'Well, you can't, because I haven't finished telling you what I wanted to.' She looked away as she took a large gulp of her own drink, hoping it would abate the heat that was pulsing through her.

When she had drunk almost half the bottle, she carried on speaking.

'So, the lady who bought the painting from me, she didn't have any cash on her, so she said she'd pick it up the next day. When she didn't show, I assumed she'd changed her mind, but instead, she sent her son. Her son, who happens to be this massive marketing guru type guy who owns loads of businesses, and he had this idea that we could do a silent auction for my paintings.'

'A silent auction? What does that mean?'

'It's a thing people do to raise money. Lots of times it's done for charities, but let's be honest, I'm a lot like a charity case right now.'

'You still haven't explained how it works.' Theo cut through, helping to keep Daisy on track.

'Sorry, you're right. So, you display all the items you want to auction off, with a clipboard underneath that's got two pieces of paper on. The top one is blank, but on the one underneath, people write how much they're willing to pay for it. Then, whoever is the highest bidder pays that amount and gets the painting.'

Theo's eyebrows rose in a manner Daisy knew meant he was mildly impressed, although not yet fully convinced.

'Okay, I like it. But where are you going to display the paintings?'

'Outside the boat. I'll get some tables from somewhere, then we'll invite all the people who come and visit the lock and canal. Christian reckons he can pull some marketing strings and give it a small announcement in a couple of local papers, that type of thing. It'll be an event. We'll make it a proper reopening for the cafe, combining the two events together. By that point, the licence should have come through, because Bex is going to lend me the money, so there won't be any issues with that. Then, fingers crossed, if the auction goes as well as Christian thinks it will, I'll be able to pay her back, and maybe have a chunk to put towards the new propellor.'

A paused punctuated the conversation as she waited for Theo to respond.

'And this Christian, who you've only just met, he's going to help you do all this?'

'Yes. I know it sounds crazy, but he's a really genuine guy. We were out at brunch today talking about it for nearly two hours.'

'The guy bought you lunch. Interesting.'

Theo lifted his beer bottle and took a long sip. Over time, Daisy had become skilled at reading his expressions, and this wasn't the reaction she'd hoped for.

'You don't like the idea?' Her voice wavered with disappointment. She couldn't deny that Theo's opinion mattered to her, and he had seemed so keen to start with.

'No, it's not that. It could work, absolutely. You know I think your paintings are incredible. And I'm glad you've figured a way to get the licence. It's just this Christian guy, coming on board to help you with all this, seems crazily fast. You barely know this man; his mother buys one of your paintings, and then he's saying he'll set this whole thing up for you.'

'Almost as fast as meeting someone and having them ask for the keys to your boat so they can help renovate it?' she retorted, raising an eyebrow.

At this, Theo's serious expression finally broke into a grin. 'Okay, fair enough, I guess. Have you set a date for when you're going to do it?'

Daisy nodded. 'Two weekends from now. That should give me time to borrow the money from Bex, get the licence, and make sure I've got enough paintings done.'

'That makes sense.'

'So, you'll help me? You know I really value your opinion on what paintings I should do. I'll be honest, I was hoping I might use the outside of your boat to display some of them, too.'

He stared out at the water for a moment, and Daisy's heart raced, as she feared he might refuse. Instead, he turned to her with a look of utter seriousness.

'Daisy, when are you going to learn that I'll do anything for you?'

## 24

When Daisy returned to the *September Rose*, her first task was to call Bex just in case she'd changed her mind since the meeting with Christian.

'Are you sure you don't mind?' she asked for at least the tenth time. Despite Bex's immediate agreement, and near elation that Daisy was accepting the offer, Daisy still felt the need to clarify a few points. 'I think we should put a contract in place. And I can pay interest if you want to. Just set out your terms.'

'My main term is that you stop going on about it,' Bex said, straight to the point.

'But you know I'll pay you back? As soon as I can. That's my number-one priority.'

'How about you just give me complete credit when you're a world-famous children's illustrator? You can dedicate every book to me.'

'You've got a deal.'

'Really, I'm glad you finally accepted help. I'll ping the money across to you now.'

After telling Bex her bank details and thanking her another

dozen times, Daisy got off the phone. It may have been early evening, but she was buzzing. How she was going to keep calm for the next two weeks while she got the auction set up was beyond her, but at least she had an outlet for the energy: painting.

Daisy remained at her desk with watercolours scattered about her until the clouds coloured the sky with the warm, rich hue of dusk. With Bex's words about her illustrations still floating through her mind, Daisy focused on her paintings – more specifically, her characters. Soon her eyes were straining to make sense of the images. She had added the first layers of paints to both an otter and a red squirrel, with two more pencil sketches ready to start: one of a mole and another of a barn owl.

She decided that, at some point over the next couple of days, she would take an inventory of all the paintings and their various states of completion. After all, the more she had, then hopefully, the more money she would make.

The next morning, Daisy awoke with an urge to leave the boat and go for a walk. Since inheriting the *September Rose*, nature had become part and parcel of her everyday life, but she didn't take as much time to actively observe and enjoy it as she could. And, given that in a couple of weeks, her early mornings would be spent serving steaming coffees, it seemed like a waste not to make the most of the clear skies.

In a plain hoodie and paint-stained jeans, Daisy headed outside. The sun had long since risen, but the sky maintained a delicate glimmer that was almost ethereal. In the distance, a wind turbine rotated lazily, while a flock of geese flew overhead, one dropping out to the side and ruining the perfect V formation. As she stood there and took a deep breath, filling her lungs with the fresh, countryside air, a deep throb ached in her chest. She may have said that she could go back to London to work, temping or otherwise, but she knew the truth. She was rooted here. Whether this place was her past or not didn't matter. Wildflower Lock was her future, and she was going to give everything she had to stay here. The days of being the Daisy who quit things were well and truly over.

After her morning walk, she started to sort her paintings. The first job was dividing them into piles of finished and sellable, finished but not sellable, and not finished but could be sellable. Once that was done, she began to tweak the ones that were not yet finished. Christian had been so optimistic, insisting they would hit her target with little to no effort. But realistically, how many paintings was she going to need? Even if thirty pounds was, as he and his mother had said, far too cheap for her work, it wasn't as if they would sell for thousands. The most she'd feel comfortable taking was a hundred pounds. That meant she needed to sell seventeen at that maximum price just to cover the licensing fee. And there would likely be plenty that didn't reach their maximum.

With sixteen paintings already in the 'could sell' pile, Daisy set herself the target of finishing ten more before the day of the auction. That would give her twenty-six, and even if she didn't make a massive amount of money on any of them, twenty-six lots of thirty pounds would still go a long way to paying back Bex for the loan.

It was late in the afternoon when she received a message from Christian.

Can you send me a photo of your boat, and a couple of your paintings too? Maybe a photo of you standing outside it if you've got one?

Daisy didn't need to think about whether she had something matching that description. She smiled to herself at the memory. It had been one of those picture-perfect days, with fluffy, white clouds and a bright-blue sky, though the wind had whipped through the trees and it took several shots to get a clear photo without her hair covering her face. The outcome had been a photo of her smiling widely in front of a freshly painted *September Rose*. It was her profile picture for all of her online accounts.

As for one of her paintings, she quickly spread out the finished pile and selected different styles to be fired off to Christian. A surge of butterflies flooded her. She didn't know what he was going to do with the photos, but she was going to trust him and pray she was right to do so.

With the task of sorting out photos done, she carried on painting, with no intention of stopping anytime soon.

For the rest of the week, Daisy followed the same routine of getting up early to walk alongside the canal and breathe in the fresh air before returning to paint, normally full of inspiration. One morning, she spotted a patch of cornflowers. The bright blues were alive with bees, and the moment she got home, she sketched out an illustration based on them. Five hours later, she was prouder of her work than she'd been in a long time.

It was Friday morning, after nearly a full week of painting, and Daisy was working on another illustration, this time involving a badger, when her mother rang.

'Have you seen the paper? Why didn't you tell me?'

'What paper?' Daisy put down her paintbrush.

'I've just seen the article. You come across very well in it.'

'What?'

'And the photographs are brilliant. You are so talented. A double-page spread. I can't believe it.'

'A double-page spread?' Daisy repeated her mother's words. 'Are you sure?'

'I'm staring straight at it. "Local Artist Unveils New Art Collection for Fundraiser".' Her mother's voice implied she was reading. 'It's in the *Standard*, but Farah from over the road messaged me to say there's a piece in the *Echo*, too. Darling, this is such wonderful news.'

'Yes, yes, it is. Look, I'm gonna have to go. I'll speak to you soon, all right?'

Daisy was already on her feet, moving towards the door. She grabbed her wallet and keys en route.

As much as she loved living in the middle of nowhere, she sometimes cursed the fact that there wasn't a shop closer to Wildflower Lock. Perhaps she could sell newspapers at the coffee shop, too, she thought as she wrestled her car out onto the road, only to dismiss the idea. That was probably a bit ambitious, considering how well her first venture had gone.

She stuck right to the speed limit the entire time, but even so, it was a full fifteen minutes before she was popping open the door to the not so aptly named Local Store.

'Where are your newspapers?' The bell still jingled above the door as the boy behind the counter tipped his head to the back of the shop.

After racing across to the row of papers, Daisy dropped to the ground and opened up the *Standard*. Her mother was right. A double-page spread.

'Local artist's latest venture makes art available in a fundraising event.' She read the words her mother had spoken to her less than thirty minutes before. The photos of the boats took up almost the entire page, and there was also a small advert in the corner dedicated to a double-glazing company, but the rest of it was all about her. 'Daisy May renovated the *September Rose*, single-handedly determined to bring the residents of Wildflower Lock a taste of freshly brewed coffee and delectable desserts.' Alongside was a quote that had apparently been given by her:

> It's such an amazing place to live. I couldn't imagine wanting to be anywhere else.

It sounded familiar, though she couldn't quite remember when she'd said it.

Still crouched on the ground, she continued to read.

> This was actually my father's boat. It's a piece of history, and I'm so lucky to be bringing it back to life again.

Daisy shook her head in disbelief. She certainly hadn't expected words from her conversations with Christian to be quoted and used in the local press, but she could hardly be cross. Not with exposure like this.

When she had finished reading the article in the *Standard*, she moved on to the *Echo*. This piece was far smaller, just two pictures and an announcement about a silent auction for contemporary art that would take place on Wildflower Lock. Contemporary art? Is that what she painted? Apparently, Christian thought so.

'Are you planning on buying one of those?' the teenager asked from behind the counter. 'This isn't a library, you know.'

'Sorry. Yes, yes, I am. I'm going to buy them now.'

With both papers in her arms, she paid up and headed outside, an insane grin fixed on her face. An artist. That was how she was being described. A local artist.

Even when she was back at Wildflower Lock, her grin was still in place. Her phone rang. She stared at the name for a second before answering.

'So? Have you seen the articles?'

She hadn't thought her smile could stretch any further, but the sound of Christian's voice did it.

'I can't believe you did that. How did you do that?'

'You're not mad, are you? I know I took liberties with some of your quotes, but what you said was so emotive, and I knew that if I showed that side of you, people would be just as taken by you and your story as I am.' His voice trailed off, before he spoke again. 'Can you forgive me?'

'Well, let me think about that...' Daisy tried to stretch out a sense of tension, but could barely keep herself from bouncing on the spot. 'Okay, I've decided: you're forgiven, you're definitely forgiven.'

Though it shouldn't have been possible, Daisy could have sworn she heard him smiling down the line.

'Well, seeing as you're in such a good mood and I'm clearly in your good books, do you fancy meeting me for lunch? I don't want to disturb your painting, but I was thinking the Ivy. My treat.'

Given the level of adrenaline pumping through her, Daisy wasn't sure she'd be able to sit still to paint. And she wanted to see Christian, if for no other reason than to thank him.

'It sounds perfect.'

'Brilliant, I'll see you there. How does twelve sound? Is that okay, or is it too early?'

'Twelve sounds great,' Daisy replied reflexively, before she considered how long it would take her to get changed and get into London. She could park at her mum's and get the bus and Tube, but she'd still need a little more time. 'Actually, can we make it twelve-thirty?'

'Brilliant, it's a date.'

## 25

Daisy's mind was a whirl as she played Christian's last words over and over in her head. *It's a date.* That's what he'd said. *It's a date.* But what had he meant by that?

As she sat on the Tube, she mulled it over again and again. It was just an expression, wasn't it? He didn't mean that their lunch was an actual date? After all, they'd had brunch together before, and that hadn't been a date. Besides, if he'd actually been asking her out, he would've suggested dinner, surely? Who did lunch dates? No one that she knew, excluding Bex – but then before Newton, Bex would have agreed to an elevenses, lunch time, teatime and dinner date all in one day if it meant she was going to meet Mr Right. No, this was just another marketing meeting, surely. Because there was no chance someone like Christian would want to date someone like her. Even though she was technically 100 per cent single.

Daisy had been to the restaurant in Covent Garden once before, to celebrate Claire and Ian's engagement, but that had been a very long time ago, and she suspected it had changed since then. She had once again spent far longer than average deciding what outfit to wear to hit the right tone. Given how warm the day was, she opted for a patterned summer dress with small purple buttons down the front. Playful, yet sophisticated, that was the look she was going for, and the one she hoped she was pulling off. Though as she stepped in through the doorway and into the restaurant, her nerves rocketed.

The restaurant was even more stunning than she remembered. For a moment, she forgot why she was even there. Her eyes scanned the decor, from the classic black-and-white checked tiles on the floor to the brightly coloured paintings on the walls. Whoever designed the place had a masterful eye, somehow creating something that was timeless, and yet modern, though it was the bar that really held her attention. She could only imagine the number of cocktails she and Bex could enjoy sitting there as they made up stories about all the men and women that milled around them. Not that she'd be able to afford more than one cocktail.

'Daisy, over here.'

Christian stood beside a small, round table with his hand in the air, though the moment Daisy clocked him, he moved away from the table to meet her.

'How is my artistic superstar doing?' Before she could respond, he had pulled her in for a kiss on the cheek. 'Come, our table is this way.' Wordlessly, Daisy followed him over to the table, where he pulled out a seat for her.

'So how many of the articles did you see?' he asked as he filled up her glass with water.

'How many? I saw two. Were there more?'

'Just a couple. Though they all say pretty much the same thing.'

Daisy didn't want to know how many more *just a couple* was.

'I can't believe it. I've had people from my old job ringing me up, saying they've seen photos of me.'

'Great, that's exactly what we need. I'm really excited about this. And I'm not going to lie. Helping you out definitely gave me some serious brownie points with my mother. She was quite taken by you.'

There was the coy smile again. The one that made her nerves rise inexplicably.

'I really don't know how to thank you enough,' Daisy said, wanting to break the tension that was wrapping its way around her.

'Well, you can thank me by telling me you've sorted that licence out already. None of this coffee shop business will work if you haven't.'

'All applied for and paid for.'

'Now, that is great news. And what about a plan for the day? Have you got all your paintings sorted?'

From there, the conversation moved from her art to Wildflower Lock, to places they had visited and places they wanted to visit.

It was only when the waitress came and asked for their order that Daisy realised she hadn't even glanced at the menu.

'I'll give you another minute,' the waitress said before disappearing back to the bar.

'I already told you this is my treat,' Christian said, as Daisy's eyes scanned down the prices nervously.

'You don't have to do that.'

'I want to. Honestly, it was even more fun than I expected helping sort those articles for you. And we've still got over a week until the auction. So, please, don't hold back.'

With a finances-related knot still twisting in her abdomen, Daisy's attention went back to the menu, although it was the lower part of the page where her attention locked.

'There are so many amazing desserts,' she said, as much to herself as Christian, before adding, 'do you think it would be wrong to have a dessert as a starter too?'

She had meant the comment purely as a joke, yet when her eyes moved up from the menu and met Christian's, a small smile twisted on his lips.

'Let's do it.'

'Let's do what?'

'Let's have three courses of dessert. I'm assuming there are three desserts there you'd like?'

Daisy didn't need to look back at the menu to answer. She had already seen the lemon meringue, crème brulé, and chocolate torte, which were three of her absolute favourites. And there were at least another four choices on the menu besides them.

'There are definitely three desserts I'd want. But we can't do that.'

'Why not?'

'Because it's not done.'

'It is now.'

It was with a flurry of excitement and nervousness that Daisy watched Christian called the waitress over.

'Are you ready to order?'

'Yes, yes,' Christian said, a glint in his eyes large enough to start a fire. 'I think we are. Aren't we, Daisy?'

Daisy's lips remained firmly fixed together for fear of laughter. She still couldn't believe Christian was actually going to go through with it. She held her breath, waiting to see if he chickened out.

'So to start with, I would like the panna cotta.' His face was completely straight, even as the waitress raised an eyebrow.

'Panna cotta. The dessert? For your starter?'

'Yes, we are having three courses of dessert today. That won't be a problem, will it?'

The woman's lips parted, as if she was going to object, but she changed her mind and offered a tight-lipped smile instead.

'Of course not. That is absolutely fine.' She turned to Daisy. 'And what will you be having for your dessert starter?'

An hour and a half later and Daisy could barely breathe, partly from all the laughing she'd been doing, and partly because three desserts – while all good on paper – were incredibly hard to eat.

'I don't know why I started with the chocolate torte,' she said, leaning back on the sofa and resting her hands on her stomach. 'I should have started with something lighter. And the champagne. We did not need a bottle of champagne after that first cocktail.'

'I think it was the extra custard I asked for with my sticky-toffee pudding that ruined me.'

'Oh, the waitress's face when you did that. It was a picture.' The laughter started again, although Daisy could barely move. When she finally stopped, Christian was looking straight at her.

'You are an awful lot of fun, Daisy May.'

'Am I?'

'Yes. You are.'

Daisy pondered the comment. She had never considered herself a fun person. Apart from when it was just her, Claire, and Bex. She was the person who avoided mingling with work colleagues, and liked to stay home with a horror film, rather than head out drinking. But something about Christian made her feel fun.

'I think it's something to do with the company,' she said.

As his eyes locked on hers, a nervous tingle began around her rib cage. The sensation had appeared several other times over the meal, like when his hand brushed against hers as he was filling her water glass. Or how, during one particularly amusing anecdote, he had put his hand on her arm, and held it there, far longer than two people who were at a business meeting would do. But then, this didn't feel much like a business meeting at all. It felt like something very different.

'I'd like to do this again. And not under the guise of talking shop.' Christian's words cut through her thoughts, mirroring them almost exactly. 'I'd like to take you on a proper date.'

He was looking her dead in the eye, and she hadn't even realised she was leaning forward until she noticed how close together they were. Their knees touched under the table and her heart had taken on a peculiar staccato rhythm. It was the champagne's fault, she tried to tell herself. The champagne that was making her think ridiculous things. Like how easy it would be to kiss him. And how she actually quite wanted to, even though it was a terrible idea.

As if reading her mind, Christian moved closer. Then, in an almost involuntary action, she could feel her own head tipping forward.

It didn't feel like it was her kissing him. It felt as if she had slipped away into some parallel universe where she drank cocktails and champagne at lunchtime over three courses, and kissed beautiful men who did wonderful, good deeds. But it was real, and the second their lips touched, she didn't want it to stop. Had kissing always been this amazing? she thought as her heart soared in her chest. Had it always left her feeling so weak in the knees, and light in the chest, and like she never wanted it to end?

Before she could consider the question, Christian broke away, leaving Daisy still struggling to make sense of what had just happened.

When she finally looked up, Christian smiled broadly. Pressing his lips tightly together, he slipped his hand over hers.

'I guess that's a yes to the date, then?'

## 26

The moment she was on the train, Daisy called an emergency telephone meeting. She positioned herself at the very end of the carriage, facing away from the rest of the passengers, and she opened up a group video call, which she had pre-empted with an SOS text. Before she had reached the first stop, the other two had joined her: Bex, in her office with the blinds down, while Claire was outside in her garden.

'Just slow down and fill us in again,' Claire said. 'I seem to have missed something here. An attractive, wealthy, handsome stranger swanned into your life to help you sort out your business and has now asked you out on a date? After you kissed him?'

'That pretty much sums it up.'

'And was it a good kiss?'

Daisy's lips were still burning with the sensation of it. The taste of three consecutive desserts and aftershave mingled to set her pulse sky-high.

'I would say it was a good kiss.' She tried to sound nonchalant.

'And you're asking us whether you should say yes to this date with the handsome, wealthy, generous, not quite so much of a stranger any more, who you've already met up with twice and kissed?' Bex added.

'Exactly.'

Her comment was met by an elongated pause, after which Bex spoke again.

'Yes, of course you have to go on a date with him. This is straight out of a novel. Besides, two dates and a kiss – you guys only need two more until you're an official couple.'

'Is that a rule?'

Daisy knew of certain 'rules' that plagued the dating world. In particular, the third date one, which she had no intention of abiding by, but she'd never heard of the four-date relationship one.

'It's my rule,' Bex replied.

Suddenly, it made sense. Yet before Daisy could respond, Claire raised the question she hadn't been brave enough to ask herself.

'Yes, but what about Theo?'

Once again, the call went silent, as Daisy's two best friends stared at her through her screen, waiting for her to answer. But what could she say? What about Theo? It was true, she already had a man in her life, even if she was refusing to date or kiss him, and something about going on a date officially with Christian just felt wrong. But she and Christian had obviously clicked. She wouldn't have kissed him otherwise. Or let him kiss her. She still wasn't exactly sure what order it had happened in.

'I don't know. I don't know about Theo at the minute. I know that I like him. Really like him. But that doesn't change the fact I still worry about him and Heather and I don't believe he can have got over their breakup this quickly. He needs time to process it first before jumping into a new relationship. I mean, I think the world of him, but I have no intention of being his rebound.'

'Okay, so what's this Christian's relationship history then?' Claire was still on the logical questions. 'You've put all these boundaries and limitations in place because Theo has just broken up with someone, but what about Christian? Do you even know when his last relationship was or how long it lasted?'

It was a good point, Daisy conceded. For all she knew, Christian might have just broken off an engagement or a marriage or have three grown-up children she didn't know about, although given his age, that last one seemed unlikely.

'I think you're overthinking this thing with Theo,' Claire continued. 'If he's the one you like, then you should be going on a date with him.'

'And if I like both of them?'

'Then you've got yourself in a bit of a pickle that you need to sort out.'

'Or you've got yourself into a really good time,' Bex said.

Daisy groaned.

'You're right. I need to get my head straight. This hasn't helped much.'

'Well, let us know what you decide,' Bex said. 'I need to head off. I've got a meeting in ten. Love you.'

'Love you too,' Daisy said, just before Bex hung up, leaving just Claire and her on the call.

'What have you got planned for tomorrow?' Claire asked, carrying on with the conversation. 'I was thinking about bringing Amelia down to the lock for a walk. Would you be about?'

'I should think so. I've not got any plans, other than more painting. Just give me a text when you think you're coming.'

'Okay, speak soon. Let us know what decision you make.'

'Will do.'

Daisy hung up the phone, no less confused than she had been beforehand. How had she got into the position that she was having to make a decision about two men? Six months ago, she'd been certain she would never find love again, after Paul, and had refused to even consider a date with someone. Inheriting the *September Rose* sure had changed her life, and not just her living arrangements.

When she got back to the car, Daisy contemplated what she was going to do next. As much as she wanted to head straight home, there was the small factor of the four glasses of champagne she'd drunk, plus the cocktail, which was limiting her travel choices substantially. Paying for a taxi or managing the array of buses it would take to get her back was out of the question. Besides, it would mean leaving her car at her mother's. Which meant she had to choose between staying there until she was back under the limit, or – her preferred option – hope that her mum wouldn't mind giving her a lift back. Then she'd brave the buses the next day to collect her car.

Hoping her mother would be in, and would want to take advantage of the chance for a catch up, Daisy used her key to let herself in, only to pause in the hallway. She could hear her mother's voice coming from the kitchen. It sounded like she was on the phone.

Daisy headed into the house, not wanting to surprise her mother, but unable to resist listening to the conversation.

'I don't know when I can get down. Soon, definitely soon.' Her mother was speaking with a full-on girly giggle. 'Don't be rude. Really, you're terrible.'

Daisy was standing outside the kitchen now. She knew it was wrong to listen, but she couldn't stop. The last thing she wanted to do was interrupt her mum, but the longer she stood here, the more she realised she was eavesdropping on an obviously private conversation.

'Well,' her mother continued. 'If that's what you're planning on doing to me, perhaps I should tell you some of the things that I'm planning to do to you...'

That was as much as Daisy could take. With a bracing breath, she stepped into the kitchen, not wanting to hear something she could never unhear.

'Hi Mum.'

Her mother's cheeks flooded with a fluorescent red tint.

'Daisy, dear, I didn't hear you come in. How long have you been there?'

'Not long, not too long. Barely even a minute. Less. Definitely not long at all. Definitely not long enough to hear anything.'

Daisy was about to continue her hugely embarrassing rambling when a muffled man's voice came through on her mum's phone. Still blushing, her mother lifted it to her ear.

'Sorry. Sorry, I've got to go. Daisy's just arrived. Speak soon.' She hung up and turned back to Daisy, a tight-lipped, strained smile on her face.

'I didn't hear you come in,' she repeated.

'Yeah, I gathered as much. So, do I want to know who that was?'

Her mother's throat bobbed visibly as she swallowed hard. 'No, it's nothing... Well, actually, that's not true. It's not nothing. I think it's something. It could definitely be something... I've been wondering how I was going to tell you, actually, but now you heard, I should just come out and say it. I've started seeing someone.'

Daisy's straight smile reflected her mother's in an exact mirror image.

'Mum, it's fine. It's not any of my business. I really don't need to know.'

During Daisy's teen years, her mother had had a habit of seeing people, and each time, she would insist they were the salt of the earth, truly generous, charming, wonderful men, but they would all end up dumping her unceremoniously after causing no end of heartache. Given her mother's track record, it wasn't hard to see why Daisy herself was so horrendous at relationships.

'I know, darling. But I want you to know. The thing is, I've started dating Nicholas.'

From the way she said the name, it was clear Daisy was meant to know who she was talking about, but nothing sprung to mind. She wracked her brain. Was it somebody her mum worked with, perhaps? There was a Nicky at the restaurant, she knew, but she was a woman, so Nicholas didn't fit there.

After a moment of concerted effort, Daisy looked at her mother.

'Sorry, Nicholas who?'

'Nicholas, on the *Jeanette*.'

Now that rang some bells. Daisy's jaw dropped as the realisation sank in.

'You're dating someone who lives on Wildflower Lock? Someone with a boat?' Daisy thought about the name. And that was when it struck her. 'Nicholas, the miserable old man who had a go at me at the coffee shop?'

Her mother's face hardened. 'I'll have less of the "old", thank you. He's only a couple of years older than me, and he's not grumpy. He just takes time to warm up to people, that's all.'

'And you are seeing him? What does that even mean?' Daisy immediately regretted her question. 'No, don't answer that. Please, please don't tell me.'

'Daisy May, stop making such a fuss. We're both adults here, and – not that it's any of your business – the relationship hasn't reached a physical level. Or at least, not at the level you're thinking. Yet.'

Daisy couldn't hear any more.

'I don't... I don't want to know.'

'Daisy, really, you're making far more fuss about this than necessary. I thought you'd be pleased.'

Daisy was struggling to keep her thoughts straight, which could have been because of the alcohol, but more likely from the fact her mother was dating someone who lived on the same canal where she had lived when she was married to Daisy's father. The same canal she had refused to visit Daisy for months.

'Sorry, Mum. I've had a bit to drink. I just came up to have a nap before I head home.'

'Of course, but Daisy—'

Daisy wasn't listening any more. She was stomping her way up to her old bedroom. This was more than she could cope with.

## 27

While a three-hour nap probably wasn't a sensible idea, Daisy felt far better when she woke up in her childhood bedroom. Physically, at least. It didn't take long before the Theo/Christian debate slipped back to the forefront of her mind, only to be joined by thoughts of her mother's new dalliance.

Thankfully, her mother was out when Daisy headed downstairs. Instead, a note was fixed to the fridge, the way it used to be in her younger years.

*Gone to work*
*Speak soon*
*Love you*

As Daisy drove back to Wildflower Lock with the last of the day's commuters, her thoughts were in overdrive.

Her mother and grumpy Nicholas Granger. It was more than she could handle at the moment. It wasn't about her mother dating; she had gotten used to that by now. It was the Wildflower

Lock issue she couldn't shake. Her mother hadn't even stepped foot on her boat yet, for crying out loud.

Stopping at a set of traffic lights, she tried to play devil's advocate with herself. It was the *September Rose* that held the memories. After all, that was where her mother had spent her honeymoon. But she had known Nicholas back in those days, too. When she was married to Daisy's father. Had something happened between them then?

Daisy's mind was already spiralling away. Was this Nicholas like all the other men her mother seemed to fall for – ones who saw her as a soft touch and quickly used her for everything she had? She wouldn't put it past him. In fact, the only positive thing she knew about the man was that he made damn fine sloe gin, but that was hardly a judge of character, was it?

On the positive side, having her mind turning her unwanted images of her mother and grumpy Nicholas had distracted Daisy from the inner turmoil she was still facing over Theo and Christian. Though it didn't stop thoughts of them creeping in now and again.

Claire was right; Daisy needed to decide how she felt about them, but that was easier said than done. When it came to Theo, at least.

With Christian, it felt more like dating. Normal dating, where you found someone you liked, and saw them for meals or drinks, and exchanged flirty text messages. She enjoyed spending time with him, and when he'd asked her for another date, she had instinctively wanted to say yes. She hadn't immediately panicked, or worried about how it could mess up a friendship or ruin a good thing she had going. But was that because she didn't know him or because she simply didn't see Theo in the same way?

Yes, she felt more comfortable with Theo than she could

remember doing with anyone in a long time. And he was the first person she wanted to go to for lots of things, like this issue with Pippa and Nicholas. But perhaps it was a sign they were better off just as friends. Good friends, but nothing more.

Whatever their relationship status was, right now, she needed to know about Nicholas, and Theo was the one person who could help her.

She parked her car and headed straight through the gate. It was later than she'd planned on getting home and the pale light reflected off the canal like a thousand shards of glass. Normally, she would have stopped to look at it, but, like every time she came through the gate, she was facing *Jeanette*, and this time, she couldn't look away.

There, on the top of his boat, Nicholas was tending his plants. As he saw her, his eyes widened, at which point, Daisy offered him the biggest scowl she could muster. The old man paled, and judging from the way he quickly ducked into the stern of the boat, he knew exactly what her look was for.

'At least you could have given me some sloe gin if you were trying to date my mother,' she muttered, not quite under her breath.

Her pulse, which had only just calmed after the car journey, was once again hammering. Hoping Theo had an extra-large supply of ales in stock, she didn't even bother going home first, but jumped straight on the back of Theo's narrowboat and swung open the back door.

'You will not believe what I just found out,' she said as she strode down the steps. 'You need to hear this. And I need a drink.'

'Daisy, hi.'

Daisy stopped dead, her feet still on the back step of the boat. Theo was there, sitting on his sofa in the same position he always sat in, but for the first time in a long while, he wasn't alone.

There, with her hand resting casually on his knee, was his ex-girlfriend.

Was it too much to hope for that, in the month since their breakup, Heather had become less attractive? Apparently so. She was flawless. Daisy had known this from the first time they met – flawless skin, flawless hair, flawless teeth. You name it; she had it in flawless perfection. But to make things worse, she was also a ridiculously kind and lovely person. She even insisted on helping Daisy when she had crashed the *September Rose*, fetching her hot drinks and making sure she was all right. It was no wonder Daisy had felt so insecure about Theo really wanting to be with her. She was wonderful.

As her temperature soared, Daisy realised her jaw was hanging wide open, and her eyes locked on Heather's hand, which still rested on Theo's thigh. That wasn't the way you'd put a hand on someone who was just a friend. No, this was an intimate touch. The touch of a couple.

'I'm sorry, I'm interrupting.'

Coming back to her senses, she moved to turn around, only for Theo to leap towards her.

'No, no, you're not, you're not interrupting. You can come in. You wanted to tell me something?' He moved towards her, but Daisy backed away up the steps.

'It's fine, it was nothing. I'll find you later,' she said quickly, before turning her attention to Heather. 'It's nice to see you again.'

Her voice cracked, and tears stung her eyes as she slammed the door behind her and jumped from the stern to the towpath. In a matter of seconds, she was in the *September Rose* closing the door behind her. The tears now escaped as she struggled to take a proper breath.

'Crap!' she said, wiping her cheeks with the back of her hand.

At least she knew one thing for certain: she definitely did not see Theo as just a friend.

## 28

Daisy held a pillow to her face and screamed as loudly as she could, hoping the sound was muffled. Her heart ached. Physically, as if it had been beating too damn hard, which it probably had been for most of the day.

How had she gone from having no love life whatsoever to having a complete and utter mess of one? Christian had already sent her messages saying how much he was looking forward to their date, asking what type of food she wanted, and had even added two kisses at the end of each one. They had set her stomach alight with butterflies, particularly when she thought about the kiss they'd shared. It had been special. He was special, and he thought the same about her. And seeing Theo there with his ex confirmed all her worst suspicions. It didn't matter how much she liked him, or how much she wanted to be in his company; she would never compare to the beautiful Heather. She was only grateful she'd kept her wits about her and hadn't fallen headfirst into a relationship with him.

Removing the pillow from her face, she took a long, deep breath in. This cleared the path for her and Christian to date, and that was a good thing. An excellent thing. It got rid of all the confusion she had faced, and the trouble of deciding which, out of these two men, to choose. It just didn't explain why her chest ached so much. Or why she felt like someone had punched her in the stomach and knocked her sideways.

Theo was back with his girlfriend. And after everything she had tried to admit to herself, about the pair of them just being friends, Daisy now knew without a doubt that she had feelings for him. Dating or not dating, it didn't change the fact that she had fallen for him hard.

'Argh!' With another thump of the mattress, she dropped back onto the pillow and was still lying face down on the bed when there was a knock on the door.

'Daisy?'

'You have to be joking.'

This time, she let out a silent scream as she chucked the pillow against the wall. Why on earth would he have come round? What could he have to say to her? Her throat tightened as she imagined the spiel he would give, making out that he was really sorry about leading her along, before he mentioned how she had probably been right after all and they were best off just staying as friends. No, there was no way she could cope with that. After all he had done, pushing her to go out with him, he could take the friendship line and shove it where the sun didn't shine.

Galvanised by a new sense of anger, she got up and marched through the boat, only to find Theo already standing inside, a large plate in his hands.

'I brought homemade sourdough?' He placed it on the kitchen counter, before turning back and closing the door, after which he looked straight at Daisy. 'So, Heather... It wasn't—'

'You don't need to explain to me,' Daisy cut in before he could continue. 'I called it. You know I did. I told you this was going to happen.'

'What was going to happen? You knew she was going to come and give me a box of things I left at her house? I don't remember you saying that.'

Daisy stopped and tilted her head. 'That's why she was there? To give you your things back?'

He nodded, a playful smile toying on the corner of his lips. He took a step towards her. 'If I didn't know you had no intention of dating me just yet, I would think you got a little jealous in there.'

'I wouldn't say I was jealous.' She was lying through her teeth, praying she could stop herself from turning bright red, though it was tough, given how he had seen right through her. And how intently he was looking at her. That look was enough to make anyone blush.

'No, what would you say, then?'

'I'd say I was surprised, that's all. You don't normally have company.'

'And when you're surprised, you turn around and run out of someone's home as quickly as possible?'

'I did not run.'

'Oh, I think you did.'

He stepped towards her, but her feet were planted firmly on the ground. As he took another step, her pulse quickened.

'You're the one who's been putting things off, Daisy. You're the one who's been playing games, making me think that maybe you're not as keen on this as you first implied.' His voice resonated through her, as if it were tuned in to her very bones.

'I've not been playing games. I've been perfectly clear about why I wanted to wait.'

'Is that right?'

'Theo, there's something I need to tell you.' Her voice cracked.

Why was it so difficult to get words out? And why was the temperature so hot? And why couldn't she stop looking into his eyes? She needed to tell him about Christian, and the kiss, and the next date. That was the decent thing to do. Even if they were just friends, that was still the decent thing to do. Wasn't it? Yet she seemed to have lost the ability to speak.

He was standing so close to her now, she could feel his breath against hers, although it wasn't Theo who had moved this time. It was Daisy. Without even realising, she had taken another step closer to him.

'Now, what is it that you wanted to tell me?' he said quietly.

Daisy couldn't think about anything other than this moment. The rest of the day so far turned into a blur. She couldn't remember any of it. She needed to tell Theo something. She knew she did. And yet, rather than speaking, she pushed herself onto her tiptoes, slipped her hands around the back of his neck and kissed him.

## 29

Daisy had no words to describe all the sensations that passed through her as she and Theo locked lips. Earth trembling. Mind-blowing. Every rom-com cliché she had ever heard swelled through her in that moment. And she never wanted it to end. Theo shifted slightly, placing his hands around her waist as he drew her closer in, though her lips stayed on his. Could he feel the way her heart was hammering? Or how badly she didn't want it to stop?

Though, no sooner had she had that thought, than Theo broke away.

'So.' His eyes glinted. 'I need to get back to the *Escape*. But I'll leave the sourdough with you. And I want you to know I'm really looking forward to when you think I'll be ready to start dating again.'

He turned around and walked out of the boat, leaving Daisy breathless as she struggled to work out what had just happened. Only when the door closed with the slightest of slams was she jolted out of her haze. Not that it helped much. Her heart was still hammering as she stood there, rooted to the spot, trying to make sense of the moment. That wasn't a near kiss, nor was it just a touch of knees and a trembling insinuation of something. It was an incredible, world-altering first kiss, and she was the one who had instigated it.

'What the hell are you doing, Daisy?'

Having finally regained control of her body, she flopped down on the sofa, only to remember the freshly baked sourdough waiting for her on the side. Hoping that a large injection of carbs might help her think more clearly, she stood back up, walked over and broke off a chunk, which she ate dry, without butter or oil. But still, of course, it was as good as the Ivy's.

The thought of the Ivy caused another groan to escape her lips. Christian. What should she do about Christian? It wasn't like the kiss the two of them shared hadn't been mediocre by any factor. It had been incredible. But Theo…

'Argh!' she screamed again, before taking a long, deep inhale through the nose. 'You can't do this. You don't have time for this. You have work to do.'

Saying the word *work* aloud was like flicking a mental switch somewhere in her brain. It didn't matter what the current state of her love life was. The fact remained, she needed to get everything up and running for the silent auction and the coffee shop's reopening.

What she needed was a good night's sleep so she could focus on what really mattered when the morning came. So, after a quick shower and another slice of bread, that's exactly what she did.

\* \* \*

When Daisy woke the next morning, she refused to give herself the chance to even think about Christian, or Theo, or her mum and Nicholas. Instead, she sat down at her dining table with a pad of paper, a pencil, and a new sense of purpose, and listed all the things she needed to sort out before the silent auction.

For years, Daisy had dreamed of having her own art exhibition, where she could display all the works that would go into her children's books. In those daydreams, the exhibitions would take place in beautiful, pristine art galleries with bright-white walls and empty spaces, ready for her to create her own atmosphere. But this would not be that kind of exhibition.

She had arranged to borrow tables from Bex's office. Apparently, they had a whole stash stored away in the conference room that no one ever used. Daisy wasn't sure whether Bex had asked permission to borrow these tables, but she wasn't going to ask. After all, she needed them. She needed a place to display the paintings, and a long row of tables right outside the *September Rose* would be perfect for that.

The clipboards and paper were going to be delivered on Monday, but she wouldn't pick up the tables until Friday, as there was nowhere else to store them.

With the bulk of the jobs done, she took out her paints, intending to finish a couple more projects, only it wasn't that easy.

Every time she paused, whether to mix a colour or clean her brush, she would find herself thinking about the two men. How different they were. How much she enjoyed spending time with each of them. How much of a mess she was making of things.

However, amid all the random thoughts, Claire's comments about Daisy knowing so little about Christian and his past relationships niggled at her. And so Daisy did what any discerning twenty-something-year-old would do in such a situation and headed straight to social media.

With the limited access she could get, she could only see his profile pictures. The current one showed him on his own, leaning against an expensive-looking sports car. There were a couple more of him on his own in an assortment of holiday destinations and one at the rugby. There were several with groups of friends, but she had to go back a fair way until she found one of him with a woman. From the way they were rubbing noses, they were clearly a couple, though the date showed the photo was three years old.

When she was content that Christian wasn't hiding any secret fiancées from her, she stopped searching and tried to decide what to do.

To start with, she debated whether she should cancel the date. It was probably the decent thing to do, but one kiss with Theo hardly meant they were a couple.

She considered calling another emergency meeting with the girls, only to change her mind. To start with, it was only 9 a.m. on a weekend, and at least one of them was likely to be in bed. Besides, she already knew how they would react. Bex would see no harm in dating both men, while Claire would likely be appalled and tell her she needed to be honest with them. It was probably better to keep this to herself.

Three hours later, she was still thinking this was the best thing to do, but then came the knock on her door.

'Daisy? You in?'

Daisy stood up from where she'd been painting and opened the door.

'Claire, what are you doing here? I thought you were going to message if you were visiting?'

'I was, but then I thought the walk would be nice for Amelia and me. And I didn't want to disturb you.' She looked across the room to where the paints were scattered out on the desk. 'See, we are disturbing you. You're working.'

'You're not. You're not, really, please come in. I need a break.' Daisy stepped back, giving Claire room to come inside, quickly followed by Amelia, who wrapped her arms around her for a quick, tight squeeze, before noticing the paintings.

'These are amazing!' she said, her eyes wide with delight. 'Can I do one?'

'No,' Claire replied immediately. 'These aren't toys. They're Aunty Daisy's work.'

'Sure you can,' Daisy said, ignoring Claire's comment and heading over to the table, where she picked up several pieces she had been working on. 'I'll move these out of the way, then I'll get you some paper of your own to work on.'

'You don't have to do that,' Claire insisted. 'We really didn't want to disturb you.'

'You're not. I'm glad you're here, actually. I need to talk to you about something. Let's get Amelia set up, and we can go into the bedroom. We should probably get Bex on a call too.'

'This sound serious,' Claire said, worry etched in her face, but Daisy chose not to reply. Better to say it once to both of them listening than having to repeat herself.

With Amelia happily sketching away on a watercolour pad, the two women headed into the cabin, where they called Bex, after which Daisy filled her friends in on the events of the previous evening.

'You and Theo kissed! The same day as you and Christian kissed!' Bex exclaimed. 'Why are we just finding out about this?'

'Bex, you're really loud,' Daisy rubbed her ears.

'I'm sorry, but this is big news. And we expect to be kept in the loop about big news.'

'It's not exactly big news. I don't know what kind of news it is.'

'Well, how's Theo been since?' Claire asked, always sensible. 'Have you seen him?'

'No, it was only yesterday. But I kissed him, and then he disappeared. That's not a good sign, is it?'

'*You* kissed him?' Bex said, emphasising the first word. 'You didn't say that you kissed him. You said that you two kissed. That's entirely different.'

'Is it? Why?'

'Because it is. You're staking your claim,' she said. 'Christian kissed you first, I assume?'

'I don't know. That was more mutual, I guess.'

Daisy's head was hurting. This was why she avoided dating. It was too complicated.

'Do you think I should cancel the date with Christian?' she asked.

'Yes.'

'No.'

The two spoke in unison, each giving the exact answer Daisy would have predicted.

'You and Theo aren't a couple.' Bex was straight in defending her viewpoint.

'No, we're not. But it doesn't feel right to go on a date with someone else. It feels like I'm cheating on him.'

'And there's your answer,' Claire said with more than a hint of smugness. 'It feels that way because you know you and Theo have something special.'

'Maybe, but Christian has been so amazing with all this silent auction stuff.'

'You can't favour him because he's helping you out. I think that's got a name.' Claire wasn't going to drop this. She was Team Theo all the way.

'It's not just that. He makes me feel, I don't know, like I can achieve anything.'

'Theo helping her with the boat was why she liked him in the first place,' Bex countered.

Daisy squeezed her eyes shut, trying to ignore the pounding behind her temples. 'So basically, you guys have been no help at all.'

A minute later, they said goodbye to Bex and hung up the phone.

With a deep sigh, Daisy looked at Claire. In times like this, Claire acted as a moral compass. A barometer for how a decent human should behave. Though Daisy wasn't sure that was even what she wanted. Not if it meant having to make a decision.

'What do you think I should do?'

'Maybe just think on it. When's your date with Christian meant to be?'

'Not until next week.'

'Okay, so you can always ring tomorrow and say something's come up. From what you've said, Christian is Mr Perfect. He's not going to hold one cancelled date against you.'

It was probably true. Delaying the decision for one more day sounded like a good thing to do.

'Right,' Claire said. 'We should get going, before Amelia uses up all your art supplies.'

'It's all right. She's enjoying herself.'

At that moment, there was another knock at the door. Even before the voice bellowed through from outside, Daisy's heart leapt and tightened simultaneously.

'Daisy?'

Daisy looked at Claire, whose expression glinted with just the slightest hint of mischief.

'Now we should definitely get out of your hair,' she said.

## 30

From the palpable tension that had wrapped its way through the room and around the three of them, Theo was well aware that he had been the topic of conversation before he arrived. Yet they all remained tight-lipped. Everyone except Amelia, that was.

'These colours look amazing, don't they, Aunty Daisy? Don't you think the colours look amazing?'

Daisy cast a glance at Amelia's developing artwork. She was busy dousing her paper in water and adding bright splotches of purple then yellow without washing the brushes first. Daisy was grateful she had moved her own paintings well out of the way before Amelia started.

'That looks beautiful,' Daisy said, still not able to ignore the tension.

'Theo, it's nice to see you. I hope you've been well?' Claire's tone was perfectly kind and neutral and didn't contain a hint of the insinuation that it could have. Another wave of gratitude struck; if it had been Bex here instead of Claire, Theo would be suffering a full-on interrogation right now.

'I'm good, thank you. Very good, actually. And that looks

fantastic.' He nodded to Amelia's painting. 'Taking after Daisy, I see.'

As he leaned over for a closer inspection, Claire and Daisy exchanged a look, which, on Daisy's part, was filled with terror. As horrendous as the tension was, it was better than having to decide what to say to Theo. Unfortunately, Claire didn't think the same. Either that, or she simply wanted Daisy to suffer.

'Come on, Amelia. I won't ask again. Get that packed away. We need to get going. Now.'

'Why?' The young girl's eyes looked up to her mother pleadingly. 'I've got loads to do. I've hardly started.'

'Well, you can leave it and come back to it another day, can't she, Daisy?'

'I don't mind if she's stays. You should let her stay.' She nodded emphatically.

'No, it's not practical. You have other things to do. Important things to do. Amelia, get that packed away, please.'

'But I thought we were going to spend the afternoon here.'

'We are – on the canal, walking.' She picked up Amelia's jacket from where she had thrown it on the sofa. 'Come on, if we leave now, then maybe we can call in on Daisy and do some more painting on the way back. Can't we?'

'Yes. Whenever you want. However soon.' Daisy's nodding still hadn't stopped. 'And maybe I'll be able to dig out a hot chocolate and some marshmallows too. How does that sound?'

With the promise of a sugar kick, Amelia stood up, leaving all her painting exactly where it was.

'Catch you later,' she said, offering Daisy a quick hug.

As the pair left, Daisy headed over to the brushes, intending to wash them off, but before she reached the table, Theo slipped his hand into hers and pulled her around to face him. The second their eyes locked, she knew there was nothing she could do.

It was like his eyes had hypnotised her. Eyes, she had recently discovered, were her nemesis.

With his free hand, Theo brushed an invisible strand of hair behind her ear before leaning closer and planting the softest kiss imaginable on her lips. It was the antithesis of the kiss the night before. All tenderness and affection, but in the same way as their first kiss, she didn't want it to end. How was it possible that it felt so damn natural? How was it so easy – effortless, even – to kiss him?

When Theo broke away, Daisy's eyes were closed, still feeling the echo of his lips and the pressure they caused on her.

A moment later, she snapped her eyes open and thumped him hard on the shoulder.

'What was that?' she asked, her tone a mix of surprise and annoyance.

Theo raised an eyebrow.

'Oh, so it's all right if you kiss me unexpectedly, but it's not all right if I do the same?'

'Maybe?'

'Maybe? I'm going to need some clarification of what the rules are here.'

His smile was so damn gorgeous that it was turning her insides into knots. All she wanted to do was lean forward and kiss him again, yet at the same time, she didn't want to. She didn't. Not until she'd got her head straight.

'What if I get really close to you, like this?' His voice was a near whisper. Deep and resonant and melting her bones into jelly. 'If I get this close, but I don't kiss you, is that against the rules?'

He was playing with her, she knew that, but it was torture. His lips were so close to hers, and the grin that twisted on them was making it near impossible to move.

She was going to go for it, kiss him again, when his head moved.

'Is that a new sofa?'

'Oh, yes. The other one was full of glass.'

He nodded and studied it for a moment, before his gaze went back to her. 'Remind me. Where was I?'

He moved towards her again and slipped his fingers into hers. Each of his movements was so small, so considered, they were setting her senses on fire.

On the kitchen counter, her phone buzzed, and her attention almost slipped, but before she could even flick her gaze towards it, Theo spoke again.

'Leave it.'

Even when the ringing tone started, she didn't move.

She was on her tiptoes, her head reaching up to him, knowing that she was playing right into his hands. But that was what she wanted, wasn't it? Yes, without a doubt, this was what she wanted.

The phone had stopped ringing now, and the buzzing shifted into her bones. She moved a fraction more. Their lips were a millimetre away from touching. He could move the last part, she thought. He could show he wanted this just as much as she did. She closed her eyes, waiting for the inevitable, when a knock hammered on her door.

Gritting her teeth, she opened her eyes.

'Damn Claire, always forgetting things.'

But before she had moved away, a voice called from outside.

'Daisy? Are you home?'

'Christian!' She jumped back away from Theo.

What the hell was Christian doing here?

# 31

Daisy jerked away from Theo, her pulse racing. Theo was staring at her, waiting for her to say or do something, but her throat had closed up, her heart having lodged its way up it.

'Wow, you are busy today. I didn't realise you were expecting someone.'

'I'm not. I wasn't. Well, I sort of was with Claire, but not Christian. I don't know what he's doing here.'

'Me neither. His timing is terrible. I'll get rid of him now.' Theo's smile twisted and a new sense of panic shot through Daisy. What would he say? That they were just kissing, and Christian was interrupting? He wouldn't. Would he?

'No, no, you can't.' Daisy leapt forward and placed her hand on Theo's chest, only to drop it again.

'Calm down, I'm just winding you up. I think you need to let the guy in, though.'

Daisy swallowed hard and tried to steady her thoughts. What was Christian doing here? And why hadn't he called or at least texted her first?

With several deep breaths, she turned away from Theo, trying to convince herself it would all be fine. After all, Christian wouldn't come straight in and start kissing her, would he? They'd only shared one kiss before. Apart from a quick second one outside the restaurant before she'd left. Two kisses, then. Exactly the same as she'd shared with Theo.

Realising that she had spent far longer waiting to answer than she should have done, she raced to the back of the boat and swung open the door. In his hand, Christian held a bouquet, equally as impressive as the ones he had sent her less than a week before. He stepped forward, leaning in. He was going to kiss her. She could see it immediately, but as he approached, she tilted her head so his lips landed squarely on her cheek.

'What are you doing here? I didn't think I was seeing you again this soon,' she said in a manner she hoped sounded neutral.

'I know, but I have something exciting to tell you. And here, these are for you. Obviously.'

While the bouquet he handed her was as large as the previous one, that was where the similarities ended. This one was full of roses, and calla lilies and peonies and Daisy couldn't help but think of a wedding bouquet.

'I thought I was being smart with the first bunch,' Christian said as Daisy took the flowers over to the sink. 'You know, a bouquet full of wildflowers for Wildflower Lock. But then I realised how ridiculous that was. Why would you need wildflowers when you're surrounded by wildflowers? So, I bought you these. But now I'm realising it's just an awful lot of flowers. Maybe chocolate would have been better.'

Daisy found it impossible not to swoon a little at the adorable response. 'You don't need to bring me any more flowers. Although chocolate is always welcome.'

Behind her, Theo cleared his throat. A strange squeaking sound shot from Daisy's mouth.

'Christian,' Daisy said, as Christian stepped forward and thrust his hand firmly at Theo. 'This is Theo. Theo, Christian.'

'You must be the marketing magician I've heard all about.'

Daisy wasn't sure if she was imagining it, but it sounded as though there was an iciness to Theo's voice.

'And you must be the handyman neighbour who's helped Daisy get this magnificent boat up to scratch,' Christian replied without the slightest hint of animosity.

'I wouldn't say that. She did a lot of work herself. I was just there to guide her.'

'Well, whoever gets to claim credit, you did a great job. It looks incredible in here. And outside too.'

Daisy's head was pounding. How could the pair of them be having a sensible conversation? She could feel her smile straining.

'Theo, didn't you say you needed to do something?' She felt entirely unfair asking Theo to be the one to leave, but he hadn't travelled far to be with her and the sooner she could separate the men, the sooner she could stop feeling like she was about to suffer a major case of angina.

'Nope, I've no plans at all, actually. Though I might go for a walk if you fancied joining me? You too, Christian, if you're hanging about?'

Daisy wanted to hit him really damn hard. Why was he doing this? She might get away with one conversation with them, but a full walk? There was no way that would work. What if one of them wanted to hold her hand? What if they both did? No, this was ridiculous. Christian wasn't interested in dating her seriously. He couldn't be. After all, the amount he had already spent on flowers for her cost more than her weekly food shop. And she dreaded to think how much you would have to splash out for a sofa like the one he bought her. He was just an incredibly generous man, that was all. An incredibly wealthy and generous man. There was no way someone with money like that would actually consider a relationship with her.

As for Theo, the fact she had kissed him didn't change how he and Heather had been looking at each other onboard the *Narrow Escape*. She was right giving him time and space. Unfortunately, none of those facts helped with her current situation.

Clearing her throat, Daisy was still trying to think of some believable excuse to make them separate as quickly as possible when Christian spoke.

'Actually, I can't stay. Neither of us can,' Christian said, with a glance at Daisy. 'I hate to do this to you, but there's an ulterior motive to me popping round.'

'There is?' Daisy thought she was going to pass out. Was he going to invite her for a weekend away, with Theo standing right there? No, of course he wouldn't. It had only been two kisses. And one of them was only short. So what was his plan?

'Don't hate me, but I was chatting with a friend who runs a local radio station last night. He happens to have a half-hour free slot on his show this afternoon, and I told him you'd fill it.'

Relief flooded through her. Christian had an entirely genuine and painting-related reason for being here, with not even a hint of romance. But the relief was short-lived.

'I'm going to go on a radio station?'

'If that's okay with you?'

'Okay? Wow. It's… It's…'

'It's a local show. I met the host at a dinner party years ago. Anyway, we bumped into each other last night and when I mentioned the cafe and what you were doing, he was more than happy to help. He runs his show from his summer house, which is a fifteen-minute drive away. But we should probably leave now. We don't want to be late.'

Daisy was struggling to make sense of what he was saying. She was about to go on the radio? There were too many confusing things bombarding her mind at once.

'It might have been a little presumptuous of me to assume you wouldn't have anything else planned.' Christian's gaze went back to Theo.

Theo was a tall guy, but there was something about his posture at that moment that Daisy had never seen before. It was as if his chest was puffed outwards.

'Like I said, it's only a local show, but he's got a pretty big following. And locals are good. It means they'll be able to come to the auction.'

'Wow, that sounds like you've got everything sorted out,' Theo said.

Daisy turned to Theo, who was staring at Christian, his arms folded across his chest. There had been a dryness in his voice that Daisy couldn't deny, but if Christian noticed it, he didn't show it.

'Well, if anyone deserves some luck on her side, it's got to be Daisy, although we should get going. You'll need to get set up before the show starts.'

Daisy turned back to Theo, only to find him still glaring at Christian. He was wearing an expression she'd never seen on him before, as if tension was radiating from his pores. It was the same static buzz she imagined you'd feel before a bar fight, a charge in the atmosphere, so electric, you could almost hear it humming.

'I'll catch you later? Tell you about it?' she said to him.

In an instant, Theo's eyes fixed back on her, and he had changed back to the normal Theo, not the alpha male she had been facing a moment ago.

'Actually, no.'

'No.'

'I got distracted when I came over. I forgot to tell you I'm going away. Tonight.'

'You're going away? Where?'

'Slimbridge.'

'Slimbridge?'

'It's in Gloucestershire,' Christian clarified. 'On the Sharpness Canal, if I'm not mistaken.'

Whether he was right about the location or not, Daisy didn't find out, as Theo carried on talking.

'There's a guy I used to work with who's moved up there now. He asked if I fancied a visit. Apparently, there are a couple of things he needs a hand with.'

'Are you going on the *Escape*? That's his boat,' she added quickly to Christian, just to show that she hadn't forgotten him standing there.

Theo shook his head. 'No, the journey would take too long. I'm going to drive and stay up.'

'For how long?'

She didn't want to sound desperate, but she hadn't been living in the *September Rose* that long, and Theo was her first port of call should anything go amiss. She always felt at ease knowing that he was there, less than a minute away, should something happen.

'It's a fair trek, so I'll spend a few nights at least.'

'But you'll be back for the auction?'

'You know I wouldn't miss it.'

As he took a step towards her, Christian stepped up to her other side.

'Don't worry, I'll make sure she's taken care of.'

Theo's lips pressed together into a thin line which twitched ever so slightly.

'Actually, Daisy, I know you need to rush off, but can I just show you something on the *Escape* quickly? The bilge gauge has been a bit temperamental, and I was hoping you could keep an eye on it while I'm away. I just want to show you how it works and where all the pump switches are before I go. You're okay to wait here for a minute, aren't you, Christian?'

Christian responded with that same perfectly serene smile he always wore. 'Sure. I can make myself at home.'

'Don't worry, this won't take long.' Theo pressed his hand to the small of Daisy's back and guided her up the stairs and out onto the towpath. When they reached his boat, he opened the door and ushered her inside.

'Okay, so what is the gauge doing?' Daisy asked as she headed towards the pump, but before she got there, Theo had grabbed her hand.

'Nothing's wrong. The boat's completely fine. I just wanted to get you on your own.'

'Theo...'

'I don't like him. I don't trust him.'

'Christian?'

'Who else would I be talking about?'

Daisy thought about the interactions she'd had with Christian so far. He had been nothing but a gentleman. A goofy, funny, generous gentleman.

'What is it you don't like about him?'

'I can't say what it is exactly. There's just something I don't like. I can't put my finger on it.'

It was hard not to think Theo's mistrust sounded remarkably like jealousy, and the thought made Daisy's stomach squirm. Could he tell that something had happened between her and Christian? No, of course he couldn't. But then, there were two bunches of flowers in her boat from him. Maybe if she'd told Theo about the incident with the sofa, it might have made a little sense, but then she'd promised Christian she wouldn't tell anyone. Besides, she doubted Theo would have told her about Heather's visit if she hadn't walked in on them.

'Theo, you have nothing to worry about. He's a good guy. I've met his mother, remember?'

'You met her once. You haven't seen her since. It could be a ruse. And all this stuff about him knowing a local radio station DJ and getting you a slot. And getting all those newspapers to do a feature on you, don't you think that's odd? He doesn't even know you and yet he's going out of his way to try to help. Just because his mum liked one of your paintings? You have to agree that's not normal.'

'Really, you have to believe me. He's a good guy.'

Theo harrumphed, not having received the answer he was hoping for. 'Just keep checking in with me. I want to know you're all right while I'm away. And try not to miss me too much, okay?'

He moved forward as if to kiss her, but Daisy put her hands on his chest.

'I kissed you once. You kissed me once. Now we're even.'

## 32

Daisy had expected Christian to have a fancy car, to go with his fancy watch and shoes, but when they reached the car park, he directed her to a beat-up Land Rover.

'I figured this was a better option than the Porsche,' he said as he opened the door.

Daisy went to laugh, only to realise he wasn't joking.

'You don't mind that I completely railroaded your day, do you?'

'To go on the radio, to promote my art and save my business? No, I definitely don't mind.'

They climbed inside the car, and Christian began to drive. Daisy had her hand resting on the edge of her seat, but less than a minute into the journey, Christian slipped his hand on top. A slight movement on her part was all it took for their fingers to intertwine. There it was, that buzzing again, as if his touch filled her with electricity.

'You know, I'm worried that when you've sold all your paintings and got a name for yourself, you won't need me any more. I'll have to find another skill to make myself useful to you.'

'Do you have lots of other skills?'

'Not that should be discussed in public.'

With her cheeks pink, Daisy twisted her head around to look out of the window at the thick hedgerows that lined the country roads. Perhaps Theo going away for a couple of days was a good thing. A chance to make her mind up about exactly which of the two men she wanted to date for real. But there wasn't time to fret about that now. She was too busy worrying over what she was about to do.

'This is where the radio station is?' she said as they approached a large pair of metal gates. A gravel driveway wove away from the road, but where it went was anyone's guess; there certainly wasn't a house she could see.

'Well, the radio station is actually in his summer house, the lodge he calls it, but this is where Dicky lives, yes.'

'His summer house?' In Daisy's mind, a summer house was a nice name for a shed at the end of the garden that had a couple of extra-large windows and a sofa in it. She couldn't imagine being able to run a radio show from one.

'Most radio work is done remotely nowadays. They hardly ever have all the presenters in one station. Dicky used to work on a national show, but he gave that up a few years ago. He decided to retire and bought this place instead. Turns out he's not so good at retiring, so now he does a weekly show for one of the smaller local stations.'

So not only was she going on the radio, but with a former national presenter. It was getting more and more terrifying by the minute.

'Thank you so much for this,' Daisy said gratefully as she tried to push down her nerves.

'Honestly, don't thank me yet. You haven't met Dicky.'

With the gate open, they drove up the gravel driveway. They

must have been at least a quarter of a mile in from the road when the house finally came into view. If you could call it a house.

The building was three storeys high and had six windows across it. While Daisy didn't know what the technical requirements for a house to become a mansion were, she was sure this made it.

'You okay?' Christian asked as he turned off the engine.

'Not really.'

'Don't worry, you'll be fine.' He opened his car door and stepped outside.

By the time Daisy had gathered her thoughts enough to reach for the handle, Christian was already opening her door and offering her a hand. Still, she took her time, trying to steady her nerves with some deep breaths, although any calm she managed to instil in herself evaporated as a riot of barking shot out into the air.

Three massive dogs bolted around from the side of the house.

'Down, down, down.' Christian rubbed the dogs' heads as he tried to stop them from jumping up. 'Are you okay with dogs?' he asked, throwing a worried glance at Daisy.

'I'm great with them.' She crouched down, letting the animals approach her. 'You don't seem like very good guard dogs,' she said as she rubbed one behind their ears. 'You're meant to scare strangers off.'

'Damn soppy mutts. Don't even know why I keep you.'

There, standing in the now-open front door, was a large man with round spectacles wearing a towelling dressing gown.

Grinning from ear to ear, Christian left the dogs to embrace the man.

'Nice to see you dressed up for our visit,' he said, when the pair broke apart.

'What do you mean? I was naked ten minutes ago.'

Ignoring the comment, Christian turned to Daisy. 'Daisy May, this is my old friend, Dicky Score. Dicky, meet Daisy May.'

'So, you're the young lady that's got her claws into our eternal bachelor here, are you?' Dicky said teasingly. 'Got him badgering me all night to get you on the show.'

'I... I...' Daisy stuttered as she struggled to gauge whether this was Dicky's idea of humour, or whether he was being serious.

'Please don't listen to what he says. I did not badger him. In fact, he was the one who said he would like to have you on the show.'

'Is that right?' Dicky said with a laugh. 'Well, perhaps I did. I can't say I remember. Anyway, Daisy, welcome to my little abode.'

He was definitely being modest, and Daisy struggled to take it all in. The oversized doorway opened up to a hall with a sweeping staircase that went in two directions before re-joining in the middle. A large and exceptionally ostentatious chandelier hung down the middle of the space, while several portraits of Dicky hung on the walls.

'So, we've got twenty minutes before the show starts. Just enough time to do a quick sound check. Anyone want a glass of port?'

'No, Dicky,' Christian said, before turning to Daisy. 'You don't want a port, do you?'

'No. No thank you.'

'Fine, just me then.'

Daisy and Christian, together with the three dogs, followed Dicky through the house and into a space that could have been a living room or a library, judging by the number of books on the shelves. There, he uncorked a decanter and poured himself a small glass.

'Right, we're off to the summer house for the radio station.'

As he opened the door, Daisy caught a flash of skin, and hurriedly looked away.

'Is he wearing any underwear?' she hissed.

Christian sighed and shook his head.

'I doubt it.'

The summer house was exactly that. A house. A full house made of bricks and glass and at least twice as big as the *September Rose*. Nothing like the small outhouse she had imagined.

'We're in the third bedroom for the station,' Dicky told them.

Had Daisy not known that she'd just walked across the garden from some great manor house, she would have thought she was in a studio in London. Unlike the rest of the house, which had appeared entirely normal, this one was fit for purpose. The walls were covered in the dense black sponge of soundproofing material, while all types of audio equipment, from mixing consoles to microphones and headphones, were arranged meticulously in the space.

After fixing himself on a large swivel chair, Dicky pointed to a second one in front of Daisy.

'Come on, let's get your sound levels right.'

For the next fifteen minutes, Daisy was asked to say things into the microphone repeatedly while Dicky pressed the assortment of buttons in front of him. Occasionally, he got out of his seat to fiddle with her microphone and chair too, only to return to his previous position. But even with all the back and forth, Daisy wasn't prepared for the moment he said:

'Three minutes to go.'

A surge of fear rushed through her.

'You know, I'm not sure I'm going to be any good at this.'

She said this more to herself than anyone in particular, but no sooner had she spoken than Christian was behind her, gently massaging her shoulders.

'Don't worry, you're gonna be absolutely fine. Better than fine. You're going to be amazing.'

Despite the car journey together, Daisy only now caught a whiff of his aftershave. The deep, musky scent flooded her nostrils as she closed her eyes and she tried to take a deep breath in.

Now that Christian's hands were on her, with their firm, reassuring grip, she didn't feel so nervous.

As Dicky counted down on his fingers, Christian offered a kiss on the top of her head before disappearing behind her.

'Now, as you guys know, we love a bit of culture in the studio.' The change between Dicky's on- and off-air voice was almost laughable. With a deepened accent, and even greater enunciation, he sounded like a caricature of his former self. Completely over the top and yet somehow endearing. 'And what's more cultured than an artist? Well, I'll tell you what: an artist who lives and works on a canal boat. And what's more, she's set up a business there. Now we are very lucky to have Daisy May in the studio. Daisy, welcome to the show.'

'It's great to be here.' She tried her best to sound confident and sincere despite her nerves.

'Now, you're a painter, and from what I've seen, a pretty fabulous one. So why don't you tell us how you got into that?'

# 33

The rest of the interview had gone by in a blur. When she wasn't talking about her art, Daisy had listened to music in her headphones while her heart drummed as she waited for the next set of questions.

When they were done, Dicky swiftly waved them goodbye before continuing with the rest of his show.

'Are you sure I sounded all right?' Daisy asked again as she climbed back into Christian's car. 'I was so nervous, it felt like every other word I was saying was um or ahh – if those can even count as words.'

'No one will have noticed. You sounded amazing. Trust me, you are going to have queues of people outside the boat next weekend.'

A level of pride rose through her that was unmistakable. The last time Daisy's heart had felt this full was when she'd finally finished painting the *September Rose*. In fairness, that high still hadn't faded completely, but all the stress of the coffee shop had tainted it a fair bit.

'So, I know we hadn't settled on when our next date was going

to be, but how do you fancy a pub dinner? Or late lunch, which-
ever way you want to think of it? Or we could head for a walk first
if you aren't hungry yet? Assuming you do still want to go for
another meal? I don't want you to feel under pressure just
because I'm here and asking you.'

The adrenaline from the radio show had not yet faded, and
Daisy wasn't ready for another surge of it, but it was impossible to
deny how calming Christian's hands on her shoulders had been.
And she had been so lost in painting that morning, she hadn't
even bothered with lunch or breakfast so her stomach had been
growling since the show ended.

'Food would be lovely.'

'Great, I was hoping you'd say that.'

A few minutes later, they reached a small pub.

'I did a bit of research while you were on air, not that I wasn't
listening the whole time, of course...' He grinned sheepishly. 'The
reviews for this place are pretty good. But I apologise if it's
terrible.'

'It smells delicious,' Daisy said as they headed towards the
bar. They were promptly shown to a table at the back.

'So, how are you feeling?' Christian asked as he pulled out a
chair for her.

'About the fact that I just did a live radio show or that I'm
reopening the coffee shop or that my art is going to be on display
for everyone in my neighbourhood to laugh at?'

'I probably should have been more specific. But I've already
told you your radio interview was fabulous, so I'm not going to
address that again. And your art is incredible, so that just leaves
the auction next weekend. Unless you want to discuss how you're
feeling about us?'

The question caught Daisy by surprise, and she hastily
ignored it.

'I'm ready for next weekend. And I've got time to do a full trip to the cash and carry to make sure I'm fully stocked with fizzy drinks and crisps and juice cartons. I'm going to have to borrow Theo's fridge for some of it, though that shouldn't be a problem.'

Daisy could have sworn Christian's face flickered slightly at Theo's name, but then his expression was back to its normal, smiley self, and she was convinced she must have imagined it.

'Great, and have you got someone to run the coffee shop?'

'To run the coffee shop?' Daisy frowned. 'That's what I do. It's my coffee shop. My job. I'll be running it.'

'I get that, but on Saturday, you want to be talking to people about your paintings. You might get some bids just leaving them out there, but really, people want the story. They need to hear you. That's the way you're going to make real money.'

Now that Christian had said it, it made sense. But Daisy hadn't considered having somebody else run the coffee shop.

'I could write little notes to go by the side of the paintings, describing where they are set and what they show, I suppose,' she said, but the moment she spoke, she knew it wasn't good enough. 'No, no, you're right. I need to be around to interact with everyone. I'll get someone to cover the coffee shop. At least for the hour when the bidding happens. And probably a bit before then, too. Then when I'm announcing the winners too. You're right. I'll find someone.'

'Do you have anyone who can run it for you? I mean, how hard can it be?'

'How hard indeed?'

Her immediate thought was her mother. After all, she was used to being on her feet all day, far more than Daisy, and she was aware of how busy the hospitality industry could get. But she worked in the restaurant, behind the scenes, and there was no way she could deal with all the different coffee types that people asked for, from their oat-milk, decaf lattes to the no-foam cappuccinos. It had taken Daisy long enough to learn them, and the only way she'd managed was with Theo testing her.

That was when it hit her. There was only one person she knew who could run The Coffee Shop on the Canal and not mess it up.

'I'm sure you'll find a solution.' Christian said, reaching his hand across to hers. 'But changing the subject and at the risk of making a fool of myself, what's the deal with your neighbour?'

'Theo?' The fact that he had been in her head the moment Christian mentioned him left Daisy more than a little unnerved, though she tried not to show it.

'That was it. Theo. He looked like he wanted to shoot daggers at me. Were you and him a thing?'

Daisy's throat closed shut. There was no animosity in Christian's voice and he seemed to have asked the question out of casual interest, rather than concern about her and Theo being together. Then again, she doubted Christian ever got jealous of other men. After all, what could they offer someone that he couldn't?

'No, not exactly,' Daisy said, finally managing to find her voice.

Christian arched an eyebrow. 'Not exactly. What does that mean? Is he an ex?'

'No, no, nothing like that. Theo and I are just friends. He's only recently got out of a relationship.'

'And now? You two aren't together?' This time it sounded a little more than just general conversation.

'No, we're not.'

She didn't know why she wanted to add a *not yet* to the end of that sentence. *Not yet* sounded much more realistic than just *no*. But it also sounded completely weird, like she'd somehow foreseen the future. And she hadn't. She and Theo weren't written in stone. Far from it. The way Heather had looked so at home on the *Narrow Escape* was probably an indication that Daisy shouldn't get too comfy in Theo's company. Besides, this wasn't just anyone she was talking to. This was Christian. Christian, who she had kissed and quite possibly wanted to kiss again. When the hell had life got so complicated?

'Good, I just didn't want to be stepping on anyone's toes,' Christian said, his eyes flashing with a smile. 'Not that I'd have been put off that easily. I reckon you're worth stepping on more than a couple for.'

She hadn't noticed until now, but their knees were touching under the table, and now that she was aware, it was shooting sparks of electricity all the way up her leg. Still, he didn't so much as blink. That heat was building again. That same magnetic attraction that seemed to be pulling her into men's lips for the last two days, but before she could even shift in her seat, her stomach growled again. This time even louder than before.

Christian grinned. 'We should order some food.'

Once again, the conversation flowed with amazing ease. They spoke about art and the boat again, but also about themselves: their youth, jobs they had done and trouble they'd got into. Christian's upbringing had been privileged, what with being at boarding school since he was eleven and a choice of any university he wanted to go to, but he had grafted too, always balancing several jobs. She learned that he had a younger sister, whom he doted upon, while his mum and dad had separated from each other, but were both now very happily married to other people.

'They've taught me a lot about relationships,' he told her as he sipped on his drink. 'It's give and take, you know. They're far from perfect, and they definitely had some rocky patches when we were growing up, but they worked through them.'

Daisy thought about her own parents' rocky patches. From

what her mother had told her, neither of them had tried to work through those.

'Sounds like you had good role models.'

'I'm guessing that you didn't?' he said. 'I don't want to pry if you don't want to talk about it...'

'No, it's fine. It is. I didn't have a relationship with my dad. And it's a shame. Turned out there were a lot of things I didn't know about him, and now I won't get a chance to. It's a bit rubbish.'

'I'm sorry.' His hands were on hers again, distracting her from the sadness that was swelling within.

'I try not to think about it, if I'm honest. It's hard, because I grew up thinking my dad was this person who didn't want to know me, and I was better off without him, but now I know that's not true. I actually think we would have got on really well. We've definitely got some similarities.'

'What about your mum? You've spoken about her before. You're close, aren't you?'

'We were. Very close, but then when I found out all these things about my dad, it was hard to keep the relationship the same. I try. Of course I do, but it's tough. Sometimes I resent her and I don't want it to be that way. She's the only relative I've got left now.'

'Families are so difficult. You know, we're normal on the outside, but we all have our issues. Believe me. I worry I won't be able to give my children the same type of life. Be the father they deserve.'

'I think you'd be an amazing father.'

Daisy didn't know when they had started holding hands, but there they were, fingers interlaced, eyes fixed on each other, and she realised how deeply she meant her comment. While she didn't know much about Christian, she knew he was generous and that his friends thought a lot of him, and if he put half as much effort into parenting as he had helping her with her paintings, that would be one lucky child.

'I should probably get the bill and get you home, just so I haven't highjacked your entire day.'

He pulled his hand away from hers and lifted it to the waiter. Daisy couldn't help but notice how cold her own hand was without it.

**34**

---

When they reached Wildflower Lock, the summer sun was resting on the horizon. The journey there had been as quiet as the one out, when they'd headed to the radio station, but this time Daisy wasn't quiet because she was nervous. She was quiet because she didn't know what to say. The more time she spent with Christian, the more at ease she felt with him. He was a man who shared her values of family and friendship and who pushed her to be the best version of herself.

But wasn't that the same with Theo? They both made her laugh, saw talent within her, and made her step out of her comfort zone. How could you choose between men like that?

When they parked up, Christian stepped out of his car and opened the door for her. Daisy scanned the car park, only to see the space that Theo usually took was empty. The wash of relief she felt was accompanied by a good dousing of guilt.

'I can walk from here.'

'Don't be silly, I'll walk you myself.'

He didn't hold her hand, like Daisy expected, but her fingers still stretched out, as if they wanted him to take them. Why was her stomach such a knot of butterflies? Why couldn't her head stop racing from one scenario to another, all of which involved kissing?

When she reached the *September Rose*, she turned to face him, waiting. Only at that moment did she realise he might expect an invitation inside. Was she meant to ask him in for a coffee? That's what normally happened in situations like this, wasn't it? But there was no way she was ready for that. Fear struck, and she stopped, keys in her hand.

'Do you... are you...' Her tongue fumbled as she struggled to speak.

As she stood there, she wondered whether it was strange that she'd reached twenty-five and never found herself in this position before. Paul had been her first and only boyfriend and they had grown up together. This, getting to know a man through dating, was entirely different. 'Were you expecting to come in for a coffee, because I'm not sure that I want you to do that.' She finally choked out the words, only to realise how rude they sounded. Thankfully, Christian chuckled.

'I only wanted to walk you to your boat. That's all. Though if I did come in, at least I know I can sit on your sofa without getting impaled.'

Daisy blushed, unsure whether she was disappointed by his response. After all, a coffee could be just that, and she had a very good coffee machine now. Still, she couldn't help but glance over at the *Narrow Escape*, with the tarpaulin pulled over the stern – another indication that Theo was definitely not in.

'I was hoping we could do dinner again this week,' Christian carried on, interrupting her thoughts. 'Maybe mid-week. I can book us a table?'

Daisy wanted to say yes, desperately, but it felt as if the

*Narrow Escape* had come alive and was staring straight at her. If only they could have had this conversation elsewhere.

'I think this week, I need to focus on the paintings. Maybe after the auction. Would that work?'

'You're going to make me wait a whole week?'

The way he spoke made those seven days feel impossibly long. After all, they had met less than a week ago, and in that time, he had purchased her a new sofa, two bouquets of flowers, three meals together and she had been on a live radio because of strings he pulled. Though she wasn't even sure that she was dating him.

'Don't worry, I'm winding you up,' he said, stepping forward and taking her hand. 'But I am going to miss you.'

She could feel the kiss coming. The way his smile lit up his eyes, and caused her stomach to flutter – and when he did finally place his lips on hers, it was with such tenderness her whole body wanted to scream.

That was, until she opened her eyes, and found herself staring directly at the *Narrow Escape*. The guilt was instant. And for a split second, she expected Theo to appear and call her out for what she had done. But even when he didn't, the guilt continued to rile around inside her. It was official. Daisy May was in trouble. Big time.

\* \* \*

True to her word, Daisy used every spare minute of the week to focus on her paintings. Well, that was between firing off messages to both Theo and Christian. The pair were poles apart; Christian sent her a midweek hamper where the only flowers in sight were edible ones, enrobed in rich, dark chocolate, while Theo sent images of cygnets he had seen while out kayaking in Slimbridge. But the closer it got to the weekend, the more Daisy panicked and by Friday night, with Theo on his way back, and Christian telling her he was going to arrive by ten the next morning for the auction, she was a mess with nerves.

'Why did we have to get up so early?' Amelia stretched out her arms without bothering to cover her mouth as she let out a wide yawn.

'We're up early because your Aunty Daisy has made a complete mess of her love life,' Bex explained helpfully. 'And your mummy and I are here to keep it all under control.'

Daisy would have liked to disagree, but it was absolutely true. How she'd got herself into such a mess was beyond her. But here she was. The day of the auction was upon them, and she was still no closer to deciding about Theo and Christian. And if that wasn't bad enough, they were going to be together for almost an entire day. Which was why she had called in the calvary, asking Bex and Claire to arrive at 8 a.m. for the sole purpose that she was never alone with one of the men, and they would never be alone with each other either.

'It's going to be fine,' she said, as much for herself as for the others. 'Theo is working in the coffee shop. He's going to be inside all day.'

'*All day*, all day? You're not going to let him have a break?' Claire's practicalities could get irritating.

'Well, of course, I'll have to give him a break at some point.'

'And who's going to man the coffee shop, then?'

'I guess I'll have to.'

'At which point you leave Christian outside to make polite conversation with everybody out there, including Theo.'

'Why don't you give me a solution, then?' Daisy raised her hands in the air. The one positive about this mess was that she had been far less stressed about the actual silent auction. The licence for the coffee shop had now come through, meaning she would be able to pay back Bex eventually. She just needed to get through today.

She had set up each of the paintings in a simple frame and, after the conversation with Christian, used her best penmanship to write a small title and note for each of the paintings.

Bex had kindly stolen several pens from work, which they had attached to all of the clipboards and made it look like an accountancy service was sponsoring the event, but Daisy didn't care.

'It will be fine when the day gets going,' Daisy said. 'It's just the set-up that's going to be tough; they need to be kept apart from each other.'

'How do you feel about me flirting with Theo?' Bex asked very matter-of-factly.

'Pardon?'

'You want me to keep him distracted, don't you?'

Daisy took a deep breath in.

'Rebecca Jones, you are an intelligent woman with a master's degree and Christ knows what other attributes and qualifications. You have travelled the world and have countless funny and interesting anecdotes to talk about. Surely you can think of a better method of keeping Theo distracted?'

The group fell into silence, which extended for longer than anyone could have anticipated. Daisy's eyes went to Claire, who shrugged unhelpfully, while Bex waited, her eyebrows arched.

'Fine, flirt with him,' Daisy said, relenting.

'And you won't get jealous?'

Daisy threw her a scowl. 'It's pretend flirting, remember? You're with Newton. Besides, Theo's sort of, kind of taken.'

'You mean like Christian's sort of, kind of taken?'

Daisy knew Bex was winding her up, but it was working. Yet before she could throw back a biting comment, the door opened, and standing there for the first time in a week was Theo. Just the sight of him, all rugged and staring straight at her, was enough to make her heart leap.

'Which one is this?' Amelia was sitting on the sofa, with a face like butter wouldn't melt.

'Amelia, this is Theo. He is my neighbour. You've met him before, remember? He's going to be running the coffee shop while I am outside doing the paintings.'

'Oh, the neighbour one.'

'Amelia,' Claire warned, before turning to Theo and kissing him briefly on the cheek. 'Theo, it's lovely to see you again. Amelia, why don't we go and set up the tables outside? Bex can help us too. Then Daisy and Theo can make sure everything is okay in the kitchen.'

Daisy noted that Amelia's lips twitched, but her need to be a know-it-all was quashed by her mum's impressive glower. Without protest, she stood and headed up the stairs, with Bex and Claire following, leaving Theo and Daisy alone.

A second of silence filled the boat.

'Why do I get the impression they were trying to give us some privacy?' Theo sidled up towards her and slipped his hand in hers. A spark of electricity shot through her.

'I don't know. I think it must be your imagination.'

Daisy's abdomen was alight with butterflies. She could feel her breath shallowing and her eyes willing themselves to close. It was only now Theo was back that she realised just how much she'd missed him. And how much she wanted to kiss him again, but before she could fall prey to herself, she jumped backwards and held her hands out in front of her, as a barricade. 'This is not the time. I can't be distracted. I need to have my head on straight.'

'And you're saying I distract you? You know, it's not me putting a delay on things, right? It's you.'

'Because you need time—'

'To prove I'm over Heather. Well, I think there are other ways I could prove it to you.'

He was infuriating. He had always been infuriating. That wasn't anything new. But now he was infuriating in the most gorgeous of ways. She could feel herself being drawn to him. Perhaps this was the sign she needed to choose him. And would one kiss really hurt?

Not if he was the one.

'Daisy, I think you've got a visitor.' Bex called from outside. 'A very attractive visitor.'

A flood of fear replaced all of Daisy's other emotions.

'Yup, I'm guessing this is Christian.' Amelia's voice was loud from outside.

Attempting to swallow despite a bone-dry throat, Daisy turned towards the door, but before she could take a step, Theo grabbed her by the wrist.

'Daisy, be careful with him.'

'Christian?'

'I don't like the way he looks at you. I know men like him. They think they can get any woman they want because they're charming and rich and always know the right thing to say. I get it. They have everything they need to make a woman feel like she's the world. But it's all just words and meaningless flashing of cash. I'd like to think you'd know better than to fall for an act like that.'

The guilt twisted within her. There was no denying it. This situation was turning her into a pretty terrible person, and the sooner she could sort it out, the better.

'Christian is a good guy,' she said, feeling the need to defend him. 'He's done everything to help me here, and he's asked nothing from me in return. I know this might be hard to believe, but you're not the only perfect guy out there.'

'I never pretended to be perfect.' Theo's stern expression surprised her. 'Trust me, the way I was thinking about you when I was still with Heather is evidence of that. But I own up to my mistakes. And, more than anything, I don't want to see you get hurt.'

She could see it was the truth, and it cut her like a knife.

'It's time we get the coffee shop open,' she said, her voice cracking. 'We can talk about this later.'

## 35

Even with all the newspaper coverage and the radio interview, Daisy had never really stopped to think about how many people were going to turn up or how much money she would make from the event. At the back of her mind, all she had been thinking about was the £1700 she owed Bex and the need to pay it back as soon as possible, while hoping to get some more for the propeller too. But at 10 a.m. when the canal was the busiest she had ever seen it, Daisy realised just how many people Christian's marketing campaign had reached. This was a proper art show.

'This is crazy.' She was standing a polite distance from the tables, watching people mill about, discussing her work. Four people seemed interested in the kingfisher painting and Daisy made a mental note to paint more of those in the future.

'What time do people start bidding?' Claire slid up next to her. 'I've had several people ask if they can buy paintings now.'

'None of them are for sale yet,' Daisy said, wishing she'd made signs to say as much. It was so far her most frequently asked question. 'The auction starts at twelve, though. So there's only twenty minutes to wait. Can you make sure they stay here until then? Or ask them to come back?'

'Okay, and what time does it end?'

Daisy turned around to see Bex standing on the towpath behind her, at which point her relative sense of ease evaporated.

'What are you doing here? You're meant to be inside with Theo.'

'Theo is a control freak. Apparently, I used the wrong milk or used the wrong jug or the wrong takeaway cup or something.'

Daisy didn't respond. Theo could be a slight control freak, but it was one of the features Daisy found endearing about him. She could image how crazy it would drive Bex, though. 'Besides, it's a nice day, and it's boiling in there. I want to swap and do an outdoor shift. Claire and Amelia can go inside and we'll swap baby-sitting duties. It's time I got to see more of Christian, anyway. You know, help me give you more clear advice on which to go with.'

'What are you ladies talking about? It all looks very suspicious.'

Daisy's stomach dropped as Christian strode towards them. While she had already introduced them all, the girls hadn't said more than a couple of sentences to him before Bex headed inside to help Theo, while Claire had got to work displaying the paintings. Wanting to keep her contact with him to a minimum, Daisy had quickly set Christian to task helping out, and they'd barely finished setting up when the first people arrived. It had been go-go-go ever since. Now, though, as Christian approached, he slipped behind Daisy and put his hands on her waist.

Feeling like the most horrible person in the world, she slid out to the side of him.

'Oh, we're not talking about anything interesting. Nothing interesting here at all. I was just saying that the auction starts at twelve. And we'll end it at half past. Hopefully, we'll get everything wrapped up by one.'

'Sounds good,' he said. 'You've got lots of interest. Oh, and I forgot to tell you, I had these made. I've been giving them out to people, in case they don't win at the auction and want to buy from you later.'

From out of his pocket, he pulled a small, clear plastic box.

'What is it?'

'Here, take a look.'

He handed the box to Daisy. Her jaw dropped at the sight.

'You made me business cards.'

These weren't just any business cards. They were printed on deep cream paper, embossed with her name and telephone number, and there in the corner was the painting of the heron. The same one his mother had bought.

'I forgot I should have asked about putting your number on them before I handed them out to strangers.' Christian's cheeks suddenly paled. 'I think most of the people are still here. I can ask for them back?'

'No, no. They're perfect. They're absolutely perfect.'

The warmth of his gesture flooded through her, and for a split second, she almost forgot where she was. Christian's eyes locked on her and he leaned in, as if he was about to kiss her, when a voice cut above the noise.

'Daisy, can I borrow you for a second?' Theo's head was peeking out of the hatch. A bright-crimson flush flooded Daisy's cheeks as she offered Christian the slightest peck on the cheek – the type of peck she hoped could be considered purely platonic. 'I better go.'

'I understand. Don't be long, though. The auction starts in fifteen minutes.'

After a quick glance around to make sure nobody needed her

help, Daisy headed into the *September Rose* to find Theo wiping his hands on his jeans. 'I need you to take over for a bit,' he said. 'Before the end of the auction.'

'Is everything okay?' Daisy studied his face for tell-tales signs of what was going on but came up with nothing.

'Yes, I'll just need a five-minute break. Is that all right?'

'Of course. Of course. You can go now if you'd rather?'

'No, I'd prefer to wait a bit.'

'Okay.'

Tension was wrapping its way around the boat, but it wasn't like the tension she'd felt earlier in the day. The tension where she had so desperately wanted to kiss him. This was pricklier.

Daisy waited, thinking that perhaps Theo was going to say something more, but only the silence remained.

'Okay, well, I'll be back to take over from you in—'

'Daisy, you and this Christian guy – is there something going on there?' The question was so direct, it felt like it had been thrown at her and the tightness in her chest returned. She couldn't lie to him. Not when he'd asked her outright.

'I've known him less than two weeks—' she started, hoping the rest of the words she needed would follow. But before they could, a face appeared at the hatch.

'Are you serving? I'd like three cappuccinos and a flat white, please.'

'Of course, absolutely.' Theo returned to the coffee machine, leaving Daisy standing mutely. 'You should get outside. It looks like it's getting busy there.'

Back on the towpath, Daisy didn't have time to think about Theo or Christian. Instead, she moved from one person to another, her cheeks aching from reciprocating so many smiles. Never could she remember receiving so many compliments about her art. Or having so many conversations about it. Many people were dog walkers who regularly passed, others had come especially for the event. She chatted and laughed, and talked about the coffee shop and even told some of them how she hoped to do children's illustrations. Less than a year ago, she hadn't even been able to pick up a paintbrush without feeling like an utter failure. It was safe to say this event had gone a long way towards curing that.

She had just announced that the auction had begun and that people were allowed to start bidding when she glanced down the towpath and saw a couple walking hand in hand towards her. Her stomach tightened.

'Is that your mum with her new man?' Claire peered over Daisy's shoulder.

'Yeah, that's him, Nicholas. I need a better name than that. Nasty Nick?'

'Been done too many times before.'

'Naughty Nick? No, scrap that. I'll think of something. Miserable Nick would be best, though it doesn't have quite the right ring to it.'

'And also, he doesn't look miserable at all.'

Daisy looked to where Nick's hand was holding tight on her mother's as they laughed away. She didn't know whether to cry or faint. How was it possible this was the same man that had come at her accusingly only a week or so before? And how was her mum looking so comfortable walking around Wildflower Lock? Thankfully, by the time they reached her, Daisy had fixed her face into a smile.

'Mum? You didn't have to come.' She squeezed her tightly, while ignoring the man at her side.

'Of course I did. It's your big day. Are all these people here to see you?'

Daisy took a moment to study the crowd, many of whom were

scribbling down their bids on the clipboards. An unmistakable flutter of pride struck.

'I think a lot of them just came to walk their dogs and stumbled past. But a couple definitely came especially for it.'

'It's amazing, darling. I'm so proud of you. Now, how do I buy one of these? I like the one with the frog.'

'It's an auction. You bid. Everyone has to put down how much they're willing to pay. Then, when the auction ends, I look to see who's bid the most, and they pay for the painting and get it.'

Daisy thought she'd given a fairly clear explanation, though her mother still looked utterly confused.

'So, I don't know how much I'm meant to pay?'

'You don't have to pay anything. If you want a painting, I'll just paint you one.'

Her mother still didn't look convinced, but Daisy didn't have time to argue. Theo was waving to catch her attention.

'I'll see you soon, Mum. I need to use this time to chat to people. Wish me lots of luck.'

'You don't need luck, my darling. I can feel it. This is going to go better than you could have even dreamed.'

And for a reason she couldn't quite explain, Daisy almost believed her.

## 36

Just as he said, Theo's break lasted less than five minutes, and thankfully, when he returned, he didn't feel the need to question Daisy about Christian again. Not that she'd have been able to answer him. She was far too busy worrying about whether people were going to bid. What happened, she wondered, if she lifted up one of the papers and found that there had been no bids at all? What if it happened on all the paintings? There would still be the extra takings from the coffee shop, so the day wouldn't have been a complete waste, but it would be so embarrassing.

When the time came, she had to clear her throat several times to find her voice. Bex had gone back into the boat to help Theo, who was dealing with a steady stream of people, while her mother and Nicholas were staring straight at her from the front of the crowd. Over sixty people had gathered – a group so big, they almost blocked the entire towpath. At the very back, Christian stood with a small, knowing smile on his lips. An incredibly calming, knowing smile.

After one more throat clearance, Daisy finally began.

'Okay, ladies and gentlemen, thank you all for waiting. I will now read out the results. This may take a bit of time. I'm afraid I'm very new to this, but I have the help of my trusty assistant.'

Claire waved to the group; it was going to be her job to sort out the money and hand over the paintings while Daisy read out the winners.

With a deep breath, Daisy began.

'My first painting from the auction is the picture of the swallows above Wildflower Lock.' As Claire lifted the painting and turned it to the crowd, Daisy took the corresponding clipboard and scanned down the numbers.

The first bid was fifteen pounds, but it was nowhere near the winner. Down the page was an increasing list of offers, which finally settled at eighty pounds.

Daisy's heart leapt with excitement. Eighty pounds was a brilliant start.

'And the winner is Mr L Cross. Mr Cross, are you here?' An old man raised his hand. 'Fantastic, thank you, Mr Cross. If you would just like to see my helpful assistant here with your payment, the painting is all yours. Thank you so much for your support.'

Daisy's heart throbbed with pride. Eighty pounds for one of her paintings. She wanted to scream, but that would hardly look professional, particularly given she had still had the rest of the auction to get through.

The second painting also went for eighty pounds, but the third was slightly less at only fifty. Daisy wasn't disappointed though, because it was Yvonne who had bought it. She did, however, feel slightly guilty that she had barely found time to speak to Yvonne today. Maybe she would do her an extra painting for free, just to say thank you.

One after another, Daisy's artworks sold, and so far, she hadn't seen anything near to that blank page she had feared so much.

'I can't believe we're getting near the end.' Daisy glanced at the emptying table before turning back to the crowd. 'And I honestly can't believe all your generosity here. It's incredible. So now, one of my favourite paintings.'

After the winning name and bid were read out, the new owners clapped excitedly as they made their way to Claire, while Daisy picked up the next painting: one of a small bridge further down the canal. The picture wasn't painted from her imagination, but a very vivid memory, as it was the same bridge by which she had crashed the *September Rose* into the riverbank and needed to be rescued by Theo and his ex-girlfriend. She had painted it after the event and every time she'd looked at it, had been reminded of that day and the fool she had made of herself. Hopefully, a nice sum of money would finally make her like that bridge a bit more.

As she lifted the paper, her eyes went straight to the largest number at the bottom of the page. 'Two hundred and fifty pounds!'

She gasped in disbelief. A series of cheers went up around her, but Daisy didn't take them in. She was already looking across the page to the name of the bidder.

'Theo?'

So this was why he had asked for his five-minute break, she realised as a lump swelled in her throat. Two hundred and fifty pounds was a large contribution to what she needed, and he had given it to her. On top of giving up all day to help her with the coffee shop. She was going to hit her target for certain and she didn't know how she was going to thank him for it.

'Theo, if you want to come and collect your painting, you can, or I can just give it to you later. That would probably be easier. Actually, yes, keep serving coffees. It's too busy for you to stop.' The people around her chuckled. 'Thank you all so much. Oh my goodness, we've got just two paintings to go. I can't believe it.'

The second-to-last picture was an illustration, which sold for the lowest price of the day at only thirty pounds, but Daisy remained ecstatic.

'Claire, how much do we need this next one to make to hit the target?' Daisy said quietly, hoping Claire had been doing the maths as they went along. She may not have been the accountant in the group, but she still had a keen head for numbers.

'Five pounds,' she said after a slight pause.

'Five pounds?'

'Yup.'

Daisy's jaw dropped. They still had one painting to go, and she had almost reached the target. It didn't even matter if this clipboard revealed a blank page, like she had feared so greatly when this all started. Adding the coffee shop takings for today to the money from the auction, she might even be able to get the propeller looked at in the next week, too. She could feel her throat thickening with tears of joy.

'Ladies and gentlemen, thank you for being here. I don't have the words to say how grateful I am that you all turned up today. Your support really has been life-changing. Now, before I get all teary about how fantastic it is to live in a place like this, and how lucky I am to have such a wonderful group of friends and family supporting me, it's time to reveal the winning bid for the last painting.'

The last piece was the biggest she had done for a very long time, and she had only started it a couple of weeks after discovering her father's art supplies on the boat. The image, drawn with a mixture of watercolours and pencils, spanned a length of the canal, including the lock and a half dozen narrow boats on either side, not to mention all the wildflowers that gave the location its name.

Considering how long it had taken her, Daisy hoped this one

wouldn't sell for thirty pounds. She'd didn't expect it to sell for two hundred and fifty, though. After all, that was Theo being overly generous, but she had spent the best part of a week on it, but even if it didn't sell, she'd be happy. Today had been a total success. She couldn't have asked for more.

She took the clipboard and removed the top sheet, revealing the series of numbers and names. As was now the habit, her eyes went straight to the bottom, to the biggest figure. Yet unlike before, she didn't read out what it said.

'Is everything all right?' Claire whispered.

'I… I think there's been a bit of a mistake.' A sudden heat was rising through her, making it difficult to speak.

'No, no mistake.' Christian squeezed his way through the group to the front. 'That's definitely the right price.'

Daisy still couldn't speak. A numbness was travelling through her, as if she wasn't quite attached to her body any more.

'Are you gonna tell us how much it's gone for?' Bex shouted from the hatch. 'The suspense is killing me here!'

Daisy tried to speak, only for her throat to emit a strained cough. Even when she said the words, her voice was barely audible. 'Two thousand,' she tried again, a little louder. 'It's sold for two and a half thousand pounds.'

A collective gasp rose from the crowd, which quickly transformed into a cheer.

'Well, it looks like we made the target,' Claire said, clapping away with everyone else. But Daisy wasn't listening; she was staring straight at Christian.

'You shouldn't have done that,' she said as he walked towards her. 'It's too much.'

'No, I think it's just right.' He was standing right in front of her now, but Daisy was still too numb to realise what was happening. All she could think about was the fact that someone had paid more than two thousand pounds for one of her paintings. She had smashed the target. She could pay back Bex, fix the propeller, and put some aside, ready for the mooring fees. It was better than she could ever have hoped.

With all those thoughts, she barely even registered as Christian leaned down towards her, his head coming down to hers, and he planted a kiss squarely on her lips.

It was a reflex action to kiss him back. After all, that was what she had done every time he'd kissed her before. It felt like some kind of daydream – this man, these paintings, this life. Only when she broke away and heard the cheers of the crowd did she realise this wasn't like the times they had kissed before. This was very, very public. And as she looked around, blushing, she saw there was one person not sharing in the joy of the moment. A person who had come out of her boat to pay for the painting he had bought, which he was now holding in his hand as he stared straight at her.

'I guess my role is done,' Theo said.

## 37

Daisy couldn't move. All around her, people were clapping, congratulating her and trying to shake her hand. There was even someone who claimed to be a photographer from the local press taking photos. Her mum was wiping tears from her eyes, while Amelia had somehow commandeered the bag of marshmallows that were meant for the hot chocolates.

And all the time, Christian was there, right beside her, holding her hand.

'See, I told you you were going to make it. These paintings are brilliant. You should be so proud of yourself.'

'I am.' Daisy choked out a couple of words, but she was scanning the crowd. Theo had gone. One scathing sentence and he had taken his painting and marched back to the *Narrow Escape*. It was enough to make her heart sear with pain.

She fought the urge to run after him. What would she say? Yes, she had been seeing Christian, but it wasn't anything serious? That they had started dating the exact same night as things started between the two of them? That she had made an utter mess of everything and she still didn't know how she was going to sort it out?

'I should probably go sort out the coffee shop.' Her voice cracked as she spoke. 'I think Theo went back to his boat. I should check everything is all right. I need to close the hatch and clear up.'

'I can come with you?' Christian offered.

'No, no, it's fine. You've done so much already.' And then, because she felt like she should, she gave him a quick peck on the lips.

Daisy hurried into the boat. As soon as she was inside, she dropped her head into her hands and let out a silent scream.

How the hell had she made so much of a mess? And what was she meant to do now?

Needing to distract herself, she headed to the coffee machine and closed up the hatch; everything was immaculate, probably more immaculate than this morning before they'd started serving. There wasn't a single coffee filter unwashed, and everything was stacked perfectly. Of course Theo had done a great job. That was just what he did. Helped her constantly. And this was how she had repaid him.

She was busy wiping down the surface one more time, when she heard footsteps in the boat.

Turning around, she saw Christian standing right there, deep furrows in his brow.

'Is everything all right?' He moved forwards and placed his hands on her waist. 'I feel like I did something wrong. Was it the kiss? I'm so sorry. I didn't think about your friends and everything. You were just so happy, and when you're happy, I want to kiss you.'

They were such sweet words, but they made her heart throb.

'No, no, nothing is wrong. I think I'm just a little over-whelmed, that's all.'

'I get that. It's been a big day. Are you too overwhelmed for celebratory cocktails? I might have been a bit presumptuous, but I booked us a table.'

It wasn't really presumptuous, Daisy wanted to say, given that by buying one single painting he had dished out almost all the money she needed. In that sense, a dinner booking was a pretty safe bet.

'Christian, you really didn't have to spend that much on the painting. It isn't worth it.'

'Yes. Yes, it is. Look, I like you. You know I do. I've liked you from the first moment I saw you and you didn't judge me for being the biggest cry-baby in the world. Daisy, you're like a breath of fresh air. Your smile, your lifestyle. The way you work at every-thing. Not to mention your determination. It makes me want to be a better person. But those things aren't the only reason I bought the painting. I bought the painting because it's good. I collect art, and the moment I saw it, I knew exactly where I wanted to hang it in my apartment. But I'm sorry if you felt like I'm rushing things or pushing things or if maybe you have some other unfinished business you need to deal with.'

There was something about the way his eyes moved when he said that which gave Daisy the impression he was talking about Theo.

'Would you mind if we give drinks a miss?' she said, avoiding his comment as best she could. 'I think I'm too exhausted after everything. A glass of wine and a film is all I really feel up to.'

'Sounds perfect. Do you want some company for that? No pressure.'

The perfect gentleman routine was making everything even

more difficult for her. Particularly as she doubted that it was a routine at all. It was just who he was.

'Do you mind if I say no tonight? I'm so shattered, I don't think I'll be the best company.'

She felt terrible, but she wasn't kicking him to the curb. Not exactly. She was trying to get her head straight.

Thankfully, Christian seemed to understand.

'Of course, there's no rushing or pressure here. I just want to make your life easier, that's all.'

Why was he so damn charming? And why did the way he looked at her make her insides melt?

'I should go outside and help.' She broke her own stream of thoughts before they could descend even further. 'Claire and Bex will whine non-stop if I leave them with all the tidying.'

'Do you want me to stay and help? I'm happy to. But I suspect you'd like some time to yourself with your friends? The day's been pretty full-on.'

'Thank you,' she said, grateful she didn't need to explain herself. 'And I'll call you.' She kissed him lightly on the lips before they both headed outside. As expected, Claire was ordering Bex around in a military fashion, and all the collapsible tables were now flattened and against the ground, ready to be carried away.

'Your mum said she'll give you a ring tonight, but she's very proud of you,' Claire said as she folded the legs on another table. 'We're all very proud of you.'

Daisy smiled, aware of Christian's presence right beside her.

'Ladies, it was lovely to meet you. I should get going. But hopefully, I'll see you all again soon?'

'That sounds great.'

'Was good to meet you too.'

With that, he turned and headed down the towpath.

Thankfully, the girls had the sense to wait until he was out of earshot before they went wild with their interrogation.

'He paid two and a half thousand pounds for one of your paintings. That's insane!' Claire said, still whispering, although Christian was long gone.

'He is pretty spectacular,' Bex added. 'I mean, that kiss at the end. I was jealous. He's clearly crazy about you.'

'I know.' Daisy's gaze shifted involuntarily to the *Narrow Escape*. The constant up and down of emotions was enough to leave her nauseous. It needed to end, one way or another.

'You know you're going to have to talk to him.' Claire squeezed Daisy's arm, the excitement of a moment ago replaced with a far more serious air.

'I know,' Daisy said. 'I just don't know what I want to say.'

'Well, you better think of something. And the sooner the better.'

## 38

Daisy waited, though she wasn't sure what she was waiting for. Bex and Claire had long gone, the space where they'd hosted the auction looked like the event had never taken place, and yet she still hadn't dared leave the *September Rose* and head to the *Narrow Escape*. Perhaps she hoped Theo might come knocking on her door with a homemade wholemeal loaf and ales he had been saving for one of their evening chats, but deep down, she knew that wasn't going to happen.

He wasn't going to come knocking on her door at all, with or without food. If she wanted to speak to him, she was going to have to pluck up the courage and go over there herself.

Christian had already messaged to say he'd cancelled the reservation and rearranged it for the end of the week. But again, he'd reinforced the no pressure and had congratulated her on a wonderful day. He had also sent a photo he'd taken of her surreptitiously. A perfect portrait of her grinning away while talking to a bidder. Underneath, he had written:

Love this.

Never in Daisy's life had she anticipated a guy like him would look at her twice. And now that he had, it felt like the end of the world.

She liked him. She really liked him, but it didn't change how she felt about Theo. Her memory flashed with the image of Theo's face after she and Christian had kissed. No, she had made up her mind. She had made up her mind before Christian even set foot on the boat.

She was dressed in her pyjamas and slippers and didn't think twice as she marched out of the boat and straight across to the *Narrow Escape*. Her heart pounded as she reached the door and as usual she didn't bother to knock, but let herself straight in. She needed to tell him. She needed to let him know he was the one.

Before she had even set foot inside, Theo spoke.

'I didn't expect to see you tonight. I thought you'd be off celebrating with your new man.' He didn't bother lifting his head up from his book to look at her.

'Theo, I—'

'It looks good.'

Daisy was caught off guard by his comment, and as she struggled to restart her sentence, something in the corner of the room caught her eye. There, hanging on the wall just above the window, was the painting of the bridge.

She took a step towards it.

'You hung it up already?'

Theo remained where he was, still pretending to be interested in the book. 'I put the nail in this morning when I knew which one I'd buy. It seemed a waste not to use it.'

Daisy's heart ached. Even after he'd seen her and Christian kiss, Theo had still hung up her painting. She didn't know if that made her want to laugh or cry.

'Theo.'

Her voice was barely a whisper, but this time, his head snapped up to face her and a glowing fury burned in his eyes.

'I think the thing that gets me, Daisy, is how well you had me fooled.'

'I didn't fool you about anything.'

'No? So you won't let me take you for dinner, but you'll let this guy you've known for two weeks kiss you in front of your friends and family and strangers. I was such an idiot. I actually believed all those things that you said about making us work, and about giving me time to get my head straight. But at the end of the day, the only thing that's been messing with my head isn't the breakup with Heather. It's you. It's you and your games.'

A burning began behind Daisy's eyes, but she shook it away. This wasn't what she'd come here for. She'd come here to make things right.

'Theo, I'm sorry you feel that way, but I've never been playing games with you.'

'Really? Do you really believe that? I consider myself a pretty patient guy, a pretty forgiving guy. But right now, I don't even think I know you, Daisy. I think you've been playing me from day one, to sort out your boat, just like you were playing with this Christian guy so he'd give you a chunk of money. To be honest, I feel sorry for him.'

There was no swallowing back the tears now as they welled in her eyes.

'Theo, please, you know it wasn't like that. It's never been like that. I'm sorry about Christian. I was confused. I *am* confused.'

'Oh, I get it, you've got to choose between the working guy who lives in a houseboat and the guy who will flash a Rolex and take you out for fancy dinners. I get it. It must be a confusing decision to make.'

A fraction of his anger shifted to her.

'It's not like that. It's never been like that.'

'Well, it's sure as hell what it looks like. And I've been such an idiot playing your games. I should have known the whole "waiting for me to be ready" was a way to avoid seeing me as more than just a meal delivery service.'

Tears leaked down Daisy's cheeks. She tried to sniff them away, but they wouldn't stop. Was that really what he thought of her? That she had been using him this entire time?

For the first time since she had entered the boat, Theo put down his book. He stood up and, with his eyes locked on her, he marched across the boat. It was the same stride he had taken when he had stormed onto the *September Rose* and planted a kiss on her lips, sweeping her away entirely. But the fire burning in his eyes now was not the same. It was furious. Even when he reached her, he didn't speak. There was no pushing herself up onto tiptoes this time. Instead, she cowered down under the weight of her guilt.

'I just didn't know how I was meant to choose.' She sounded weak and pathetic, and she hated herself for it. 'I'm sorry. I got it wrong. I got it wrong, Theo. Please, I'm sorry.'

She reached out her hand to take his, but he snatched it away.

'Well, I guess that's something. You don't have to make a decision now.' He turned around and headed back to the sofa, where he sat down and picked up his book without offering her so much as a second glance. 'Now, please get out of my home.'

## 39

Daisy May wanted her mum. No, Daisy needed her mum. She needed her mum to make her a cup of tea, the way only she could, and wrap her arms around her and tell her everything was going to be okay. She needed to hear her mum say how she was going to get through this, the way she had done after the breakup with Paul. She needed to be told she wasn't the worst human in the world, because that was how she felt.

Brushing away the tears that continued to stream down her cheeks, Daisy picked up her phone and called her mother.

'Mum? Are you home?' Daisy's voice wavered. It was only a slight quiver, but more than enough for her mother to pick up on.

'Daisy, darling, what is it? Is everything okay?'

'Are you home? I just thought I might come and see you for a bit?'

'No, no, I'm not. But where are you? Are you on the boat?'

'Uh huh.' Daisy couldn't even bring herself to speak in full sentences.

'I'll be there in a minute.'

She had assumed her mother was speaking figuratively, but around sixty seconds later, there she was knocking on her door.

'What happened?' Her mother scanned Daisy's tear-stained cheeks before brushing them with her hands. 'I thought today was a good day. It was, wasn't it?'

'Why are you still here?' Daisy realised the answer to the question before she had even finished saying it. 'You were spending the night at Nick's?'

'I wasn't staying the night. He was just cooking dinner, that's all. He makes a wonderful courgette ravioli. Anyway, we're not talking about me. What's wrong? What happened?'

Daisy had kept the ins and outs of hers and Theo's relationship private from her mother. Partly because she had been so objectionable to anything boat-related but also because there was the issue with her mother lying about Daisy's father, and Daisy hadn't felt ready to open up to her so soon afterwards. Besides, she didn't want her to get invested in the thought of her finally settling into another relationship when she wasn't even sure herself whether she wanted one.

However, the irony was: now she knew for certain. Just like she knew she'd blown it.

\* \* \*

'He's so mad at me, and he should be mad at me.' Daisy sniffed and wiped her face with the back of her hand. She had just finished talking her mum through the entire Theo and Christian debacle, all the way back to her and Theo's first near kiss and the splinter Christian got from her sofa. 'I deserve it. And Christian thinks everything is great between us. You saw what's ridiculous is that everything is great. It would be, if it wasn't for Theo. and I don't know w

'What does your heart tell you?'

'It's never been a great judge of character...'

'Yes, well, you've never given it much of a chance. One bad relationship doesn't mean you're destined to be hopeless in love your entire life.'

'I've got a 100 per cent failure rate so far.' Daisy was refusing to be pulled out of her slump.

'Stop it,' her mother said with a firmness she rarely used. 'Now, maybe it's my fault. Maybe with all the useless louts I've dated, you think that's what all men are like, but it's not. And you wouldn't know that because you refuse to put yourself out there. And maybe you've not gone about it the best way with these two men, but you're young. Young people make mistakes. Trust me, I know. Now tell me about Christian.'

Given how little time she'd known Christian, Daisy had far more to say about him than she would have expected. From the sofa to the flowers and the three courses of dessert. It was quite an impressive testimony to the type of man Christian was.

'But how well can I really know him? I mean, it's only been a fortnight,' she said, feeling the need to reinforce this point to her mother.

'I know, but does it seem like a lot longer?'

'I guess. Yes. It does.'

'Well, that's a great sign. And you two have things to talk about. You don't run out of conversation?'

'No, we don't. He's incredibly easy to chat to, actually. And he bought me the sofa you're sitting on now.'

'He bought you a sofa? That's not your normal romantic gesture, but I guess it's something. And it is comfy.'

She pushed down on the springs with her hands.

Daisy stayed quiet. As much as she was grateful that her mother was there to talk to, it wasn't making things any easier.

'He's not from my world. You saw that. Two and a half thousand pounds for one of my paintings? That's crazy.'

'Darling, money doesn't make a person. It's how he makes you feel that counts.'

Daisy considered this. It was hard not to feel a strange, warm fuzziness when she thought about Christian.

'He looks at me like I'm amazing,' she said eventually. 'And that makes me feel amazing. But then Theo looks at me the same way. When he's not having a go at me for putting my feet up on his coffee table, and he's my neighbour, he's pretty much one of my best friends, and now I've messed it all up.'

She didn't even know why she was having this conversation. Theo said there was no chance for them now. He said the decision had been made for her and wasn't that what she wanted after all? To not have to decide?

In the silence, her mum rested her hand on her leg.

'Look, love, I know people say what's meant to be will be, but don't believe that. If you want something, you've got to make it happen. It's not going to fall in your lap. Now, I think you've got a good thing going with Christian. He seems like a lovely guy, and he obviously thinks the world of you. And you think a lot of him too. But if he's not the one, and you're sure this Theo is, then you're going to have to fight for him. You'd want a man that would fight for you, too, so it's only right you'd do the same for him.'

Long after her mother had left, those words stuck firmly in her mind. Who was she willing to fight for? And who would she want to fight for her?

\* \* \*

The next morning, when Daisy opened up the coffee shop, she had far less time to worry about the dire state of her love life than she'd expected. Dog walkers and day-trippers were out in hoards.

'This is a wonderful idea,' one person said as Daisy handed them the change for their green tea. 'You know, I've been saying for years that somebody should do something like this along here. I'm so glad that you did.'

'Thank you.'

'And next time, I'll have one of those cakes too.'

'Any chance we can pre-order drinks for when we get back from our hike?' another person asked. 'We'll want eight cups of tea and eight scones. We can pay for them now.'

Learning to make scones had now gone to the top of Daisy's priorities, along with getting the propeller fixed. Walkers, it appeared, loved their scones.

Still, it was hard to forget about the men entirely. Any time there was a lull in the queue, she found herself staring at the *Narrow Escape* absentmindedly. She'd had the hatch open since eight o'clock in the morning, and so far, there had been no sign of Theo. Was he going to stay in his boat forever? He would have to leave at some point, even if it was just to refill his water tank. But she could hardly hang around waiting for that to happen. Once again, her mother's words sunk into her head. It wasn't just whether she was willing to fight for it; it was whether he was. And the more time that passed, the more she doubted that was true.

Finally, just as she was about to close for the day, the back doors to the *Escape* opened.

'Theo!' She yelled his name with such force that the customer she had served only a moment before jolted with surprise and almost spilled their cappuccino. But Daisy didn't have time to apologise. Instead, she was racing out her boat and onto the towpath. By the time Daisy was on solid ground, Theo's back was facing her as he strode away, but she wasn't deterred. After all, she considered, there was a good chance he hadn't heard her.

'Theo, can you wait a second. Please?' She watched as his step faltered only momentarily before he carried on without so much as a backward glance. That time, she knew he had heard her.

A new level of heat rose in Daisy. Rather than calling him, she sprinted down the towpath, before coming to an abrupt stop just in front of him.

'Can we talk?' she said, as she turned to face him.

*Can we talk?* They were three little words. Words she should have said to him before things got this far. The tension grew tighter and tighter with every moment of silence.

Daisy stared up at him, trying to think of some way to break the moment. Something she could say that would make the last couple of weeks disappear into nothing. But she couldn't. Not unless he was willing to hear her out. She stood there, her heart hitching further and further up her throat, when he finally opened his mouth.

'No,' he said. 'There is nothing I want to say to you.'

By Tuesday, The Coffee Shop on the Canal had been open for a record four consecutive days, and if the takings carried on as strong as this throughout the whole of summer, she would be set for winter too.

She had received six text messages from Christian, just checking in on things, and asking her to let him know what days she was free for a date. While other than their less than pleasant meeting on the towpath, there had been zero word from Theo. Absolute silence. If it hadn't been for the fact that she saw his light on at night, she might have thought he had actually moved out.

'It's ridiculous,' she said on the phone to Bex that night. 'The whole point of not dating Theo was because I didn't want things to get awkward between us. Now we're not dating and things are awkward anyway.'

'So maybe you need to talk to him. Especially if he's the guy you want.'

'I tried to talk to him. He didn't want to listen. If he won't even have a conversation with me, I don't know what I'm supposed to do.'

'And what about Christian? Where do you two stand?'

'He sent more chocolates. And flowers.'

Daisy gazed at the bouquet sitting on her dining-room table. These weren't like the flowers he'd bought her before the radio show, or the ones the previous Sunday. Sunflowers, yellow roses and carnations created a bouquet of pure sunshine, which had been delivered on Monday, just to say congratulations for the silent auction.

'He wants to know when our next date is going to be.'

'And what have you told him?'

'That I'm pretty run off my feet with the coffee shop. Which is true. And that I do want to see him again. I just feel so bad.'

'Why? You like this guy, and it's not like Theo is making any effort. If anything, it's making him look like a fool. I'm glad we didn't go on our double date.'

Daisy let out a small chuckle.

'Can I say something else?' Bex said, with an uncertainty she rarely displayed. 'And don't get mad at me.'

'Why do I get the feeling I'm not going to like this?'

'I think maybe you're glad about this whole disaster thing.'

'What?'

'Well, it means you don't have to commit to either relationship. Let's forget about Theo for a minute. You've got an amazing guy wanting to take you out. A man who is charming, funny, handsome, not to mention someone you like. I don't see why you're making this so difficult on yourself. Or maybe I do. You haven't been with a guy since Paul. That's a long time. It's fine if you're nervous about it.'

'Who says I'm nervous?' Daisy could hear the doubt in her voice.

'Anyone would be nervous. But at least give the guy the chance he deserves for all the effort he's putting in.'

Daisy thought about her mother's words again. However much she deserved it, Theo had gone out of his way to make her feel bad about the situation, and though she might not know him as well, she could never imagine Christian doing the same. Even if she had hurt him. As much as she hated to admit it, Bex may well be on to something. With a deep breath in, she felt the resolution settle within her.

'Okay, okay, you're right. I'm going to give me and Christian a proper go.'

**40**

---

Daisy wouldn't have thought it was possible, but she was more nervous about this date with Christian than she'd been for their initial meeting about the silent auction, and possibly even the radio interview. She had tried on several outfits and had to reapply her makeup twice, having initially thought that red lipstick would be a good idea. One quick application reminded her she looked more like a circus clown than the Dior model she'd envisioned, and so she wiped it off and opted for a clear lip gloss instead.

Christian had planned the date. Dinner and a show.

Daisy couldn't remember the last time she had been to see a show. At school, they had been on several theatre trips. *Blood Brothers*, *My Fair Lady*, and a couple of Alan Ayckbourn plays that she struggled to remember the names of. But when she left school and started working, she had saved all her money for a wedding and a house that had never happened. When she'd lived in London, the West End had been right on her doorstep, and she always wanted to go and watch some of the big musicals, but there had always been something more vital her money needed to go on, like a holiday with Bex or a service for the car. Now she realised what a good opportunity she had wasted. A trip to London now was far more effort, and with the coffee shop to run single-handedly, there was no chance of seeing a weekend matinee.

At the restaurant, Christian was waiting at the bar, looking like he was posing for a magazine shoot. Two of the bartenders were fluttering their eyelids at him. Another pang of nervousness struck. Of course people would flirt with him. Who in their right minds wouldn't?

Daisy was still lingering on the edge of the bar, wondering if she was making a huge mistake, when Christian noticed her. Immediately, he was on his feet.

'You look amazing.' He kissed her on the cheeks.

'So do you. And you smell incredible.'

He laughed. 'I do my best. Come on, shall we go to the table?'

As they sat down, the waiter handed them the menus, though the minute he stepped away, Christian placed his down on the table.

'You know, it feels like ages since we did this.'

'I know. I'm sorry.'

'Don't be. You're busy. You have your own life. That's important. You must be pleased about how the auction went?'

'Yes, very. Absolutely.'

'And you paid your friend back?'

'It was the first thing I did.'

Daisy paused. She didn't know if it was her imagination, but it felt as though there was a stagnation to their conversation that hadn't been there before. Perhaps she just needed a glass of wine.

'I need to thank you again. What you did was way too generous. You shouldn't have bid that much.'

He waved the comment away. 'Stop it. If you don't stop going on about it, I'll return the painting. I've already told you how much I love it. It's already hung on my wall.'

'Really?'

Daisy's cheeks rose in a large smile.

'So, have you been here before?' He gestured to the restaurant.

'No. Have you?'

'No.' The pair fell into silence, before Daisy finally broke it.

'That ended that conversation quickly, didn't it?' she said.

Christian laughed. 'I'm sorry. I don't know why I'm feeling really nervous tonight. It feels different, for some reason.'

'I know exactly what you mean,' Daisy said, a wash of relief flooding through her. 'All the other times, we've been talking about the paintings and the auction. Now that's done, and I was panicking that we wouldn't have anything to talk about.'

'I was exactly the same.'

Another short chuckle followed before Christian placed both his hands flat on the table. 'Well, I know about the painting, and I know about the houseboat, so tell me something different. Tell me about your friends.'

'You want to know about my friends?'

'I want to know all about you and they are obviously important to you.'

There was something about that comment that warmed her from the inside. It was said with such complete sincerity. And as for her friends, well, Daisy never ran out of things to say there.

'To start with, we've known each other since school...'

After that, dinner went by in a whirlwind of laughter, food and cocktails. After Daisy had finished telling Christian about Bex and Claire, he repaid the favour by telling her all about his group of friends, those he had gone to school with, and those he had gone to university with. Not to mention those he worked with.

After which, it was time to get the bill and get moving.

'We'll get a taxi,' he said, as they left the restaurant. 'I don't want to be late for the show. They put on such a spectacular display at the beginning.'

'I don't think I know what show it is we're going to see?' Daisy said, feeling a slight hint of embarrassment. 'Did you tell me? I think I might have forgotten.'

A smile toyed on the corner of his lips, accompanied by the brightest twinkle in his eye.

'I think it might have slipped my mind. Tell me, have you ever seen Cirque du Soleil?'

It was unlike anything Daisy could have imagined. The costumes, the set, and the people hanging from the ceilings who were nothing more than a blur as they swung back and forth. And the seats they had were phenomenal – only four rows back from the front. Daisy gripped Christian's hand with fear as a man balanced on a ball on top of a swing. One false move and he would tumble straight on top of them. But of course, he didn't. The entire show was a masterpiece of music and gymnastics, of dance, musicality, and imagination.

'It was when they were hanging down from the ceiling that terrified me the most.' Daisy's heart was still racing madly as they queued for the cloakroom. 'How could they hang upside down like that for so long? Surely the blood must have gone to their heads. And I can't believe there wasn't a safety harness on the woman with the bike. How come she didn't fall?'

'My answer would be years of training.' Christian was grinning. It wasn't his normal grin, though. It was wider, more mischievous.

'Why are you looking at me like that?' she asked as she

handed the man in the cloakroom her ticket. 'It makes me feel nervous. Like I've done something wrong.'

She couldn't recall anyone ever staring at her so intently before, and she wasn't sure whether it made her want to shrink into herself or stand up even straighter.

'I just love being able to make you smile. You have an incredible smile – you know that, don't you?'

He was going to kiss her again, and she was perfectly okay with it. She wanted to kiss him.

Matching his grin, she pushed up on her tiptoes.

'Your coat.'

The pair broke away before their lips even touched, and Daisy blushed as she took her long, cream jacket from the man.

'Well, that was terrible timing,' Christian said, but rather than turning towards the exit, he took her hand and pulled her out the side of the queue, before slipping around the corner, so her back was pressed up against the wall. There, he brushed a strand of hair behind her ear.

'Sorry, I can't wait until we get outside.'

There was no one to interrupt them now, as his lips pressed against hers. It was such a tender kiss, so gentle, and so natural, yet still exciting. As if they had been doing it for years. She was enjoying kissing him, and why shouldn't she? Theo had made his opinion on her perfectly clear. She could kiss who she wanted.

Daisy jerked away from Christian, acutely aware that Theo had been in mind while she was kissing him. Even if it hadn't been a positive thought, it still didn't feel right.

'Is everything okay?' he asked.

'Yes, fine. I was just thinking how I need to get back, that's all. It's Saturday tomorrow. The coffee shop is bound to be busy.'

Christian nodded, but didn't move. He was staring at her with his intense gaze again, though this time his expression was far more serious.

'I know it's probably too soon to make this offer, and you have to get back to work for tomorrow and everything, but you're welcome to stay at mine tonight if you'd like?'

## 41

Daisy hadn't been naïve enough to think that the night couldn't end up like this, but at the same time, she hadn't fully considered how she would react if it did. One thing was certain, though; Bex was right about her being nervous. The way her stomach was currently ravaged by butterflies confirmed that.

Trying to steady the drumming in her chest, she pressed her lips together tightly.

'I rushed things, I'm sorry, I rushed things.' Christian's hands were around her waist. 'Please forget I said anything. I'm sorry.'

'You didn't rush.' Daisy shook her head as she tried to find the right words. 'Well, I think maybe it wouldn't have been a rush for other people. But I've not been in a relationship for quite a long time. Two and a half years, to be exact.'

She expected him to react to that comment. Ask her why, perhaps, or else look at her like she was insane. Though instead, the corners of his lips twisted upwards.

'That's a while. Although I can beat you. It's been five years since I've had a girlfriend.'

Daisy's jaw dropped. 'Five years?'

This guy looked like a model, had money streaming out of his pockets and the manners of a saint. How the hell could he have been single for five years?

He chuckled at her response.

'That doesn't mean I've been an angel. I'll be honest, there've been plenty of flings. Probably too many. But it's been five years since I felt anywhere close to the way I feel about you, or at least, how I think I'm going to feel about you. I think this thing is real and I hope you feel the same way.'

That was a lot to take in, not just the five years single and the number of flings – probably with women who all looked like supermodels – but the fact that he'd been so open and honest about it. And about how he felt about her. One thing was certain: she definitely wasn't a rebound.

'Five years,' she said after a pause. 'That can't have been a normal breakup. I would know. Whatever happened must have been pretty rough. Can I ask why? What happened?'

She was worried she had pressed too hard, but if he was serious about wanting to go all in with her, she needed to know.

'Yes, you can ask. I'm okay talking about it now, I guess. It was a typical thing. Been together for a long time, thought it was forever, then I found her in bed with my business partner. That was the end of that relationship. Well, both relationships.'

Several dots joined in Daisy's mind. 'That was the business you set up? The one you didn't want to talk about when we first went for breakfast?'

'And now you can see why.'

'I'm so sorry you had to go through that.'

'I wasn't telling you to gain sympathy. I was telling you because I want you to know it's okay. I don't mind waiting. I've had my years of fun and playing around. And I want more. And I think you could be that for me.' He suddenly shook his head.

'Sorry, this was way more full-on than I planned on tonight being. Come on, let me accompany you back to the Tube.'

They held hands for the entire walk, their steps perfectly in sync. Would other people passing be able to tell they were such a new relationship? Daisy wondered, only to dismiss the thought. Of course they couldn't. But it was, wasn't it? Bex had been right about her avoiding any form of commitment, but if there was anyone to get into a relationship with, surely Christian, who knew even better than her what it was like to get your heart broken, was the right person?

When they reached the Tube station, they stopped outside the barrier.

'I've had an amazing night.'

'Me too.'

They kissed briefly, before separating with matching grins.

'I thought that over the weekend, I might head down to the countryside for a bit. Stretch my legs. I hear there is this marvellous coffee shop on the canal down there.'

'You might score yourself a free coffee, too.'

'You reckon?'

'Perks of knowing the owner.'

They were talking in between kisses, in a cutesy way that would have made Daisy feel nauseous if she'd seen someone else doing it, but with Christian, it felt completely natural.

'This is probably going to sound really cheesy and everything, and I can't believe I'm going to say it, but Daisy, would you be my girlfriend?'

'Your girlfriend?'

'I know. I was hoping it sounded better aloud than in my head, but I know I came across like a ten-year-old. It's just, I'm not interested in playing games. That doesn't mean I want to rush things. We can take things at whatever pace you want, but I want to know you're with me. To quote the Americans, I want us to be exclusive.'

How did he make everything sounds so simple? Daisy wondered momentarily. There was no blurring of lines here. No wondering where she would stand in two or three or six months' time. In fact, when she thought back to it, from that very first, ludicrous gift of a sofa, Christian had made it clear he was interested in more than just friendship.

The fluorescent lights of the Tube station hummed overhead, casting a cool glow on the worn tiles and metal railings, while the distant rumble of approaching trains echoed through the tunnels. It shouldn't have been romantic, not with the smell of smoke and fumes that filled the air, and yet somehow, it was magical.

Daisy's eyes locked on Christian's as she spoke.

'Yes, okay. I'll be your girlfriend.'

All the way home, she replayed the evening over and over in her head: the circus, the way their fingers interlocked when they were squeezing each other's hands in moments of combined fear; the dinner, where he wiped a smudge of food from the corner of her mouth with his thumb; and those kisses. All those kisses.

She got a taxi from the station back to the canal, her heart light until she reached the boats.

If only she could have reached the *September Rose* on another path. But there was no way. She had to go past the *Narrow Escape*. Desperately trying to ignore the dimming state of her happiness, she noted the bedroom light glowing brightly from her neighbour's home, and envisioned Theo reading away, probably scowling.

For all his talk of wanting to be with her, she'd not heard a single word from him since the auction. On one hand, she got it; he was hurt. But then again, what was it Christian had said about her? That she was worth stepping on a couple of toes for? Obviously, Theo didn't think the same. One thing she knew about Christian is that he was prepared to put up a fight for her, and if Theo wasn't willing to do that, then clearly he had never been the right person for her in the first place.

Daisy shook her head clear. She would not let Theo ruin these thoughts, or ruin this evening at all.

She and Theo were definitely done. It was Christian from now on out.

## 42

'So, when are you seeing him again?' Bex said on the phone.

As expected, the weekend was manic, so much so that Daisy had messaged Christian and told him to delay a visit to the lock. It wasn't that she didn't want to see him, but she didn't want to gain a reputation for the coffee shop being closed at random hours when they had only just opened up. By the time the evening had come around, she had collapsed onto the bed without even getting undressed, all the messages she had been sent left unanswered.

But now it was Monday, and when Daisy had a lull in customers around midday, which coincided with the time she knew Bex was on her lunch break, she used the chance to fill her friend in.

'Honestly, I'm not sure when we're going to meet up next,' she said. 'I'd like to say as soon as possible, but I'm so shattered by the time the evening comes, I don't think I could hold a proper conversation. Honestly, I'm gonna have to get a stool behind the counter.'

'Aren't you, like, three metres away from your living room?'

'I know, right? But I can't just lie on the sofa and wait for customers. I'll probably fall asleep.'

'Just put a bell and say, "ring for service".'

It wasn't a bad idea. After all, running the coffee shop was taking up all her energy, leaving her no time for her life admin. She still hadn't looked into how she was going to get the propellor fixed, but that probably had something to do with her avidly avoiding her go-to boat person. Maybe she could ask Yvonne, although she had a sneaking suspicion that Yvonne would just say to go talk to Theo.

'Well, I'm glad you're happy.' Bex's voice cut her thoughts short.

'I think I am. It's hard to explain, but I feel I like he's good for me. Like maybe we're good for each other.'

'And on your next date, you're going to stay the night? I mean, that is the rules.'

'Will you stop going on about these rules? There are no rules. Christian and I are taking things at a pace that works for us. Besides, staying the night is a pretty big jump and he knows I'm not ready for that. Honestly, I still worry he's way too good for me.'

'Any chance of getting any service around here?'

Daisy's muscles tensed as she turned back to the hatch, a sudden, cold wave wafting through her. She knew that voice, but she hadn't expected to hear it again at the coffee shop for a long time.

'Bex, I've got to go,' she whispered into the phone.

Theo was there, staring straight at her.

Her cheeks coloured as she worried whether he had heard the last part of her conversation.

'Double espresso.' He omitted any form of *please* or *thank you*.

'What happened to your coffee machine?'

'Getting serviced.' He reached into his pockets and pulled out three pound coins, which he slammed down onto the countertop. It took every ounce of strength she had to force her lips into a smile.

'No, there is no charge. I still owe you for running the whole day on Saturday. You've got free coffees here for life.'

She thought he might object, but he slid the change off the counter into his hand, then dumped it in the small jar marked *tips*.

'And I've got my own cup.' He promptly dropped a small espresso mug in front of her.

Daisy's smile strained further still.

'Thank you.' She placed the mug on the coffee machine, which whirred as it poured out its measure of rich, black coffee, with steam rising from it in dense plumes. Still, it wasn't enough to alleviate the silence that thickened between the pair of them. For some reason, it was dripping so damn slowly, and each passing second was making it harder and harder for her to deal with the tension.

'So, how have you been?'

'Are you two officially a couple, then?'

Their words came out at the same time, and Daisy shrunk inwards. Ignoring Theo's gaze, she took the coffee and placed it on the countertop.

'Not that it's any of your business, but if you're talking about Christian, then he has asked me to be his girlfriend, yes.'

'He asked you to be his girlfriend? What are you, seven?'

She had tried being nice. She had tried taking the higher ground, but he was making it really damn hard.

'It doesn't have to be like this, you know. We can go back to being friends.'

'I don't know what you're on about. As far as I'm concerned, everything's perfectly fine.'

He picked up his mug and turned back onto the towpath, only to take two steps, and swivel back around.

'Actually, no, it's not fine.' He was staring her in the face. 'I get it. You've made your choice, but you made the wrong one, you know that? And that stuff you were saying on the phone just then, I call bullshit.'

'Sorry?'

'He is not too good for you. There is no man in the world who is too good for you. And the fact that you even think that for a split second is how I know he is not the right person for you. Actually, the fact he's made you feel that way is a pretty clear indication that the guy is an idiot.'

Daisy's patience snapped. It was one thing being rude about her, but she would not take him attacking Christian when the guy had done nothing but be the perfect gentleman.

'For starters,' she said, 'you know nothing about him, and I'd ask you to not eavesdrop on my conversations.'

'That's pretty damn hard when you're practically shouting about your love life to the entire canal.'

'And as for him being the right person—' Daisy ignored the comment and carried on. 'Are you actually trying to convince me that you are? You haven't even messaged me since the auction. You haven't said one word. If you really wanted to be with me, you would've put up more of a fight.'

'Put up more of a fight? Are you joking?' He marched back and slammed his coffee down on the counter, causing the coins to jangle in the tip jar. 'I have been waiting for you, Daisy. What do you think that has been, if not fighting for you? I've been doing nothing but fighting for us.'

Daisy could feel her cheeks burning.

'You said you weren't ready. You said another five months.'

'You have to be joking. *You* said that. Not me. I didn't think you were serious. Daisy, I've been ready and waiting for you since the day I met you.' He looked like he was about to turn around, only to carry on with his tirade. 'When Heather showed up and said she wanted to get back together, I told her it was over. I told her I wasn't interested. And she knew the reason. She knew the reason, and she told me I was a fool. She told me I was hanging on for something that would never happen, and guess what, you've gone and proved her right. So I'm sorry you didn't think I was fighting hard enough for you, Daisy. But I fought the only way I knew how.'

With that, he took his coffee and left.

# 43

Daisy sat on Bex's sofa, sipping red wine. Red wine was her least favourite drink. She preferred ales, lagers, gin and tonics. Then white wine, rosé, and then, finally landing on the red.

But she had turned up unannounced and that was all Bex had to offer.

'Wow, he laid it on thick.'

'It's hard to think about. Honestly, every part of me hurts. My head hurts, my heart hurts, my feet hurt. God, my feet hurt.'

She had already kicked off her shoes and was sitting with her legs up on the sofa, massaging the tender soles of her feet.

'The thing is, even though it's exactly what I wanted him to say, I'm even more angry than ever, because it means he lied to me.'

'What do you mean he lied to you?'

Daisy took another sip of her drink. Hopefully, the next glass wouldn't taste so bad.

'When Heather came round to his houseboat that time wanting to get back together, he said she was just there dropping off his things. He knew all my insecurities hinged around the two of them, and yet he hid her reason for being there. And if he's willing to lie like that before the relationship even started, then there's no relationship at all.'

Bex stayed silent for a moment, chewing on her nails before speaking.

'I see where you're coming from, but—'

'But what? I thought you were Team Christian all the way.'

'Technically, I was, but now I'm reconsidering.'

'I don't want you to reconsider. He lied to me outright.'

'Yes, but he spent an entire day manning the coffee shop for you, and he lied for the right reason. He lied because he wants to be with you. We know you can get a little stressed when it comes to relationships. And he came round right after, right? He ran out after you while Heather was still there, despite the fact she'd just asked for him back. That's a sign of commitment. I mean, he really slammed the door in her face with that one.'

Daisy could hear what she was saying, but she couldn't take it in. She didn't want to believe it.

'No, no. If he'd told me outright that Heather wanted him back and he'd chosen me, that would've been enough. More than enough. But it's Christian. I chose him, and I'm sticking with my choice. I'm sticking with the one who doesn't lie to me. It's Christian.'

'Okay, then. I take it you're staying the night? I can put some sheets on the bed.'

Daisy didn't need to think about it for long. The weather forecast for the morning was terrible, and Bex was up so early for work, she wouldn't have a problem getting back to Wildflower Lock before the walkers arrived.

'Yes, but can we please go and get something better to drink?'

\* \* \*

When Daisy had been with Paul, they had seen plenty of each other. It wasn't really difficult, given that they went to school together. Then, after they finished school, they only lived three streets away, so a quick walk and they could be at each other's houses enjoying the other's company.

Dating as an adult was entirely different, particularly if you were just setting up a fledgling business and learning on the fly, and your boyfriend was a busy man, running his own businesses too.

So, for the first week of their official relationship, all Daisy could do was speak to Christian on the phone.

'Favourite board games?' she asked him.

'I'm an adult. I don't play board games.'

'You're joking, right?'

'No, I mean, I used to play them. I liked Cluedo.'

'I'm definitely going to teach you some new board games when I see you.'

'Really? I'm sure people are meant to stop playing board games when they hit their twenties. Unless they're one of those geeky, role-playing types.'

Daisy bit her tongue. In her opinion, board games definitely weren't just for geeks, unless that meant she was one, though she didn't have long to ponder the thought before Christian spoke again. 'Okay, my turn. How many kids do you want?'

Daisy let out a deep breath. It wasn't the kind of question she had been expecting. More like, what breed of dog is your favourite, or seaside holidays versus city breaks? How many children seemed very serious, so early on.

'I can't say I've thought about it. Two maybe. Yes, I guess I would've liked a sibling growing up.'

'Fair enough.'

'Is that the right answer?'

'To be honest, I just wanted to see what you'd say. I didn't know if you were one of these women who had decided everything already – how many, what the age gap would be, their middle names – all before you were even engaged.'

'No, that's definitely not me.' The word *now* probably should have been added to the end of that sentence. After all, she had been exactly like that with Paul. But she had also been young and foolishly naïve; she would not fall into that trap again.

'Great. And boarding school at eleven, or would you want to wait until they're fourteen?'

'Boarding school?' The words caught in her throat. She may have considered some aspects of her theoretical children's life when she was with Paul, but boarding school? How was that even a possibility? She lived on a boat and ran a coffee shop out of her living space. People like that didn't send their children to boarding school. That was reserved for people like Christian.

'Okay,' she said, wanting to steer the conversation back to a topic that didn't give her heart palpitations. 'Who's your favourite comedian?'

The nights went by the same. They chatted together on the phone until one of them yawned enough for the other to suggest bed.

Daisy groaned as she rolled over and glared at the clock.

'I need to get some sleep. I can't believe I'm going to be awake and working again in less than six hours.'

'You should really think about employing someone,' Christian replied. 'You can't work seven days a week by yourself.'

'It's not that bad. I'm going to put a bell on the counter so I can sit in the living room, and people can ring it when they want a drink. Bex suggested that last week.'

'And the fact you haven't had time to get it yet should tell you something.'

It was true. Days were pretty rushed, but that's what running a business was supposed to be like, wasn't it?

'I don't want to be condescending or anything, but you've only been open full time for two weeks, and you're shattered. Why not see if you can get someone part-time?'

'Maybe next summer, but I've only got three months before the peak season is over. Realistically, there's not going to be any point in me opening up during the week in the autumn and winter. I'll just be open on weekends then. So I'll see how I get by this summer, then look at it again next year.'

'So what you're saying is, in September, I might get to see a bit more of you?'

'That's exactly what I'm saying.'

The following Monday, the schedule was finally aligned for them to see each other. Through their extensive conversations, Daisy had learned that not only did Christian have a complete lack of knowledge about current board games, but had also never enjoyed some basic childish luxuries, such as Laser Quest or bowling. She decided she should warm him up gently by heading to the bowling alley for a date. It was hardly the type of luxury he'd shown her, but if he was serious about their relationship, he was going to have to get used to not every meal coming from a Michelin-starred restaurant. Besides, it was amusing to see him in blue-and-red bowling shoes, as opposed to the designer shoes he normally wore.

'You have to be joking. You have definitely done this before.' Daisy lifted her hands in defeat as he hit his third strike in a row, and it was only their first game.

'I swear. I haven't. At least not that I remember. I'd like to say perhaps my parents took me and my sister when we were young, but I thoroughly doubt that.'

While he'd been happy to talk about his sister, Christian had been less forthcoming when it came to his parents. In fact, other than being divorced and happily remarried and the fact that his mother had purchased one of her paintings, she knew close to nothing about them.

'You can tell me I'm butting in, but it feels like you and your parents didn't have the best of relationships? Or the happiest of childhoods?' Daisy swung her ball down the alley, only to hit two pins. She was sure she was getting better.

'I could hardly say I had an unhappy childhood,' Christian said, picking up a ball and waiting for his turn. 'We had the works. The nanny, the private school. The new car when we turned seventeen.'

Daisy remained silent. She'd never had a brand-new car in her life, let alone one when she was seventeen years old, but she could tell from the way Christian spoke that it hadn't made up for everything.

'It wasn't that bad. Mum and Dad spent enough time working apart that they didn't have to face the fact they didn't like each other until we were both in our teens. Then they threw in the towel and got divorced. My sister's wedding at the end of the year is going to be the first time they've been together in the same room for an extended period for over five years. Why she thought it would be a good idea to have them staying in the same villa is beyond me, but it's a disaster waiting to happen.' He smiled apologetically. 'Sorry, this isn't the cheeriest date conversation, is it?'

Daisy threw her second ball straight down the middle. After watching to see that only two pins remained, she turned back to him.

'I think it's perfect. I like learning more about you,' she said, reaching up and kissing him. As she did, she slipped another ball down the lane.

Twenty minutes later, Christian had thrashed her.

'Do you want to play again?' He smirked.

'No. Never, actually. I think this is the last time I'm ever going bowling with you.'

'You're not sulking that I beat you on my first go, are you?'

'No.' Daisy pouted, but it was only in play, and as he slid up towards her, the corners of her mouth twitched into a smile.

'I looked at the weather forecast, and tomorrow is meant to be horrendous – raining all day.'

After the incident with the storm, Daisy had added two extra weather forecasting apps on her phone to compare and contrast. In the last week, Christian heard the weather reports daily in their evening conversations, and concern flashed on his face.

'I'm guessing that's not good? Maybe it'll clear up. Or maybe you might get some local customers.'

'Actually, I was thinking that if it's going to be bad, then there's no point in me opening up at all. And if I'm not going to open up in the morning, then I don't need to go back to Wildflower Lock tonight.'

Christian frowned slightly before he tipped his head to the side. 'Are you saying what I think you're saying?'

'I packed a toothbrush in my handbag, just in case you said yes to me staying the night.'

Christian squared up to her, kissing her firmly on the lips. 'Yes. Yes. Absolutely yes.'

## 44

Nervous tension filled the air between them, tightening Daisy's muscles as she walked.

She had made this decision before they'd even got dinner. After all, this was date number four – wasn't it? She didn't know and truthfully, it didn't matter. All the conversations they'd had on the phone were like hours they had spent together, and it felt right. Being with Christian felt like the right mix of exciting and calm.

'This is me.' They had arrived at an apartment block which looked straight out over the Thames. Large, darkened windows broke up the sleek, black brick. The building couldn't have been more than a couple of years old, and with its location, she dreaded to think what the price tag would be.

Downstairs, they waited for a lift, where once inside, Christian pushed the seventh-floor button.

'Are you okay?' He lifted her hand and kissed it gently. 'You've been very quiet.'

'I'm fine. Just thinking, I suppose.'

She was thinking, definitely, about how much her life had

transformed in the last year. She had gone from being single and refusing ever to date again to being here with an actual boyfriend, going to see his apartment, which she had a feeling was going to be spectacular.

When the lift stopped and the doors opened, Christian turned to the left and opened his front door with a key card.

'Welcome home.'

Floor-to-ceiling glass windows offered views of the river and city which disappeared in the distance. A thousand lights twinkled and a thousand more reflected on to the water. It was like a painting itself. A constantly changing canvas from which to see the world.

Daisy stepped towards the window, only to remember there was an apartment to look at too.

As she'd expected, everything was modern: white walls, a kitchen island and an open-plan living–dining area with a large, deep fireplace. The size and simplicity could easily have looked bare and sterile had it not been for the rest of the decor.

Large, bold works of art, some six feet high, hung on the walls. Abstract prints in too many mediums for her to take in sung out. It could've been chaos with so many clashing colours, but it wasn't. It was absolutely perfect.

Daisy stared at one piece. 'This is beautiful. Who did this?'

'Now that's one of my favourites. I bought it at an auction two days after I bought this place. It was the first piece I hung in here.'

With an arm around her waist, he moved her across to another piece of work. A large geisha, although modern, it was painted in a pointillism style. The effect was mesmerising.

'What about this one? Where did this one come from?'

'It's beautiful, isn't it? Actually, this belonged to a friend, but the first time I saw it, I fell in love. Then I basically badgered my friend until he agreed to sell it to me. Does that make me a terrible person?'

'No, that makes you a person with wonderful taste in art and a determination to get what he wants.'

'I knew there was a reason I liked you so much.' He leaned in and kissed her, but it wasn't like the kisses they'd shared before. Not like the ones in restaurants or outside the Tube station, or even after Cirque du Soleil. This was a kiss in the privacy of his home and one that neither of them had any intention of stopping. Yet, as his mouth was pressed up against hers, another thought suddenly struck.

'So, what about my painting? Where did you hang that?'

Christian's eyes were still closed as he responded. 'I gave it to my mum. I thought I told you that?'

He moved in to kiss her again, but Daisy took a step back.

'I thought you said you'd already hung it?'

'Yes, she has.'

His eyes were open now, and he was looking straight at her.

'You don't mind, do you? You know she loves your work. And it's not that I don't think it's incredible, but it doesn't really fit in with my aesthetic here. That's all. That's why I thought it was better there.'

Daisy looked around the room. There were all sorts of different styles on display, but she couldn't deny that he was right. Her quaint little picture hardly fitted with the modern vibe of the place, but that wasn't what she minded.

'You definitely told me you'd hung it in your flat. That you'd picked out a place too. Why would you say that if it wasn't the truth? I wouldn't have minded if you just bought it as a gift for your mum.'

Christian moved back from her and took her hands. 'Baby, I'm really sorry. I didn't think this would be an issue. I guess I wasn't thinking properly when I said that to you. I probably just didn't want to upset you by saying it wouldn't fit in here.'

'You just lied to save my feelings?' She spoke the words to herself as much as to him, but he was looking at her, confused.

'Is this a problem? I'm so sorry. I would never do anything to upset you deliberately.'

He continued to apologise, but Daisy was only half listening. She had stepped away, her mind filled with an image she couldn't erase.

Theo was right, she realised as she stood there against the backdrop of the Thames. It had never been about Theo being ready for another relationship. It had been about her. And when she'd finally realised she was ready to open up her heart again, it had been with the wrong man.

'I'm so sorry. I need to go.'

'Honestly? I didn't mean to upset you. You know that's the last thing I'd want to do?'

'I know, I do. And thank you, because you've made me see things clearly. You've helped me so much.'

He frowned. 'Why don't I feel like that's a good thing?'

She rested her hands against the side of his cheek and stared up into those incredible, dark eyes.

'Christian, you are so wonderful. I'm not going to say you're better than I deserve, because as a friend told me, I deserve everything, but so do you. You deserve someone who is with you 100 per cent. Not someone who couldn't make up her mind whether it was you or someone else she wanted to be with.'

'Theo?'

Daisy would've liked to have spared him the truth, but it was lies that had caused all her problems. So she just nodded.

'I'm so sorry,' he said. 'I would never have started this if I thought you really liked him like that. I assumed you were just friends.'

With a deep sigh, Daisy dropped her head onto his chest. 'You are the most ridiculously perfect man I've ever met. And I'm probably insane.'

'I won't disagree with that.'

When she lifted her head back up, Daisy could see the hurt in his eyes, and the way he tried so desperately to hide it made her want to take back her words even more. She wanted to go back to an hour ago. To when she was going to spend the night with him, but she couldn't.

'Do you want me to walk you to the Tube?' he asked, finally stepping back and releasing her.

'No, no, it's fine. I'm good.' She reached up and kissed him on the cheek before bolting to the door.

## 45

Never had a train journey felt so infuriatingly slow. Daisy stared out of the window, her feet tapping anxiously against the floor as if it might somehow speed up her trip. She had already tried ringing Theo and sent messages, but the phone calls went unanswered, and the messages all remained unread. Still, it didn't matter. This wasn't something she wanted to do on a phone call.

When she reached the station, she raced to the taxi bank, beating the others off the train to grab the first taxi waiting.

'As fast as you can.' She slammed the door shut and scooted across into the seat.

'Everything all right, luv?' The cabbie looked at her in his rear-view mirror. 'You look a little stressed.'

Daisy didn't want to get into small talk with a taxi driver. She didn't want to talk to anyone unless it was Theo, but the driver was looking at her with an air of concern.

'Everything is good. Really, really good. I hope. I just need to get to Wildflower Lock.'

'Right you are.'

The entire ride, Daisy's body was alive with nerves and excitement. Nerve-citement, she thought. It was a word she was going to use from now on. That flurry of excitement combined with absolute terror. But really, what did she have to feel worried about? Theo felt the same way about her as she did about him; he had told her as much. She just had to hope he could forgive her for not seeing sense sooner.

A set of temporary traffic lights had her gripping her hands in frustration. Had it not been so late at night, she would have considered getting out and walking the rest of the way. It would have been faster to cut across the fields than to drive along the roads the way the taxi had to take them. But even then, she would likely arrive as a mud-coated mess, and that wasn't the look she was going for right now. Not that Theo would mind. He had seen worse.

Her purse was out and ready before the taxi driver had even taken the Wildflower Lock turning.

'Thank you.' She tapped her card against the machine. 'Thank you so much. And have a great day. Night. Evening. Life. Have a great life.'

She slammed the door behind her, leaving the amused taxi driver in her wake.

When she reached the towpath, all the lights were on in the *Jeanette*, and Daisy was sure she heard a laugh that sounded distinctly like her mother's, but she didn't even stop to glance at the silhouettes behind the curtains. There was only one person she could think about now. Only one boat she needed the lights to be on inside.

By the time she was standing outside *Narrow Escape*, her heart was lodged high in her throat and when she took that first step onto the stern, the first flicker of doubt rose within her. How was she supposed to go inside? Before Christian, she could always march straight in with a single knock and drop on the sofa or help herself to a beer.

But that was before. Now, he might well have locked the door to stop her coming in, or worse still, throw her out if she tried.

With her thoughts still muddled, Daisy knocked on the door, slightly harder and faster than she anticipated.

'Theo, are you in?' She strained to hear the sound of footsteps padding towards her as she knocked and spoke again. 'Theo, please. I need to come in. I need to speak to you.'

Her heart was hammering now, but there was no disguising the sound of Theo's feet marching across the inside of his boat.

'Daisy, is that you? Do you know what time it is?'

'Please, Theo. Can you let me in?'

The door creaked open, revealing Theo backlit by the lights inside the boat. Once again his hair was loose, while deep creases wrinkled his forehead as he looked at her.

'Daisy, is everything all right?'

'No.' She shook her head. 'No. It's not. I've been a complete idiot.'

She didn't say any more, but instead planted her lips straight on his. A thousand bolts of lightning struck through her as he responded to the kiss without a moment's hesitation. Then, without warning, he hoisted her up, so that her legs wrapped around his hips. Why had she thought she wanted to wait for this? She must have been insane.

Theo carried her through into the boat and only when they reached the living room did he drop her down onto the sofa.

'Daisy, I thought... You and Christian—'

'Like I said, I'm an idiot. A complete idiot.'

She moved to kiss him again, but he stopped.

A pang of fear shot through her. 'I'm too late. You've changed your mind. You don't want this any more?'

'Oh, I want this. I want every inch of this, believe me, but—'

'I'm not here to mess you around. I promise. I'm so sorry for how I behaved before. I don't need to wait to see if you're ready. I don't want to date anybody else. I just want to be with you. So I'm hoping that you want to be with me too?'

Never could Daisy remember putting her heart so openly on the line, and it was terrifying, yet somehow freeing too. If Theo rejected her right now, it was going to break her heart, that was for sure. But she would know she only had herself to blame, and at least she had fought for what she wanted.

As she waited for an answer, Theo bit down on his lower lip in a way that made her heart tremble.

'I definitely want this more than anything. But—'

'No buts right now,' she interrupted, rising on her tiptoes to kiss him again. 'We've waited long enough for this.'

## 46

Daisy woke to a soft drumming. A constant, repetitive beat tapping outside the window.

The sound of rain hammering on the roof probably should have given her a feeling of anxiety. After all, it meant she wouldn't be opening the coffee shop, at least not early in the morning. Rather, it gave her a deep sense of peace. It meant she could stay here, wrapped up in the thin sheets, feeling the comfiest she could remember in weeks. If not years. Even when she knew she was awake, she kept her eyes closed, not wanting to succumb to the realities of the morning.

The whole evening had felt like a dream, so much so that if she thought about it for too long, it almost gave her palpitations. After all, she had started the day with one boyfriend, and now, although she and Theo hadn't put a name to their relationship, they were definitely something.

Daisy rolled over and stretched out her arm, expecting to find Theo's warm body next to her. Instead, she found the empty side of his bed. The peace that she had been feeling only moments ago vanished.

'Theo?'

She sat up, trying to recall if he had said he was going somewhere. Their entire night had been incredible, a constant stream of fireworks, interspersed with love and tenderness and, a fair few times, laughter too. But maybe when she'd fallen asleep, he'd changed his mind. Maybe he had decided the debacle with Christian simply wasn't forgivable. She reached her arm down to the ground, searching for her top.

'You're not planning on leaving, are you?'

Theo stood in the doorway with two mugs of coffee in his hands. Daisy blushed as she dropped her top back to the ground.

'I was worried you'd changed your mind,' she said, deciding after all they'd been through so far, truth was probably the best option.

'About last night? No chance. But you might if you see what I get like without my caffeine.' He handed her one of the mugs. 'Annoyingly, the coffee shop next door is shut this morning, so I had to make it myself.'

Daisy took the mug and blew the steam off the top before placing it on the bedside table to cool.

For a moment, neither of them spoke.

'So... with all this rain, there's no point in me opening the shop...'

She smiled coyly, hoping Theo might use the words as an invitation to kiss her again, or perhaps even climb back into bed. But instead, he remained where he was. All the warm fuzziness Daisy had felt since waking up seeped away at a drastic speed.

The night before, he had barely been able to keep his eyes off her, but now he couldn't even meet her gaze. And every passing second felt as though a knife was twisting in her heart.

She tried to keep her voice steady as she spoke.

'You regret it, don't you. You regret what happened last night.'

'What?' Theo put his coffee down beside hers. 'No, in no way do I regret it. Last night was incredible, Daisy. It was everything... more than I could have dreamed. No. I don't regret it at all.'

A slight wash of relief ebbed over her, but it wasn't enough to ignore the niggling feeling in her stomach. If last night had been so incredible, why hadn't he kissed her since they woke up? Morning breath aside, he could have at least offered a peck on the forehead. Instead, he continued to stand just out of her reach.

'Daisy, I need to talk to you about something.'

The nerves surged again. 'Theo, you're acting strange, and it's freaking me out.'

'I'm sorry. I just don't know how to tell you this. If last night hadn't happened, I was thinking about not telling you. But I can't now. You need to know the truth.'

As he paced back and forth, Daisy's mind shot to Heather. They had got back together while she was with Christian. They had got back together during this last week, and now she had barged in and taken another woman's man to bed.

This was horrendous. This was worse than she could've imagined. She felt sick. Appalled at herself.

'I've been offered another job,' he said, severing her stream of thought.

'Another job?' She shifted in the bed. 'What sort of other job?'

'It's a good position, a management position. I'll be overseeing over a dozen locks. It's a pretty big responsibility.'

She didn't know much about canal life yet, but she could tell it already sounded important. And something Theo would thrive doing. What didn't make sense was why he didn't sound happier about it.

'I don't get it. That's great news. Isn't it?'

He didn't reply. There was something about the way he still couldn't look at her that gave Daisy the distinct feeling that there was more to this than he had first let on. Why wouldn't a new job be a good thing? Surely he wouldn't have applied for it if it wasn't what he wanted to do. After all, he loved his current position.

That's when it hit her like a lead weight.

'You're moving away, aren't you?'

## 47

Neither of them spoke. Theo was still staring at his feet, and Daisy was staring directly at him.

As the seconds ticked by, she took his silence as a confirmation.

'When you came and kissed me, then left for a few days, that was where you went,' she said, putting the timeline together as she spoke.

'I know, but honestly, I didn't realise I was going for a job interview back then. My friend asked me to come up and help him with some work on the canals. And I'd got leave from my job to use up, so it seemed like a good thing to do. It wasn't until the second day that he told me why he'd actually invited me. Even then, I wasn't sure if I was going to take it. But after the auction, I accepted.'

'You mean after you saw me and Christian kiss?'

The reality made her feel sick. This had been her doing. If she'd just stopped messing around and been so fixated on what the right thing to do was, she and Theo could have already been together. And then he probably would never have considered taking the job. Instead, she had practically pushed him into it.

'So, where does this leave us?' Next to her, the coffee was slowly going cold, but she didn't reach for it. She didn't feel like she could swallow anything. 'I've just paid all this money for the fixed mooring licence. And I haven't repaired the propeller. And the coffee shop is really taking off.'

'I know. I know all this. But I don't know what I can do. I don't want to sound harsh, but this is a great opportunity for me, Daisy. And I've already handed in my notice. I can't take it back.'

Daisy reached out her hand and placed it on his arm. She could feel the warmth of tears pricking behind her eyes, and for once, she didn't pretend they weren't there. She simply let them fall.

'This is my fault. If I hadn't been an idiot...'

'I'm not going to deny that. This is entirely your fault.'

The tiniest of smiles flickered on the corner of Theo's mouth, lighting up a spark of hope in Daisy. It was the first hint of optimism she'd felt since he'd come back to the bedroom.

'So, where is this job?'

'Slimbridge.'

She raised her eyebrows. 'And where's that exactly?'

Theo's smile broadened by a smidgen. It was nice to see, even if it was at her horrendous geographical skills. 'It's in the Cotswolds. A really beautiful part of the country, actually.'

'Okay, and how far away is that?' Daisy knew the Cotswolds were west of where they were, but that was where her knowledge ended.

'About a three-hour drive away. Or a week if you're going to take the boat.'

Daisy thought about the implications. She was going to lose Theo from Wildflower Lock. There was no way around that.

What mattered now was whether she lost him from her life, too. And having only had him properly in it for one night, that wasn't something she was prepared to give up on.

'Three hours.' Daisy nodded as she spoke. 'That's doable. It's not ideal, but it's doable. I can check the weather report and come up on days when it's raining.'

'At the weekends, you're going to need to be here whether it's raining or not. And that's the time I have off.'

'Well, in that case, you can come down and help me with the coffee shop. You can be my employee.' Daisy forced herself to smile, although her heart didn't feel like it. 'We can make this work. If you want to, I know we can. We've just got to fight for it.'

The terror of the night before, and the fear he might reject her once again, returned. Long-distance relationships could be tough. She knew that from first-hand experience with Paul.

But Paul wasn't Theo.

'I want to fight for this,' he said, dropping onto the bed by her feet and taking her hand. 'More than anything. But I'm worried it won't be easy.'

'Maybe not, but it will be worth it.'

At some point, her fear had dropped, and now she was smiling again. So much so that her cheeks were aching from the force of it.

Theo was the same. She could see it. The glint in his eyes. The excitement at what the future would hold. A future they were going to spend together.

As he looked at her, she bit down on her lips, before taking his hand and pulling him in to her.

'Well, now that all that's decided, can you come back to bed? You know this rain won't last forever.'

# ACKNOWLEDGEMENTS

So much work goes into bringing these books to life and I am so grateful to every person involved. Thank you to the fantastic team at Boldwood Books; you are phenomenal. With particular mention to Emily Yau, who always knows how to get the best out of my stories. Thank you to the staff at Paper Mill lock, who patiently answer all my questions, and thank you to my readers, who have been on so many journeys with me, whether it is to a boat on a canal, a sweet shop or an ancient world. I am so grateful for all your support. I would not be able to do this without you.

Lastly, to my family, in particular Jake, John, Chrissie and Elsie. You are my support team and I am so lucky to have you in my life. Thank you for everything.

# ABOUT THE AUTHOR

**Hannah Lynn** is the author of over twenty books spanning several genres. As well as signing a new romantic fiction series, Boldwood is republishing her bestselling Sweet Shop series inspired by her Cotswolds childhood.

Sign up to Hannah Lynn's mailing list here for news, competitions and updates on future books.

Visit Hannah's website: www.hannahlynnauthor.com

Follow Hannah on social media:

facebook.com/hannahlynnauthor

instagram.com/hannahlynnwrites

tiktok.com/@hannah.lynn.romcoms

bookbub.com/authors/hannah-lynn

# ALSO BY HANNAH LYNN

**LOVE NOTES**

*LOVE IN EVERY CHAPTER*

WHERE ALL YOUR ROMANCE
DREAMS COME TRUE!

THE HOME OF BESTSELLING
ROMANCE AND WOMEN'S
FICTION

 WARNING:
MAY CONTAIN SPICE

SIGN UP TO OUR
NEWSLETTER

https://bit.ly/Lovenotesnews

# Boldw**oo**d

Boldwood Books is an award-winning fiction publishing company seeking out the best stories from around the world.

**Find out more at www.boldwoodbooks.com**

Join our reader community for brilliant books, competitions and offers!

Follow us
@BoldwoodBooks
@TheBoldBookClub

Sign up to our weekly deals newsletter

https://bit.ly/BoldwoodBNewsletter

Made in United States
Troutdale, OR
01/22/2024

17071339R00162